Tracks in the Brass

Jim Ross Lightfoot

$19.99
ISBN 979-8-218-65116-9
51999>

DEDICATION

This book is dedicated to the men and women in law enforcement who take the oath to "Protect and Serve."

The story in this book is fictional. However, many of the characters are based on real people, people I know and have worked with; only their names have been changed to protect their privacy. Their hard work and dedication make our world a safer place to live and work. Thank you to the thin blue line for all you do. I will sleep well tonight as I know you are on duty to protect my neighbors, my family and me.

ACKNOWLEDGMENTS

I am profoundly grateful to my law enforcement and professional friends for their unwavering support and dedication. Their invaluable contributions ensured the accuracy of the law enforcement aspects of this fictional story. I deeply appreciate their years of service in keeping us safe and their help with this book. They are, in alphabetical order:

ATF Special Agent Jay Dobyns

ATF Special Agent Pete Gagliardi

John Magaw, Former Director United States Secret Service and ATF

Robert Walsh, founder and owner of Forensic Technology, INC. (FTI)

The Men Who Helped.

Jay Dobyns was a United States federal agent for twenty-seven years investigating America's violent crime.

He achieved worldwide notoriety as one of history's most daring undercover operators by playing a contract-killer hitman, mob debt collector, and gunrunner. He is best known for his landmark infiltration of the notorious Hells Angels motorcycle gang.

Jay has been featured in over a dozen film and television shows and is the author of two best-selling books, **No Angel, My Harrowing Undercover Journey to the Inner Circle of the Hells Angels**, and **Catching Hell, A True Story of Abandonment and Betrayal**.

A criminal defense attorney once described Jay as: *"...a government-trained 'Predator' repeatedly sent on seek and destroy missions in search of drugs, guns, and violence with instructions to succeed at any cost without regard for the agent himself or those he crosses paths with."*

Jay was an All-Pac10 conference / All-American candidate football player at the University of Arizona, coached high school football for 15 years, and is an adjunct professor at the University of Arizona.

Pete Gagliardi has over 50 years of experience extracting useful investigative information from crime guns and related evidence in the public and private sectors. Sixteen of those years he served as the Senior Vice President with Ultra Electronics Forensic Technology Inc. and its predecessor Forensic Technology Inc. the developers of the Integrated Ballistics Identification System (IBIS).

Thirty of those years were in law enforcement most of it focused on firearms and explosives-related crimes with the United States Bureau of Alcohol, Tobacco and Firearms (ATF).

He has served as ATF's principal liaison to Congress, the Deputy Assistant Director of Science and Technology, the Deputy Assistant Director of Law Enforcement Programs, and the Chief of Strategic Planning.

In 1999, Pete retired from ATF as the Special Agent in Charge of the New York Field Division.

In 2010, Pete authored the book: *The 13 Critical Tasks: An Inside-Out Approach to Solving More Gun Crime.*

He is a life member of the International Association of Chiefs of Police (IACP) and served for many years on the organization's Firearms Committee.

John Magaw is a distinguished former American police officer and administrator who has made significant contributions to public safety and security. He served as the Director of the Bureau of Alcohol, Tobacco, Firearms and Explosives (ATF) from 1993 to 1999, where he introduced the IBIS ballistic identification system and pushed the National Integrated Ballistic Information Network (NIBIN), greatly enhancing crime gun identification.

Before his tenure at ATF, John was the Director of the United States Secret Service (USSS) from 1981 to 1993, overseeing all protective operations for the President and the First Family.

John began his career in public service as a state trooper with the Ohio State Highway Patrol in 1959, after earning a Bachelor of Science degree in education from Otterbein College in 1957. He later became a special agent with the USSS in 1967, serving in various key roles, including deputy special agent in charge of the Vice Presidential Protective Division and head of the Washington field office.

In addition to his roles at ATF and USSS, John was appointed as a senior advisor to the Federal Emergency Management Agency (FEMA) director for terrorism preparedness in December 1999 and later served as the Under Secretary of Transportation for Security, where he helped establish the Transportation Security Administration (TSA) following the events of September 11, 2001.

His dedication to public service has been recognized with the Presidential Rank Meritorious Award in 1991 and 1999, as well as the Presidential Rank Distinguished Award in 1995.

Robert Walsh, innovative engineer, inventor, and entrepreneur. Crime shows have captured the imagination of millions of people, offering viewers a sneak peek of life inside a forensic lab. Robert Walsh is the man who helped create one of the most critical innovations used every day in real life. His Integrated Ballistic Identification System, or IBIS, has changed how crimes committed with firearms are investigated and solved in over 88 countries. In short, his pioneering work has helped make the world a safer place.

Mr. Walsh didn't start in the criminal justice sector. He's an engineer by trade. After graduating from Loyola College in 1963, he studied mechanical engineering at McGill. He founded Walsh Process Control in 1969 to specialize in applying automation and process control technologies to increase profitability in manufacturing.

In 1991, he took a leap of faith. He started a pilot research project to automate the matching of spent bullets and cartridge cases to the weapon from which it was fired. His efforts paid off.

A year later, he started a new company, Forensic Technology Inc. (FTI), to focus on his newly developed passion, crime-solving technology. The Montreal-based enterprise quickly established itself as a world leader thanks to its IBIS ballistic identification system.

Worldwide, Forensic Technology has helped authorities trace over 100,000 gun-related crimes by allowing the sharing of information between labs, cities, and even countries. Over 10 million cartridge cases and bullets have been acquired into IBIS from hundreds of crime laboratories

Mr. Walsh is a member of the Ordre des ingénieurs du Québec, bringing to the company his technical expertise and 44 years of management experience. In addition to its headquarters in Montreal, Forensic Technology has offices in the United States, Ireland, South Africa, and Thailand, employing a team of professionals in engineering, forensics, and law enforcement.

Among many awards, Mr. Walsh was honored by Ernst & Young in 2002 with the Québec Entrepreneur of the Year Award and became a Fellow of the Canadian Academy of Engineering. Forensic Technology won the 2002 Mercuriades Award for technical innovation, research and development and was named one of Canada's best 50 managed companies by Deloitte and Touche and CIBC for two years running. The following year, the company was awarded the Canada Export Department of Foreign Affairs and International Trade Canada Export Award

FORWARD

Congressman Lightfoot was the member of the United States Congress who was the chairman of the committee that was charged with the responsibility of looking critically at the Bureau of Alcohol, Tobacco and Firearms (ATF) after the deadly incident that took place in Waco, Texas. He and his bi-partisan committee were tasked with the responsibility of determining the root causes and shortcomings of ATF that contributed to the tragedy at the Branch Davidian Compound in Waco, Texas in 1993.

As newly appointed director at ATF, my responsibility was to meet with Congressman Lightfoot and other members of the committee that oversaw ATF. It was my responsibility to identify the shortcomings at Waco and their root causes including structure, hiring, training, policy, procedures and discipline, if necessary, and share them with the committee. Congressman Lightfoot was strong, constructive and critical, but at the same time he listened as I answered probing questions from members of the committee. As the weeks and months of investigation passed, I had constant contact with the chairman about the status of the progress. His respect for law enforcement was apparent as we worked through the issues and needs of ATF.

So, when I was asked to pre-read Congressman Lightfoot's first book "Tracks on the Brass" I did so with pleasure and honor. As a long-time law enforcement officer, I read this mystery through the lens of an investigator and was impressed with the knowledge he possessed about the procedures law enforcement must follow and the intrigue of the mystery.

CONTENTS

CHAPTER ONE

Ah, the golden years, filled with promises of relaxation, golf, and time with the grandkids, unless, of course, an unknown assailant shatters that dream with two bullets to the base of your skull. Seventeen years later, the mystery remains unsolved, and the shadows of the past still linger. Moving from small-town Iowa to the bustling city of Santa Ana, California, might not seem like the best idea, but how else can you spoil your grandkids when they are 1,589.6 miles away?

Hershel Harper, a gentle soul adored by everyone who met him, spent his life cultivating not just his beloved roses but also the friendships that blossomed in his small town. His passion for golf was rivaled only by his dedication to helping neighbors in distress, a trait that earned him the nickname "the town's guardian angel." Leaving their entire life in Iowa was going to be emotionally challenging and extremely difficult. His wife, Ethel, a talented seamstress and exceptional cook, missed her daughter and the grandchildren as much as Hershel did. Together, they made the exciting decision to retire in sunny Santa Ana, California.

The comforting aroma of freshly brewed coffee mingled with the soft, rhythmic ticking of the old grandfather clock.

Cherished family photos adorned the walls, each frame a window into a treasured memory. As they sat in their cozy Iowa living room, the warmth of the room contrasted with the chill of their impending move. Their daughter, Marlene, son-in-law, Troy, and three grandchildren had moved west after Troy received a promotion and a new job. The Harpers were happy for Troy but missed the grandchildren and wanted to be close to them. They decided a move west, following Marlene, Troy, and the grandkids, was the logical solution to their desires.

Since retiring as President of the Fifth National Bank in a small, friendly rural community, Hershel spent his days puttering around the garden, tending to his beloved roses. When the weather was right, he was known to slip off to the county-owned golf course for a round or two. Hershel was the pillar of his community, always there to help anyone in trouble or contribute money and labor to a community project. Everyone loved and respected him. Every morning and afternoon, you could always find him visiting with folks at the little café, two doors down from the bank, during coffee breaks and lunchtime.

Ethel stayed busy with club activities and social work for their church. She loved their home, the townspeople, and those living on the surrounding farms. She was known for her sewing machine skills. Many winning blue and purple ribbons from the state and county fairs hung in her sewing room. Ethel loved young people and was deeply involved in all youth activities, which included 4-H Clubs, school activities, and her church. Like Hershel, everyone loved her, and she loved everyone.

Hershel was sitting on the couch, gazing out the large picture window at the cornfield across the road. The tall, green plants, their tassels swaying gently in the breeze, filled him with a sense of gratitude.

He loved watching the growing season unfold. From the little corn plants poking their heads up through the beautiful dark soil in the spring, growing all summer until they reached fall and then turning brown at harvest time. He enjoyed watching the farmer move through the field with his nearly million-dollar combine as it picked the ears of corn from the plant, removed the tiny kernels from the cob, and saved them in a bin on the combine.

The now bare cob and any other pieces of the corn plant gathered during the picking process were ejected from the rear of the combine onto the ground. Hershel was always fascinated with the birds that would follow the big machine looking for a quick meal if the combine missed a little of the grain and sent it out to the ground. Their hunt was useless as the big green machine seldom made a mistake.

And then the snow would come and put a beautiful white blanket on the field. An occasional rabbit could be seen hopping across the snow, and sometimes, the footprints of a coyote or fox painted a picture on the white landscape canvas.

Spring would arrive, and the process started all over again. Hershel sat staring out the window as these thoughts rolled through his mind. *Yes, I love this show God puts on every year. It breaks my heart to leave it.*

Hershel and Ethel pondered their future. The idea of a hassle-free apartment or condo with no yard work or maintenance seemed like the perfect solution to their retirement dreams. And in southern California, the wonderful wintertime gift of no snow to shovel was an added bonus.

Taking a drink from his coffee cup as he turned away from his daydreaming look out the front window at the field across the road, in a sad voice, he said, "As crazy as it may sound, I'm going to miss looking at that corn field."

"I know, Hershel," she replied, "but we need to go since Troy, Marlene and the kids moved out there. If we don't, those grandchildren are going to grow up, and we will miss it."

"Yeah, I know, but all our friends are here. Other than Troy, Marlene, and the kiddos, we don't know a soul out there."

"Oh, Hershel! We have decided to go. Please don't change your mind now," Ethel almost pleaded as she set her coffee cup on the coffee table in front of her.

Hershel took a beat and another sip of his coffee. "No, sweetheart, I have not changed my mind. I bet I can make a lot of new friends on the golf course. In fact, I'm looking forward to knocking that little white ball around a golf course every day. Isn't that what retirement is supposed to be all about?" Hershel told Ethel as he slid closer to her on the sofa and gently kissed her cheek.

Ethel patted Hershel on his knee and returned his kiss. "Thank you, I know it will be a huge change for us, but we will be able to watch those wonderful children grow up!"

"And we can spoil them rotten," Hershel added with a big smile. Glancing at his wristwatch, he said, "Hey, it's getting late, and we have a big day tomorrow. There are a lot of things I still have to do before we leave."

Hershel and Ethel's conversation about the move ended. There were bags to pack, a few errands to run, and a grueling day lay ahead. In the morning, they had an early 60-mile drive to Omaha to catch their flight to California. Both were filled with excitement and a degree of nervous anticipation. What would it be like to live in a big city compared to the peaceful, small farming community where they both grew up and which had been their home since they married 46 years ago? Little did they know, their new life in Santa Ana would bring challenges and surprises they could never have imagined.

They were about to find out.

The next morning, the alarm went off on time. They grabbed a quick coffee at McDonald's on their way to Eppley Airport in Omaha. An excited Mr. and Mrs. Harper boarded their flight just in time. Settling into their seats, three hours and thirty-three minutes later, after a smooth flight, the airplane touched down at John Wayne Airport in Santa Ana, California, only five minutes behind schedule.

The Harpers checked into a small hotel they had picked for their home-hunting visit. Hershel contacted a realtor he had seen advertising in a real estate brochure he received in the mail. The agent agreed to meet them at 9:00 a.m. the following morning to show them several apartments available for rent or lease.

"This is a good start, Ethel. We got us a realtor on the first call."

"Yes," Ethel responded with a smile in her voice. "What a great way to start our house hunt, but I can hardly wait to see the kids."

"Me too," Hershel agreed. "I think Troy and Marlene are supposed to get back from that conference late tonight or early tomorrow."

The realtor was on time and met them at nine. The hunt to find an apartment began. Sadly, the adventure was a complete disappointment. After a long, tiring day, not a single apartment caught their eye, and the realtor's indifferent attitude only added to their frustration. The realtor seemed only interested in collecting his commission. They needed another realtor who cared about the customers first and worked to satisfy their needs.

Back at the hotel, tired and discouraged, the Harpers sat in their room discussing the past eight hours.

"What a terrible day! That guy was a real self-centered jerk!" Ethel proclaimed in a disgusted voice as she thumbed through a newspaper with little interest in what she was doing.

"You have that right," Hershel responded. "We need a different realtor. Maybe Troy and Marlene know someone. You know we aren't acquainted with this area at all." Ethel shook her head in agreement. In a happier tone, Hershel continued, "We get to see the kids tomorrow night. Maybe they can help us with a new realtor."

The next day, the Harpers decided to take the day off and just rest. The long flight out west, moving through two time zones, and the bad experience yesterday had taken a toll. Old man time had removed their younger resilience, and they were learning they had reached a point in life where "slow down" was acceptable. Acceptable? No, it was required.

Tonight, for the first time since arriving in Santa Ana, they would visit Troy, Marlene, and the grandchildren for supper and get their recommendations for housing. Hershel wondered why he had not done this before leaving Iowa!

When Troy and Marlene moved to Santa Ana for Troy's new job, they purchased a home in an older neighborhood. They found a house they fell in love with. The appliances were all updated, and it had a large, enclosed backyard. It is a perfect place, pleasant and safe for the kids to play.

Filled with excitement about seeing Troy, Marlene and the grandkids, the Harpers ordered a cab to take them over to the kid's house. The cab took them without problems, which was both a treat and a concern.

"I don't know about this cab thing," Hershel said quizzically. "We didn't have these things where we used to live."

Ethel giggled, "No, I think the only cab I have ever ridden in was when I hitched a ride with Eddy Anderson in his old pickup to go to the county fair."

The nearest Yellow Cab to their hometown in Iowa was 60 miles away.

The cab ride was fun, but Hershel worried about the cost of getting around. He hadn't planned for this expense.

Hershel forgot about the taxi cost as soon as they arrived at Troy and Marlene's home when the kids met them at the door.

It was great seeing the grandchildren again. They were greeted with hugs, kisses, laughter, and much love. Once in the door, they went straight to the dining room table. A tour of the house would come later. They arrived on time as Marlene had prepared an excellent meal. Everyone enjoyed delightful food and a great time together.

Hershel and Ethel had a hundred questions for Marlene and Troy, such as where they shopped, where Hershel could get a haircut, and whether a doctor was nearby. Ethel wanted to know where they bought their groceries. Marlene explained that the neighborhood had a small shopping mall. The mall had a grocery store, a series of small shops, a combination beauty-barber shop, and a very small place to grab a sandwich. The grocery store had a pharmacy and bakery.

"Hershel," Troy said with a mischievous look in his eye, "I like going with Marlene to that grocery store. The bakery in there is to die for! One of the best things they make is your favorite donuts. I think they are bigger than the ones you used to get in Iowa."

"Really?" Hershel exclaimed, "I might make a few extra trips over here for those good donuts, if they are like you say."

Troy laughed, "Have I ever lied to you?"

"No," was the reply delivered with a good-natured pat on Troy's back.

The fun is over; it is time to get down to business.

Hershel recounted the frustrating experience with the first realtor. "Troy, do you know any good realtors in the area? We have decided that an apartment is not our style. What do you think about us finding a good condo nearby?"

Troy and Marlene agreed that a condo was a much better idea than an apartment. Some of Troy's colleagues had recently moved and used realtor Sharon Green. Green had been named one of the top realtors in Santa Ana several times. She specialized in condos, and Troy's friends believed she lived up to her good reputation.

"What do you think?" Hershel asks Ethel.

"Sounds like a good idea to me. Let's see if we can reach her in the morning."

The conversation turned back to fun. What had the kids been doing? Did they like their new school? Were people friendly, and had they made any friends? How is Troy's new job going? And the list goes on and on. They had a lot of catching up to do.

Time seemed to fly! It was almost 10:30 p.m. when Hershel called a cab, and he and Ethel returned to their little hotel. The time with the family felt like it went by at warp speed.

Safely back at their hotel it was way past their normal bedtime. They quicky went to bed. Joyful talk concerning the evening's activities would not let them close their eyes. It had been such a wonderful evening.

Talking quietly about the happy time with the kids finally led to a great night of sleep. Too soon, the alarm signaled the start of a brand-new day.

Ms. Green was in the office when Hershel called as early as he thought feasible the next morning. She sounded very professional and friendly on the telephone. After asking about their needs and desires, Sharon said, "I have several newer condos in the area that are fairly close to the family's address you gave me. There are also some lovely parks convenient for taking the grandchildren."

Sensing a good opportunity, "This just happens to be a day when I have no appointments." With a little giggle in her voice, "That happens now and then. I can meet you in twenty minutes to visit some of them if you like."

The response was a cheerful "yes," and they met Sharon Green at the entrance to their hotel. Hershel noted that it had been precisely eighteen minutes since he hung up the phone after talking with Ms. Green. Hmm, he thought. *She said twenty* *minutes. This lady does what she says. This may **be a good** day.*

As an experienced realtor who knew the area well, Sharon selected some newer condos to show them. All the units they looked at were very nice but expensive and located some distance from the part of the city where their three grandchildren lived.

As Realtor Green, known for her cheerful chatter, drove Hershel and Ethel from one condo to the next, a mysterious and noticeable change occurred. As they set out to see the last unit they would inspect today, Sharon's demeanor grew more somber during their walk to her car.

Twice, Sharon took a wrong turn, and they ended up at a dead end or a cul-de-sac before arriving at their next stop. She became mysteriously quiet as they finally neared an older condo, pulled in, and parked in front of unit #102.

Hershel and Ethel had a sense that something dire was wrong.

With a bit of nervousness, Sharon said, "You folks are really going to like this place. I admit it looks like the old girl needs a good coat of new lipstick, but she is as solid as the Rock of Gibraltar.

"The condo association maintains the place at a high level. All major items, such as air conditioners and kitchen appliances, have been replaced with newer, more efficient units. Unseen items such as sewer and water systems were updated two years ago." Sharon was now shifting back into her saleswoman persona.

"As you can see," she said, pointing, "all the shrubs and lawn are perfect. I will admit, a good coat of paint would give the property much better curb appeal."

Sharon took a beat, a deep breath, and continued. "I do not know how well you know this part of the city. I did not want you to know where we were until we arrived."

Green continued, "I was dishonest with you on the way

here. When I told you I was lost and we wandered around through some of those strange streets, I was not being honest, just a little mischievous. I was not lost. I didn't tell you the truth, as I wanted to hide something from you."

Hershel and Ethel looked at each other uneasily. *Have we gotten ourselves into a bad situation?* Hershel thought. He could see the fear in Ethel's eyes.

As I said before, I don't know how well you folks know the city, so I was attempting to be confusing on our route from the last condo we looked at to here. This is something special I want to show you."

Agent Green pauses and takes a deep breath. Then, she points out her car's back window, "Do you see the sign for that little mall about four blocks down the street?"

Hershel and Ethel turn in their seats, look down the street, and nod their heads in the affirmative.

"Look a little beyond that shopping mall where you see the sign sticking up. Well, the entrance to your family's neighborhood is two blocks further down the street," Green said excitedly.

The car goes totally silent.

All you can hear is the three of them breathing. Hershel is first to speak, "You are kidding me?"

"No," replied Sharon. "I want to get you as close to those grandkids as possible. When I shuffled quickly through the papers on my desk this morning before leaving to meet you, I saw that this unit had just come up for sale. My first thought was 'no,' as this is an older neighborhood, and you are looking for something newer. Anyway, I stuck the listing in my briefcase," she said as she opened the lid of her briefcase on the seat beside her and removed the listing.

"During our conversations today in the car, you talked glowingly about your grandchildren. We had looked at some newer units that didn't fit your needs."

A sparkle came into Sharon's eyes. "The address you gave me earlier rang a bell. I know this place is nearby. I have worked with their management company for years and know they are good people. It is a bit old but well-maintained, so it is worth looking at."

"Let's go look at #102," Sharon says as she opens her car door.

Ms. Green takes them into unit #102 at the Sunshine Casita Condo Complex. They are pleasantly surprised. It is much nicer than the exterior indicated. The appliances are upgraded, the carpet is new, and there is a faint smell of new paint and varnish. The layout of the rooms is excellent.

The Harpers take a good bit of time as they walk through the unit two times, discussing everything in sight. And then they do it again. After completing their final walk-through, they pause in the doorway for a brief discussion.

Wearing big smiles, they cease their discussion, walk into the kitchen where Sharon is looking through some of her papers, and, almost in unison, exclaim, "We will buy it!" Hershel continues, "It is close to the neighborhood mall, where we can do our grocery shopping, but, most importantly, visit the grandkids just down the street."

Much happiness fills the room.

Sharon asks if they want to drop by the office on the way back to their hotel and do the paperwork. "No," answers Hershel. "Can we do it in the morning? We must leave for the kids' house in about an hour."

"Sure," Sharon responds, reaching into her briefcase on the kitchen counter.

Sharon is ready with the "Intent to Purchase" papers. Ten minutes later, everything is signed, and the Harpers agree to come by Sharon's office in the morning to finish the paperwork and write a check.

As Sharon put the signed "Intent to Purchase" papers in

her briefcase, she had one more surprise for Hershel. During their conversation today, Hershel talked about his successful bank in Iowa. Sharon listened with interest to his every word. An idea formed in her mind. She had worked with the Sunshine Casita Condo Complex's management company for several years, helping find prospects to purchase units. In her success, she built a high degree of trust with the company. She knew they had a need to fill.

With a smile, she makes Hershel an offer she thinks he cannot resist: "Mr. Harper, we need a manager for this property, and you appear to have the credentials to do it—no heavy lifting. Just supervise the two full-time maintenance people, handle complaints, and collect the monthly condo fees. It will not take much of your time. You are 100% free most days."

A little shocked, Hershel says in a neutral voice, "Interesting. But I'm not sure I want to take on a work responsibility. That's the reason I retired. I want to play golf, not sit in an office all day."

"Oh, you won't sit in an office all day. Remember, I told you most of your time would be 100% free," Sharon injects.

Hershel pauses a few seconds in deep thought. Did he have any desire to go back to work? This was supposed to be retirement time, the golden years, time on the golf course, and plenty of time with the grandkids. In the end, curiosity finally won the battle of thoughts.

"How much does it pay? You know, a couple of retired folks can always find the use for a few extra dollars, especially when you have extra special grandkids to spoil."

"Nothing," Sharon delightfully exclaims and then takes a beat to let her comment soak in. "Instead of a paycheck, we will provide your unit free of all condo charges, including any special assessments that occasionally come along. How does that sound?"

Hershel pauses a moment, turns his head to look at Ethel, who is standing behind him, and sees her expressions of surprise and intrigue. She responds out of Sharon's direct line of sight with a look that says, "Go ahead and do it," quietly mouthing the words to him.

Hershel turns his head back to face Sharon. "Ok, I will take the job. When do I begin?"

"Right now!" Sharon exclaims with a huge smile.

Not only are Mr. and Mrs. Harper the new owners of Sunshine Casita Condo Complex unit #102, but Hershel is also the on-site manager. They have one major project left to do: fly to Iowa, call the moving company, and start their new adventure in Santa Ana, California.

This is shaping up to be a marvelous way to enjoy retirement and create fantastic memories with the grandkids! With a playful grin, Hershel can't help but think, *It truly doesn't get any better than this!*

Maybe it did not. But if Hershel only knew what fate had planned for his future.

CHAPTER TWO

As the moving van from Iowa arrived, Hershel Harper felt a mix of excitement and apprehension about their new life in California. The sun cast a warm glow over the Sunshine Casita Condo Complex, and a gentle breeze carried the scent of adventure. Hershel and Ethel eagerly began unpacking the boxes, ready to start their new chapter with the grandkids.

"Ethel," Hershel remarked with a nostalgic smile, "you take this box, and I'll take the next one. Remember how we used to do this every summer when we moved to the lake house?"

"Alright," Ethel replied with a chuckle. "I just hope we didn't leave behind anything important in Iowa. Remember the time we forgot the camping gear on our trip to Yellowstone?"

Hershel nodded in agreement, though his mind was racing with thoughts of the new responsibilities and the uncertainty of their future in a new city.

Following the advice of a friendly retired neighbor back home in Iowa, they simplified their belongings, creating a more efficient packing process. Now, it was time to see if they had followed his advice correctly.

"Here." Hershel handed Ethel two framed pictures of the grandkids from the box he was unpacking, his hands trembling slightly with excitement.

"Here are two more," Hershel said, handing Ethel more

framed pictures from the box. "These are the ones from our vacation in Montana with the grandkids. I'm sure anxious to see those little buckaroos!"

"Oh, me too," came Ethel's happy reaction.

After hanging her favorite picture, Ethel admired the wall with the keen eye of an art critic. She looked at the framed warm photo of the grandchildren with a horse at the farm, admiring it. "Hershel," she exclaimed, "isn't that just beautiful? I love that picture."

"I know you do," came the heartfelt response.

"I think we are supposed to go over to the kids' place tonight or tomorrow. Marlene said she wanted us to get settled in first," Ethel exclaimed, her voice filled with excitement. After all, there were grandkids to spoil.

"Look, Hershel," Ethel exclaimed as she held up a beautiful antique flower vase from which she removed the packing paper. "Not a scratch or a crack. It made the trip in fine shape. I think I will sit it on that little buffet by the door. That way, everyone who comes in will see it. There are so many memories in this old vase."

Things were working out well. Their furniture from Iowa fit perfectly into the condo.

Ethel was a huge TV buff; it ran all day as she worked around the house. Several years ago, Hershel, who did not care much for TV, dubbed the big flatscreen television "Ethel's boyfriend."

"Hey, sweetheart, let's hang your boyfriend on this wall," Hershel suggested with a playful grin. "If we put your boyfriend up here, when we sit on the sofa and watch the TV, we can see that beautiful view out the patio door. Sweet!"

"Well, Hershel, it was a lot of work, and I hated giving up some of my stuff, but I think we did the right thing," Ethel said as she stood with her hands on her hips, surveying their unpacking handiwork. "And you have a golf course about a mile away. I will probably never see you again!"

Hershel did not answer, but he had a big smile on his face.

They had planned everything meticulously, and their new space felt like home within days.

Hershel started his new career as a condo manager. He enjoyed his few hours in the small office near the visitor parking lot. Yes, Hershel thought Realtor Sharon Green was correct when she told him his time would be nearly 100% free. As the first of the month approached, Herschel's duties as manager became busier. The condo occupants would pay their monthly condo fees and lease charges. With only a few days of activity, Herschel's schedule was manageable, allowing him to focus on his golf game or spend time with the grandkids.

During the week, Grandpa and Grandma Harper spent as much time as possible with the grandkids. Of course, they squeezed in a golf game or two. Hershel was teaching Ethel how to play. The beautiful weather in California helped convince them they had made the wisest decision in the world.

"Ethel, do you remember all that snow I used to scoop?" Hershel said as he gazed at the beautiful green grass on the fairway to the ninth hole.

"Yes, Hershel," she answered. "But it's too bad you don't have a place to raise the flowers you love so much."

"Aw, I was getting tired of being on my knees. Standing up and playing golf is better," he said with a huge smile. "And I got to throw that darned snow shovel in the trash!"

Although small, Hershel's office had a nice window, providing a pleasant view across the swimming pool and the courtyard. When working, he would open the window and welcome the fresh outdoor air to visit.

Herschel enjoyed managing the complex far more than he had expected. He loved interacting with people, and the job allowed him to connect with others while still having time for himself. When residents came in to pay their lease or rent, it typically included a friendly conversation lasting 10 to 15 minutes. Over time, Herschel became familiar with the residents' names, their families, and where they had lived before moving to Sunshine Casitas. Despite coming from different parts of the country, he found it interesting that many retired and relocated there just as he and Ethel did.

Collecting the monthly money was far more of a pleasure than a chore. Yes, sir, Herschel thought, Ethel and I made the right choice to move here. This cheerful thought assuaged some of the negative vibes Hershel had been feeling.

Supervising the groundskeeper and the maintenance man also took little time. Hershel seldom talked with the groundskeeper, who cut grass and trimmed hedges the entire week. He kept the complex looking neat and well-maintained.

Although the buildings, other than the paint, had been taken good care of, the complex was 15 years old and showing its age. It would look much better if only a little new paint could be applied. Proud people lived in the complex, and he thought they would probably like to spruce up the place with a new coat of lipstick, as realtor Sharon had said. Hershel believed this might be a project well worth undertaking. Yes, this might be a good project for me to tackle.

The gardener, Juan Rodriguez, came to the office on the first of every month. He presented Herschel with the bills for gasoline, mower parts, and anything else he needed to do his job, and he also picked up his paycheck.

Juan was a legal immigrant from Mexico who brought his family to the United States for a better life. Hard work and honesty were part of his DNA. Even though their contact was brief each month, the two men became friends, or as they say in Mexico, "amigos."

The other person Herschel supervised was Carlos Morales, Superintendent of Maintenance. Carlos and his family lived in a modest, neat little house about two miles away in a predominantly Mexican neighborhood. Carlos' skills in everything from plumbing to electricity led him to the building maintenance business. Carlos was considered one of the best. He was known for purchasing the latest model Chevrolet as soon as it came on the market. He loved red Chevrolets. The sportier the model, the better!

Carlos stopped by the office every morning to find out the latest complaint and where he had to go to fix it. On the days when Herschel played golf or went to see the grandkids, Hershel left a note for Carlos taped to the glass window in the door. It was a list of the jobs Carlos was expected to do.

Carlos had a key to the office, so the list could have been left inside. However, it was easier and quicker for him if Herschel taped the list to the door's window. Carlos could walk by, take the list from the window, and head to work.

One sunny morning, Hershel relaxed in his cozy little office. Everything was going smoothly, and he leaned back in his chair with a contented smile. His thoughts wandered to the bank he once managed. It was the best in the county and everyone's favorite, clearly shown by the impressive number and total amount of deposits. Yes, the bank operated like a well-tuned machine. The tellers and officers collaborated beautifully, much like great musicians in an orchestra, with him as the conductor. He loved that metaphor!

His condo orchestra had only two musicians, and he wanted it to function smoothly and play beautiful music, just like it did at the bank.

Beyond being the condo manager, he anointed himself as the "chief cashier."

Herschel found an old cash box in the desk drawer, but no key was sighted. He purchased a new one and paid for it with his own money. He believed the complex had treated him well, so why not treat it the same way? It was 1980. Condo residents made their monthly payments with cash or checks. Credit cards had not yet replaced these two forms of currency.

Herschel held the money and checks until the middle of the month and then made the condo complex's deposit at the Pan American Bank.

When it was built in 1965, the Sunshine Casitas Condo Complex was the biggest in the city. With over 100 units, the monthly condo fees, lease payments, and rent amounted to a sizable amount. Herschel locked the monthly fees in the green lock box in his desk drawer, keeping them out of sight from prying eyes. Only he had a key to the drawer and his new cash box inside.

Absolutely! Hershel and Ethel were as happy as two bugs in a rug. Having downsized, the furniture they brought to California fit their condo like a handsome leather glove. Even better, their grandkids lived just a few blocks away! They were pleasantly surprised when Hershel received the manager position; this additional income meant more opportunities to spend on the grandkids. Plus, California's weather was gorgeous!

Hershel had no idea that a change was stirring just around the corner—not in the weather, but in the ways of life itself. Something was coming that would turn his and Ethel's world upside down, bringing more challenges than they ever expected, like dark clouds rolling in on a sunny day.

CHAPTER THREE

Everything seems perfect in the Harper household. As two, three, and eventually four years pass, the Harpers settle into their Californian life, treasuring almost daily visits with their grandkids. Hershel also improves his golf game, shaving a stroke or two off his score. Unfortunately, Hershel is about to score a colossal mulligan, which will not be on the golf course.

One beautiful day, following a round of golf, Hershel and his friends discussed the game they had just finished and talked about going to lunch. With a twinkle in his eye, Hershel told his golf buddies, "I think that was more luck than skill!" He referred to the two strokes he shaved off his golf game that day. His friends laughed, knowing Harper's modesty hid his actual skill. "I guess that means you guys are buying me lunch," Hershel exclaims with a massive smile. 98 is the best score he has ever made. To celebrate, his golf-playing partners agree to buy him lunch. They are the happiest and noisiest group in the golf club's dining room.

After his golf game, lunch, and the short drive back to the condo, Hershel parks in his designated spot in the garage and heads for unit #102. His walk is enjoyable, with the warm California sun casting long shadows on the pavement. As he walks past the office, he realizes this is *condo fees bank deposit day*. Hershel thinks it will only take a moment to step into the office and pick up the money. He is anxious to tell Ethel the good news about his golf game. She loves hearing his golf stories, although she sometimes believes Hershel might embellish them a bit.

He fumbles for his keys momentarily, then opens the office door and steps in.

As Hershel steps into his office, a chill runs down his spine. The room feels colder, and the air is thick with tension. He cannot shake the feeling that something is wrong.

Hershel settles into his chair and turns on his small desk lamp. Since entering the office, Hershel's uneasy feeling persists as he opens his desk drawer. It is locked as usual, but he wants to put his mind at ease. Today is his day to make the monthly bank deposit. He plans to do that before going home.

Hershel opens the desk drawer with his key and quickly discovers the source of his unease. The drawer is empty except for a few papers. The green cashbox is gone!

Hershel's hands tremble as he grabs the phone and dials 911. His voice is shaky as he reports the burglary to the 911 operator, "My office has been broken into, and the cash box is missing!" To Hershel's surprise, within minutes, a patrol car pulls in and parks in the small, reserved parking area in front of the office. A younger police officer exits the patrol car and enters the office through the open door.

Seeing Hershel sitting at his desk, he inquires, "Sir, are you the one who called 911?"

"Yes," Hershel responds, his voice trembling slightly. "My office has been burglarized. I was out golfing with my friends, and when I returned to pick up the bank deposit, I found the cash box missing!"

The officer asks pertinent questions regarding what Hershel sees, what is missing, and how he discovers the theft of the money. While the officer is questioning Harper, an unmarked vehicle drives up and parks in the other reserved space in front of the office.

Hershel peers over the officer's shoulder. He spots a husky man in a rumpled brown suit stepping out of the driver's door, his eyes scanning the surroundings with a practiced gaze. The gentleman enters the office, glancing around, approaching the uniformed officer and Hershel.

"I'm Detective Sergeant George Kennedy," he says, showing his badge in his left hand while extending the other for Hershel to shake.

"Hershel Harper," Hershel replies, shaking Kennedy's hand firmly. "Thanks for coming."

"Yes, Sir, Mr. Harper," Kennedy says, eyes scanning the office. "I'm here to ask you a few questions about what happened today. But first, I want to look around the office."

Starting with the door, Detective Kennedy quickly inspects the office, looking for obvious clues. Cell phones had just hit the market, and the city had not yet purchased any for municipal use. They were too expensive.

Kennedy asks Hershel to borrow the office telephone and notifies the Crime Scene Investigation Unit to come to the scene.

Hershel decides Kennedy is through with his physical inspection of the office and offers him the guest chair.

Suddenly, the small office seems even smaller to Hershel.

"What time did you arrive here?" is the detective's first question.

Hershel glances at his wristwatch momentarily and replies, "I would say around twenty to twenty-five minutes ago."

"Is the office unlocked? I didn't see any marks on the door that somebody broke in. What did you see first when you walked into the office?" Kennedy asks.

"The door was locked when I stopped by after my golf game. After coming in, I walked around behind my desk and sat in my chair. The drawer is locked," Hershel explains in a shaky voice, although his conversation with the two police officers has started to bring him back to near normal. He continues, "This is the day I go to the bank to make the monthly deposit, so I opened the desk drawer to take out the cash box. It was gone!"

"What did you do then?" Kennedy asks.

"I called 911."

Hershel takes a breath and continues, "Since someone unlocked the door and entered the office, I became concerned that whoever got in here knew about the monthly money I collect, and they wanted to steal it."

Hershel pulls open the empty desk drawer. "This is where I keep the money in a green tin cash box." Hershel is still stammering a slight amount.

"When I unlocked and opened the desk drawer, the cash box I keep there was gone. I use the box to hold the monthly lease and condo fees until I go to the bank and make a deposit." Now more frustrated and upset, Hershel tells Kennedy, "Today is the day I normally go to the bank and make the deposit."

"How much money is there in the box?" Kennedy inquires as he jots notes in his notebook.

"$9,157 and fifty cents." Hershel quickly explains, "I was a banker for over forty years in Iowa before I retired, and we moved here. It is a habit of mine to always keep track of the amount money I am responsible for."

Kennedy sees no evidence of a break-in, or the desk drawer being forced open, so he asks, "Who has keys to the door and your desk?"

"There are only two keys to the door," Hershel answers. "I have one, and our Superintendent of Maintenance has the other. The corporate office has one, but they are in Dallas, Texas."

"Who is your maintenance guy?"

"Carlos Morales," Hershel answers. "He has been here several years. He's a good man."

"Does Mr. Morales also have a desk key?" comes the next question.

"No. I'm the only one with a desk key."

Kennedy's next question seems a bit strange and catches Hershel off-guard. "Can you describe for me exactly what you did yesterday evening? Did anything unusual happen?"

Hershel scratches his head, trying to remember the previous day's events. "Well, I came to the office to prepare Carlos's job list. We have a routine arrangement we use for his daily work list."

"It is just me in the office; anyone with a problem calls me or drops a note in through the mail slot. I make up Carlos's job list in the late afternoon or evening. I tape it outside on the door window for him to pick up when he comes to work in the morning. That saves him the trouble and time of coming into the office to get the list. I should add it keeps me from having to come to the office," Hershel says. "Carlos is an early riser and is always here before 7:00."

"That's a little early to start going to your resident's units, isn't it?" Kennedy inquires.

"Yes, but he goes to his shop and works there until people are up and stirring around."

"So, there is no one here other than you?" Kennedy asks as he makes more notes in his little book.

"No."

"Okay," Kennedy says, making another note on his pad. "And you discover the missing cash box when you arrive at the office today?"

"Yes," Hershel replies. Getting a little frustrated, Hershel starts to repeat himself. "But like I said earlier, Carlos usually comes by early in the morning to pick up his list, but he seldom ever comes in the office. As I said before, he's a bit of an early riser. I didn't find the empty desk drawer until after today's golf game." He glances at his watch again and adds, "That was about an hour ago."

Kennedy raises an eyebrow. "You said the office door was locked, and your desk drawer was locked too when you arrived, and there is no indication of a break-in. So, Mr. Harper, how did someone steal your cash box?"

Detective Kennedy sits quietly for a minute to let Harper roll his question around a time or two. Then, his eyes narrow slightly as he prepares to scrutinize Hershel's reaction. His question is direct and unexpected, "Did you stage this as a theft to make it look like someone with a key other than you stole the money?"

Hershel's face turns confused, and he feels a wave of defensiveness in response to the question. "What are you implying, detective? I would never do something like that!"

Kennedy leans forward; his expression calm yet serious. "I'm just trying to gather all the facts here, Mr. Harper. Is there anyone else who might have access to the office and the desk?"

Hershel shakes his head. "No one else has a key to the desk." Still troubled by Kennedy's earlier question, he says, "I can assure you, detective, that I am incapable of...whatever it is you're thinking."

The silence between them is palpable, and Hershel can feel the tension in the air. He knows he has to tread carefully if Hershel wants to convince Kennedy that he is telling the truth.

Finally, Kennedy stands up, his expression still a mystery. "I believe I've gathered enough for now, Mr. Harper. However, I'll reach out again soon."

Kennedy turns without saying another word and quickly leaves the office.

As Hershel watches Kennedy leave, unease washes over him. The detective's probing questions and intense scrutiny make him feel like he is being accused of staging the theft.

What will this mean for my reputation and my future? He wonders if his friends and family will believe him.

A fundamental process among detectives is not to rule out anyone at a crime scene until all the facts are gathered. Kennedy is a skilled detective. Over his 20 years on the force, he has solved numerous cases. Kennedy does not dismiss Hershel Harper as a suspect.

Kennedy's notes indicate that Harper has full access to the office and the keys to the desk drawer. Mr. Morales, on the other hand, only has a key to the office door and is unaware of the amount of money in the cash box. This discrepancy raises further questions about his involvement. No one had broken into the desk. However, Mr. Morales knows the size of the condo complex and could assume a large amount of money is in the box each month. Does Mr. Morales possess a key that Mr. Harper is unaware of?

There are many questions to answer. Mr. Morales is next on his list to question.

As he walks across the sidewalk, Kennedy stops momentarily to speak with Officer Baker, the head technician from the Crime Scene Unit, before entering his car. The crime techs dust the desk for fingerprints. Kennedy watched them while he questioned Harper.

Baker confirms the mystery: the office door and desk drawer locks have not been forced open. They were picked by an expert or opened using a separate key for each. Only Mr. Harper has that set of keys.

An obvious question: Has Mr. Harper staged the office to make it appear like a theft? Is Mr. Morales involved in the staging, or is Mr. Harper trying to establish Mr. Morales as the primary suspect?

Since there is no evidence of a break-in, this event will go down in the official report as a theft, not a burglary. Detective Kennedy has much to mull over as he drives away from

Sunshine Casita Condo Complex. Kennedy thinks *both of these guys are high on my suspect list*. Now, I must find out if anyone else knows about the money, has access to the office, and knows Mr. Morales and Mr. Harper are the only ones generally there. It is time to canvass the residents, which is a long and sometimes challenging job.

With the police gone, Hershel leaves the office.

As he walks to unit #102, Hershel's thoughts race. The detective's questions echo in his head, making him question everything.

Wow, this will be a wild story to tell Ethel, but a pang of worry hits him. *What will she say? Will she believe me?*

As he reaches the turn on the sidewalk only a few yards from home, a dark thought preoccupies his mind. The detective's tone, manner, and type of questions make Hershel feel like Kennedy suspects him of staging the theft and trying to pin it on Carlos. The thought gnaws at him, creating a knot of anxiety in his stomach.

Will the theft of the money appear as a robbery I attempt to pin on Carlos?

Hershel has also learned something else that disturbs him.

Since moving to California, he has been astonished at the racial attitudes toward people of Mexican descent. In Iowa, Mexicans come in the Spring to work the nursery fields through Fall in the southwestern part of the state. They are honest, hardworking men who earn money to send home to their families. But here, even Mexican Americans are not trusted and are seen primarily as cheap labor. The difference in attitude bothers Hershel a great deal.

Hershel worries that this attitude will lead Kennedy to blame Carlos for the burglary simply because of the color of his skin. The thought weighs heavily on him.

After all, Carlos is the only other person with a key to the office. He comes early in the morning before anyone stirs to pick up his work orders, and he always has that tricked-out new car.

What happens next? Hershel wonders. *Am I going to be investigated? Will they arrest me? What will people think? Will this story get back to Iowa? What impact will this have on the grandkids? Will they be harassed at school by other kids saying their grandpa is a thief?*

Maybe telling Ethel the story will not be as easy and fun as I first thought, Hershel thinks. He feels a mix of confusion and fear as he inserts his key into the lock of unit #102 and slowly turns it to unlock the door.

What will I find on the other side of this door? runs through Hershel's troubled mind as the door lock clicks unlatched, the door swings open, and Hershel Harper steps into unit #102.

CHAPTER FOUR

Hershel enters condo unit #102, his heart heavy with the day's events that add to the feeling of foreboding he fights to keep far in the background. *Was today a forerunner of the future?* hangs over Hershel like a dark, black cloud.

Ethel, his ever-supportive partner, sits on the couch, watching something on the "boyfriend's" big screen hanging on the wall. Her presence always brings him a sense of calm. Despite his negative feelings, he puts on a happy face.

"Hi, sweetheart. What kind of thriller are you watching?"

"Gunsmoke," Ethel responds with a chuckle. "Old Festus is opining to the Marshal about what he needs to do."

"Yeah, old Festus is quite a character. He and Miss Kitty make a great pair," Herschel responds.

Herschel kisses her on the cheek, the familiar scent of her lavender perfume calming his nerves. He heads to the kitchen. As is his habit, he kicks off his shoes as soon as he walks through the front door. The cool tiles under his feet are a stark contrast to the warmth of the living room carpet. He pours a glass of iced tea from the pitcher they always keep in the fridge, and the clinking of ice cubes makes a soothing sound.

What am I going to tell her? swirls in Herschel's mind. *Is she going to think I am trying to pull something on her after all these years? Put on a happy face, Harper,* he tells himself.

With the glass of iced tea in one hand and a big red apple he spots on the kitchen counter in the other, Herschel returns to the living room and sits down on the couch beside Ethel.

"Man, did I have a fantastic golf game today! Best score I've ever shot," he brags.

"That's wonderful!" she answers with a glow in her voice. "Have you had anything to eat for lunch? How come you are so late getting home?"

"I had a great lunch at the club. The guys bought mine for me to celebrate my new low score," Herschel says as he takes a bite of the apple.

"Well, I can't believe that bunch of tightwads bought you lunch! They are the stingiest group of men I know. Certainly nothing like your friends back in Iowa," Ethel says.

Herschel laughs, "I guess I shamed them into it!"

He doesn't answer her question about being late coming home. He still does not have an answer he is comfortable with.

Then, he falls silent for a few minutes, pretending to be interested in Gunsmoke. "That old Festus is the best character on the show."

Ethel chuckles, "That he is."

Herschel's heart races as he decides he cannot wait any longer. Ethel needs to know, but how will she react? He takes a big drink of his iced tea, wishing it is something stronger, then starts to tell her the story.

"Something happens that is not as good as my golf game," Herschel begins nervously. "Somebody gets into the office and steals the cash box out of my desk. It has the receipts for all of last month in it. I was going to go to the bank to deposit them this afternoon."

Ethel's eyes widen in shock. "Oh no! Who do you think did it?"

"I don't have the vaguest idea." Herschel slumps in discouragement.

"I wondered what the police car was doing here. I happened to look up and see it drive in. I thought maybe there was a small fender-bender in the driveway I couldn't see from here," Ethel says in a concerned voice.

Herschel continues telling Ethel about the incident, his words tumbling out in a rush. He recounts every detail, from Detective Kennedy's stern demeanor to the crime scene unit's meticulous work and the neighbors gawking at the police officer and the tech team. Each detail adds to the tension, making the reality of the theft sink in deeper. He tells her that some clues could possibly identify the thief.

Herschel continues, his voice steady despite the turmoil inside. "Another big question I have is how the burglars open the desk drawer without damaging it. They have to pick the lock or use a key or something like that." As far as Herschel knows, he has the only key to the desk drawer and the locked cash box inside. Carlos has a key to the office door but not to the desk.

"Oh," Hershel adds, "I said burglars. The detective said that since there was no forced entry it would go in the records as a theft. I've never heard that before. It doesn't make any difference to me; the money is gone whether it's a burglary or a theft."

This causes more significant questions in Herschel's mind, *who could have opened the desk drawer without damaging it? Is it an experienced burglar who knows how to pick locks? Or does Carlos have a key he has never told me about?*

Herschel's mind races with possibilities. *Could Carlos be involved? After all, those new, flashy automobiles he drives cost much more than his salary at the condo complex would allow him to afford.* Herschel makes a mental note to keep an eye on Carlos.

Hershel's curiosity about another desk drawer key drives him to action. There is one way to find out for certain about the key. Herschel picks up the phone, checks the little

44

notebook he carries with all his contacts in it, looks up and dials Carlos's number.

Cell phones were extremely rare in the 1980s, but Carlos had one of the new bulky portable units, thanks to Hershel.

Herschel decided to use some of the Condo Complex operating money to buy one of the newfangled Motorola portable phones. The first commercial unit came on the market on September 21, 1983. It was known as the "Brick," the name relating to the size of the unit. It was not a simple telephone to carry with you. The talk time was approximately 30 minutes, and it took 10 hours to recharge the battery. However, it did provide you with telephone service away from your landline.

Herschel had purchased a unit for Carlos to use at the condo complex. Since Carlos worked at various places on the sizeable property and there were times it was extremely important to find him, it seemed like a logical tool to use to contact him. It would certainly be faster than locating the condo unit he was working in on foot as they were currently doing.

The phone listed for $3,999, a hefty price to pay. However, Hershel calculated the Condo Association would save more than the cost of the phone as related to the time lost over a year trying to find Carlos.

Carlos's, new portable phone the condo company has given him rings several times before he answers. This is not unusual, many times he is working on an air conditioner or some other project and can't grab his phone and respond instantly.

When Carlos finally answers, before Herschel can say anything, Carlos asks in an excited voice, "Señor Harper, do you know police have been here? Detective ask many questions. He found me working on #165-unit air conditioner."

"Yes, Carlos, I assume you know someone stole all the

money from the office," Herschel says. "Did you see anyone hanging around the compound? Someone who isn't supposed to be here?"

"No, Señor Harper, I no see anyone not belong here. I know all garbage men and others come service our community, no, no one strange."

"No one, I don't know," Carlos continues.

"Carlos, do you have a key to the desk drawer in the office?"

Carlos quickly answers, "No."

Carlos continues, "Before you move here, Mr. Fisher in charge of the office. He bad man; we not get along well. He force me give him my key office door. I get key back after he sell his unit and move away. For me, feliz…. happy day when his moving truck pull out driveway."

"He leave key on desk. I pick up and close office. When people from condo company big office come collect monthly payments, tell me keep key and use office if I want."

"I no use office key till you come; all my work outdoors. People leave complaints for me in maintenance shed. No, Señor, I no have key to desk."

Herschel believes Carlos is telling the truth. However, he feels it would be better to talk to him face-to-face and probe a little deeper. He also wants to see if there is anything he has missed that Carlos may have seen or knows about.

"Carlos, how about if I come over to your maintenance shed and we talk about this a little more?"

"Si, Señor, I be 10 minutes. I finish plumbing repair Mrs. Cartwright's kitchen."

Hershel hangs up and turns to Ethel, "Sweetheart, I'm going to meet Carlos in the maintenance shop. I'll probably be back in an hour or less."

"Don't be any longer, as I will have supper ready by then," Ethel responds.

Hershel gives Ethel a soft kiss on the cheek as he goes out

the door to meet Carlos.

She knows he will be ravenous after his day on the golf course, plus the excitement of the theft of his office. Ethel decides, no frozen TV dinner tonight. *I have a chicken I bought to fix for Sunday dinner when Marlene and the kids are coming over. I will surprise him with his favorite meal: fried chicken with mashed potatoes and a big dish of chocolate ice cream for dessert. After the stressful day he's had, that should bring a smile to his face when he gets home after talking with Carlos. Yes,* Ethel tells herself with a satisfying smile. *It is going to be a great evening.*

Little does Ethel know that fate has a special dessert planned for her, one that does not have a cherry on top or taste good and will change forever, everything in her life.

CHAPTER FIVE

As the clock ticks past 6:00 p.m., the mouth-watering aroma of fried chicken and creamy mashed potatoes fills the cozy condo. However, Ethel's anticipation gradually morphs into a gnawing unease with each passing minute of Hershel's unexplained absence. Where is he?

Ethel has worked hard to prepare the meal. She wants it to be perfect. She smiles and thinks, *Yes, it will be a great meal and an exciting evening discussing all that happens today. There will be plenty of good conversation. Hershel will be speechless when he gets his first whiff of the surprise supper I fixed for him.*

Ethel sits on the couch for a couple of minutes, then gets up and walks over to the patio door. From there, she can see the sidewalk leading to the door of unit #102. It is empty. There is not a person in sight.

6:45 p.m. passes, and Hershel has yet to return from the meeting with Carlos. The fried chicken was ready to eat half an hour ago. Ethel's fingers drum on the table, her eyes flicking to the clock every few minutes. She tells herself not to worry, but the knot in her stomach tightens with each passing second. Hershel is often late, but not this late. She wonders what he and Carlos are discussing. She reassures herself he will be here soon, trying to shake off the growing sense of unease.

"Hershel, where are you?" Ethel asks the flowers in the vase she is messing with for no particular reason. A whiff of the fried chicken takes her attention to the table. *I worked hard on this special meal for you and don't want to lose it.*

As an occasional trip to McDonald's is their idea of "eating out," this meal is unique. "Darn it, Hershel Harper! Where are you? I'm never going to McDonald's with you again," Ethel says in aggravation at the beautiful meal before her.

She cannot help but feel a pang of worry and frustration.

Ethel leaves the table, walks over to the glass patio door, and peers out again. The sidewalk leading to unit #102 is still empty.

By 7:45 p.m., Hershel is still gone, and Ethel's frustration has blossomed into full-blown worry. Her anxiety spikes, and an unshakable feeling of dread settles in her chest. She waits, her patience wearing thin. She covers the chicken, potatoes, and other cooked food on the table and moves it into the refrigerator. *I don't want to lose this meal; I can warm it up when Hershel comes home.*

You are never this late. You have never done this to me before! Ethel's fear turns into panic. Dark thoughts consume her mind, and her heart races more every second.

Ethel can hear the clock hanging on the wall tick, each second bringing more agony as she walks around and around the empty table where her beautiful meal had rested in wait for Hershel. Each time she circles the table, it brings her to the patio door, filled with diminishing hope. She stops, looks out, and down the sidewalk; there is still no Hershel each time.

It has been three long hours since Hershel left for his meeting with Carlos; still, there is no sign of him. The air in the condo unit seems to vibrate with tension as Ethel's desperation turns to torment. *I can't stand this much longer! If I don't hear from you in a few minutes, I am going to see if I can find you. You just have never treated me like this. I hope you're OK, sweetheart.*

As the clock ticks past 9:00 p.m., Ethel's worry turns into determination. She has to find Hershel. She knows he and

Carlos are supposed to meet in the maintenance shop at the back of the condo complex property, but something feels terribly wrong. Now it is dark outside. Nerves on edge, she grabs a flashlight out of a cabinet drawer in the kitchen and leaves unit #102.

She feels uneasy about walking to the shop. *I'm going to drop by the carport and pick up the car.* Walking down the sidewalk, she thinks driving to the shop will be faster and safer.

Ethel enters the carport and sees an empty space where the car should have been parked. *What? Hershel's car should be here! Where is it?* This adds more panic to her already high-tension condition. With a mounting flutter of worry in her chest, she wonders if Hershel has taken the car to his meeting with Carlos. *But that seems like a strange choice for him. He loves to walk.*

There was only one way to find the answers to the many questions now swirling in her mind. Those answers were in the maintenance shop. Without a car to drive, there was but one way to get there: walk.

Ethel takes a deep breath to help some of her anxiety subside. *Well, here I go!* With her flashlight in hand, she begins walking to the back of the condo complex. The first portion of the walk is down the sidewalk, running the depth of the complex buildings. The accent lights mounted high on the sides of the complex buildings illuminate it well, and additional light comes from the nearby streetlights.

This isn't as spooky as I thought it would be. It's enjoyable. Constantly checking everything around her, something she has learned since moving to the big city, Ethel becomes more comfortable with each new step. *This could be fun if I just knew what's going on with Hershel.* The sidewalk ends at the back of the building. She must now walk across the nearly deserted, dimly lit rear service parking lot. The maintenance shop is at the very back of the property, backed by heavy shrubbery separating the complex from a service road. It is in a dark and spooky place.

Ethel flips on her flashlight. *Oh gosh, this thing isn't as bright as I thought it would be!* Her footsteps on the asphalt echo hauntingly off the nearby dark buildings.

Wow, those footsteps sound like someone is walking along with me. I don't like it, Ethel thinks. Her apprehension rises to number ten on her nervous scale.

She gives a sigh of relief as she reaches the door to the maintenance shop. Looking through the window at the door, *What? There is no one here! Not even a night light! Where are those guys?*

The shop is as dark as a tomb! She grabs the doorknob and twists it. Locked! She sees no sign that Carlos or Hershel are in the shop.

Where are they? They should be here talking. What do I do? I don't have Carlos's phone number. I need to get out of here and return to our unit, she tells herself in near panic.

Fear rapidly escalates to pure terror! She is alone at the back of a dark parking lot. Carlos and Hershel are nowhere in sight. Hershel's car is not there. Suddenly, she hears a rustling noise in the shrubbery behind the shop; something big is moving back there! *Man, or beast, is that thing coming after me?*

What in the world is it? I need to get out of here! There have been reported cases of women being attacked when they walk in this neighborhood at night. Now in full terror mode, Ethel starts running across the parking lot to the safety of the lighted sidewalk on the other side. Approximately halfway across the lot, her left shoe flies off, but she ignores it and keeps going.

The heck with that shoe! I need to get to that lighted sidewalk! Her heart is pounding so hard she feels like it will burst. *Yes, only about twenty yards to the safety of the lighted sidewalk,* she tells herself. And then it happens. Ethel's foot strikes an unseen object in the dark! As she falls to the asphalt, the skin rips from her right knee. Her flashlight flies out of her hand, landing under an old pickup parked in the lot. She feels warm blood running down her arm. There is no time to worry about that; getting to the relative safety of the lighted sidewalk is all Ethel can think about.

Ouch! Where did that darn flashlight go?

I gotta get out of here! Ethel rolls over, jumps to her feet, and runs again. She ignores the intense pain in her knee and the burning injury on her arm, where a long piece of flesh is torn away. *I have to get to that lighted sidewalk,* keeps racing through her mind. She detects a metallic taste in her mouth. Blood has started to seep from a large cut caused by her cheek being smashed against her teeth when she hit the ground during her fall. The only thing that matters to Ethel is getting to that lighted sidewalk.

The few minutes it takes Ethel to cross the parking lot seem like an eternity to her. She reaches the start of the lighted sidewalk. *Yes, the lighted sidewalk! I'm going down there to that bright spot and get someone to call the cops!* Ethel, winded, bleeding, exhausted, and with her heart pumping 90 MPH, drops onto the grass strip between the sidewalk and the building, directly under the powerful accent light mounted high on the complex wall. As her heart rate returns to something near normal and she catches her breath, Ethel assesses her condition.

Oh my, where is my left shoe? There is blood running down my right leg, and, oh my goodness, the knee is swollen and look at that big old bruise! I must have fallen harder than I thought, Ethel tells herself. She becomes aware there is more damage to examine. Feeling a burning pain in her right arm, she discovers a place approximately 10 inches long, from the elbow nearly down to the wrist, which is missing skin. Feeling around inside her mouth using her tongue, *Ouch, there is a cut on my cheek; that must be where the blood is coming from. Yuck! I hate that copper taste! At least I don't feel any broken teeth,* she says to herself as she continues her damage check.

And then she looks at her dress. There are three rips in it. *Oh well, this is an old one I am cooking in, so that's no big loss. And I think the flashlight rolled under that old truck. Hershel can get it tomorrow;* her thinking continues as she finally approaches the end of her damage assessment.

Out of pure habit, she had grabbed her purse when she hurriedly left the condo. The purse did more than carry lipstick and perfume tonight. It landed where her left knee would have contacted the asphalt when she fell. Her knee landed on the purse. This undoubtedly saves her from damage to that leg. Ethel picks up the purse to look inside and see if all its contents are intact. "Oh, no, no!" she exclaims. "Look at the terrible scratches in the leather! Oh no!" she sobs as she holds her brand-new Calvin Klein purse to her chest with both arms. She has saved for months to buy it as a once-in-a-lifetime treat.

However, Ethel is not concerned about herself. *Where is Hershel?* Sitting on the ground with her back against the building, Ethel thinks, *how will I call the police? I know there isn't a phone booth anywhere close. What am I going to do?*

Ethel sat under the lights for five to ten minutes. She decided she needed to return to their unit as that was the nearest phone she could think of.

With a great deal of effort, she struggled to her feet. As Ethel attempted to walk away from the building, she nearly fell. Everything hurt, and she was very dizzy. She stood steadying herself against the building.

"Ethel! Ethel, is that you?" came a female voice behind her.

Ethel turns to see a friend who lives only four units down from #102. She is out walking her dog.

Rushing to steady Ethel and then help her sit back on the ground, "What happened to you?"

Ethel stammered a bit as she told Mrs. Donato the story of the evening and what led her to be sitting on the ground next to the building, all beaten up and bleeding.

"Will you call 911 for me?" Ethel asks.

"I certainly will, my dear," Mrs. Donato responds. "You stay right where you are, and I will be right back. Don't move!" With that, she and her dog take off down the sidewalk as fast as she can walk. Mrs. Donato wants to call 911 as fast as possible. Her friend Ethel is hurt.

Ethel does her best to get as comfortable as possible. She leans her head back against the wall of the building. Ethel's mind starts to race.

Something has happened to my Hershel. He has disappeared; I can't find him! Where is Hershel? Why has he disappeared? Has someone done something bad with him and Carlos? Why is all of this happening when everything has been going so well?

Serious questions, but will Ethel ever get the answers?

CHAPTER SIX

Mrs. Donato walks as fast as she can to her condo unit. Her dog seems to enjoy the livelier pace. Arriving at her unit, she quickly unlocks the door, unsnaps the dog's leash, and heads straight for the telephone.

"What's the big hurry?" her husband asks. Tony Donato was sitting on the couch watching TV. Two years ago, he retired after a 30-year career with the Bureau of Alcohol, Tobacco, and Firearms, or ATF, as most people refer to the agency.

"Oh, Tony, as I was coming up the sidewalk, I found our neighbor Ethel leaning up against the building. She was all beat up from falling while running across the back parking lot. She asked me to call 911; what I will do right now!" Mrs. Donato answered as she grabbed the phone and punched 911.

Their telephone is mounted on the wall in the kitchen. Tony gets up from the couch and stands near his wife. He wants to hear what she has to say and perhaps help her. Thirty years, carrying a badge and a gun sharpened his instincts, and he would immediately recognize trouble.

"911," the 911 dispatcher said. "What is the address of your emergency?"

"My name is Amina Donato, and we live in unit 109 at the Sunshine Casitas condo complex. I found my friend Ethel Harper sitting on the sidewalk beside our building. She has been hurt, and she needs the police and an ambulance."

Following a couple of questions, the 911 dispatcher tells Amina that the police and the ambulance are en-route to their address. Amina hangs up the phone and turns to her husband, "Tony, I'm going back to stay with Ethel until the police arrive."

"I'll go with you," Tony says as he puts the dog in its kennel.

As the Donatos leave their condo, Ethel's thinking is abuzz with questions

Where is Hershel? What could have caused him to vanish so suddenly?

Determined, Ethel gets up from the condo wall she is leaning against. She has to find her husband of 46 years, no matter what it takes.

Ethel paces back and forth along the sidewalk as best she can with her damaged knee. Her mind races with questions. Something is terribly wrong. *Hershel has never disappeared without a word.* A chill runs down her spine as she glances at the darkened parking lot where the maintenance shed is out of sight. The shadows whisper secrets she can't grasp.

What if he's in trouble? She thinks, her heart pounding. Little does she know that the events of the following few days will reveal more than she could ever imagine.

Where are the police? Ethel feels as though Amina left to call 911 an hour ago.

What is going on? What has happened to my dear Hershel, and why does it feel so important for the police to be involved?

The questions swirl in a vortex of uncertainty, leaving Ethel feeling lost and alone. She can't shake the feeling that she is missing something crucial; *there is more to this situation than meets the eye.*

Her thoughts are suddenly pulled away from all the questions regarding Hershel's disappearance as Mrs. Donato approach her.

"Amina, oh, thank you so much for calling 911! And Tony,

I appreciate you coming to help me, too. I know it hasn't been very long, but it feels like you found me an hour ago!" comes Ethel's nearly tearful, grateful answer.

Tony attempts to add a little cheer, "Ethel helps on its way." He glances at his wristwatch, "Amina made the call seven minutes ago. Can you tell me what has happened to you?"

Ethel tells her story as Tony listens with an attentive and wise ear. He hopes to pick up some clues from her recollection that will be helpful to pass along to the investigating officer.

The flashing blue and red lights pulling into a parking space at the end of the sidewalk are a welcome sight.

Why does he park with those headlights in my eyes? Ethel thinks as the police car parks.

Ethel hears a car door shut. Holding her hand up to shield her eyes from the police car's bright headlights, she sees a tall, muscular young man wearing a perfectly pressed uniform appear out of the lights.

"Are you Mrs. Harper?" he asks.

"Yes," she says with relief, "I am the one who called you. Well, it wasn't me but my friend Amina."

In a deep, mellow voice, he says, "I am Officer Hunt. Can you tell me what happened? Are any of these people involved?" as he sizes up the Donatos.

Before she can answer, Tony introduces himself and explains that he is a retired ATF Special Agent. His wife accidentally found Ethel leaning against the building; the three of them are friends. "And my wife made the call to 911."

Officer Hunt acknowledges Tony and his remarks and thanks him for being there. He once again turns his attention to Ethel. "Mrs. Harper, can you tell me what happened?"

Ethel hesitates momentarily, begins to shake a little, and starts to cry.

"That's OK, ma'am. Take your time and tell me what you

can."

"Well, this all started when my husband came home and told me the money had been stolen from his office. I guess whoever stole it didn't break in," Ethel stammers.

"I don't know how they could do that. Do you?"

"No, ma'am," Officer Hunt answers. "What else can you tell me? Why are you out here all messed up?"

"My husband and Carlos had a meeting in the maintenance shed back there," Ethel points into the darkness of the back parking lot. "My husband didn't come home, and the shed is dark, and I heard a noise in the bushes; I got scared and ran across the parking lot to the light here. I fell down," Ethel stammers to Officer Hunt."

"Who is Carlos?" Officer Hunt inquires."

"Carlos? Oh, he is our maintenance superintendent here at the condo." Ethel informs Officer Hunt that Hershel left for a brief meeting nearly five hours ago. His car is missing. She repeats her story regarding where he was supposed to meet Carlos, which is dark and empty.

Officer Hunt asks for more details.

"All I know is someone robbed the office today. My husband was playing golf and discovered it when he returned from his game," Ethel begins in a voice that sounds more settled than she feels. "Hershel told me a detective came to Hershel's office because the office had not been broken into, but all the money was gone. The detective wanted to know who had the keys, and he told him it was just him and Carlos Morales, the maintenance superintendent."

"After Mr. Harper came home, why did he leave the house?" Officer Hunt inquires.

"I think he wanted to talk to Carlos about the keys."

"Why would he want to do that?" Officer Hunt inquires.

"I'm sorry, officer, I'm a little rattled. I don't think they were both at the office at the same time. I think Carlos came up after he left, or maybe he was there before Hershel showed up and left. I, I don't know," Ethel answers. The pain from her knee, arm, and jaw is starting to be felt as the adrenaline wears off.

"All I know is my Hershel wanted to meet with Carlos at the maintenance shed and talk about the theft of the money," Ethel says, almost crying.

Tony has positioned himself out of the way yet in a position where he can hear clearly every word Ethel speaks while observing her reactions to Officer Hunt's questions. As he listens, he thinks, *This officer is very good for a patrol officer. I would not be surprised if he became a detective very soon.*

Noticing her torn dress, bleeding arm, and missing shoe, the young officer asks her, "Ma'am, were you attacked or in some kind of an altercation?"

"No," she says. "I fell running across that darn parking lot in the dark. Something was chasing me. I don't know; I guess I stumbled over something and fell. My flashlight flew out of my hand and slid under an old truck. I just got up and kept running as hard as I could until I got here."

As Ethel answers Officer Hunt's questions, he can't help but think how much she reminds him of his Mother. Her voice is very similar; she talks in the same speech patterns, and her anxiety over Hershel is much like the time his dad did not come home when he should have.

Ethel's anguish and reaction to this occasion are exactly like Officer Hunt's Mother's. They did not find Officer Hunt's father until the following day. In a freak accident, a tire blew out just as he pulled onto an old bridge. The blowout caused his car to swerve violently to the right. It quickly crashed through the ancient guardrail and into the river below. The vehicle is totally submerged and difficult to see. A week after his father's funeral, his Mother passed away from a cancer she had been fighting for years.

Yes, the longer he talks to Ethel, the more she sounds like his Mother, who he lost only six months ago. The grief is still raw, and Hunt turns away from her several times so she would not see him wipe away the occasional tear that comes to his eye.

Officer Hunt saw the blood dripping down Ethel's arm when he first pulled up. Now he looks at her severely bruised knee, which is badly swollen. In addition, the tears in her skin drip blood down her leg.

A second police car rolls into the parking lot.

The car's driver is Hunt's Sergeant, who had been patrolling a few blocks away. Sergeant Steinmeier's practice is to cover the patrol area of an officer under his supervision to permit them to take a break. This allows the four patrolmen under Steinmeier's supervision to take a break while keeping the entire Adam district covered with an officer at all times during the graveyard shift. Sergeant Steinmeier believes this is the best way to protect all the people throughout the night.

The Adam district is a densely populated eighty-one-square block area with a few residences, small businesses, and a three-block strip of door-to-door bars. On Saturday nights, it is a busy place. Eighty-one square blocks are plenty of real estate with all they have to keep track of. The Sergeant and his assigned four officers have their hands full, especially on Saturday night.

Officer Hunt asks his Sergeant if he would radio for an ambulance. Mobile two-way radios that could be worn clipped to an officer's belt did not flourish in the law enforcement community until the late 1980s. In 1984, the only method to contact the central police station was the two-way Motorola Radio mounted in the patrol car. They are big, clunky, and work most of the time.

"That won't be necessary," Tony speaks up. "My wife did that when she called 911."

Steinmeier turns to where Ethel is still sitting, her back against the building. He joins Hunt and asks questions.

As the two officers question Ethel, she hears their words tumbling in a blur. Her mind struggles to keep up. She tries to piece together the events of the past few hours, but her thoughts are clouded by fear and uncertainty. All she knows is that she has to find Hershel quickly.

Officer Hunt inquiries about the relationship between Herschel and Carlos. Did they work together well? Were there any problems between the two? Did they share any common interests? Was there anything unusual about them or their relationship? Why are they having this meeting? Did they have a favorite bar where they hung out? Where did Carlos live? Did she have Carlos's contact information? And the list goes on.

Ethel does her best to answer the police officer's questions. It is difficult, as her worry about Herschel is paramount. *Where did he go? And why did he go?* These questions keep circling in her brain, making it difficult to think clearly. She hopes she is giving the officers the information they need.

As the policemen finish their interview, an ambulance enters the parking lot. With all the flashing lights, for just a moment, Ethel thinks this place looks like a circus. The commotion has also drawn a few onlookers.

Once the ambulance has parked two people emerge and head up the sidewalk to where Ethel is sitting.

"Did you fall?" asks the nurse.

"Yes," Ethel answers.

The nurse looks over all her wounds.

She cleans the dried blood off of her knee and arm. She applies clean bandages. The ambulance driver notices a few cuts on her head hidden in her hair. A small amount of blood has coagulated barely inside the hairline over her left eye.

Due to the cuts, which indicate her head had probably struck the asphalt when she fell, which could cause a concussion, plus the rapid swelling and discoloration of her knee, the nurse tells Ethel they are taking her to the hospital. She needs proper observation and treatment. Ethel resists, saying she is OK and needs to return to her condo to see if she can locate Hershel and Carlos.

"Besides," she says, "I do not have a way home from the hospital. Hershel has the car, and I don't have enough money with me to pay for a cab. No, I'm not going!"

Officer Hunt had been standing unnoticed near the back of the ambulance while Ethel was being cleaned up and bandaged. As a result of his becoming attached to Ethel because of her close resemblance to his Mother, Hunt does something totally out of character and probably against department regulations on impulse. He says, "Mrs. Harper, I will take you home during my coffee break, which I have not yet taken. The hospital is right on the edge of my district, so I will have plenty of time."

Ethel turns toward the young officer to protest; however, before she can get a word out of her mouth, Sergeant Steinmeier steps into the light at the back of the ambulance and tells her in a stern voice, "Yes, you are going to the hospital, and I will bring you home. My schedule is more flexible than Officer Hunt's. As soon as you are cleared to be released, I will come by the hospital to pick you up and take you home. I want no arguments. Enough has happened to you tonight."

Steinmeier has an ulterior motive. He believes after the initial excitement of the evening subsides while Ethel is at the hospital, she will quiet down. Perhaps she could remember more about what happened that night.

Steinmeier knows he can question her in a more relaxed and quieter environment in his police car on the way home. Any information he gathers will be passed along to the detective assigned to the theft, Detective Kennedy.

Ethel leans back on the stretcher and relaxes a little as the EMTs push her inside the ambulance. The doors close, and the ambulance rolls away from the scene. It is after midnight.

One thing is evident in this chaotic, disorienting world: Ethel has to find Hershel. *But where has he gone? What has happened to him?*

Little does she know what the next few days hold for her. Herschel's disappearance will be more shocking to her than anything that has ever happened in her life. Ethel has some tough days ahead, days far more difficult than she could ever imagine.

CHAPTER SEVEN

Following a night filled with fear and uncertainty, Ethel's relief at the hospital's findings is fleeting. The gnawing worry about Hershel's fate overshadows any comfort she might feel. As she lies in the sterile hospital bed, her mind races with questions. Where is Hershel? What has happened to him? Despite the bumps, bruises, and abrasions, Ethel checks out fine at the hospital. There are no broken bones, but the emotional scars run deep. The unanswered questions and the haunting memories of the night before left her feeling more fragile than ever.

"Mrs. Harper, all your x-rays and the MRI came back fine," says the nurse standing at the foot of Ethel's hospital bed. "The doctor wants to keep you overnight just for observation due to the concussion you have suffered. Okay?"

"I don't want to spend the night here," Ethel tells the nurse in no uncertain terms. "I'm fine, and I'm going home!"

"I don't think that is a good idea," says the nurse sternly. "You've had quite an experience tonight. You have several injuries, and the worst one is the concussion from your fall. It's just one night. This isn't the Conrad Hilton, but we will make you comfortable."

"There is no reason to stay here," Ethel protests. "I can go home."

She swings her feet out of bed and prepares to stand up.

That's when she gets the message. Everything in her body screams when she moves. Ethel doesn't remember ever hurting this bad, even when she had played basketball in high school and had taken some hard licks.

"Okay. I think I will stay," Ethel says as she starts the painful process of getting her feet back in bed. The nurse comes around the side of the bed to help her. Ethel slowly lies back and stares at the ceiling for a few moments.

After several minutes of wiggling around, Ethel finally gets herself as comfortable as possible. She can see out the window if she turns her head to the right. Ethel thinks the lights of the city are beautiful. She then turns back to talk to the nurse, who hands her a small paper cup containing two pills. "Well, aren't these cute," Ethel says in an attempt to be funny. "And would you look at that! They are color coordinated." One is a white capsule, and the other is a large blue pill. "I guess the big blue pill must be the guy, and the little one is his date. Hand me the water, please, and I will send these two off on their little swimming date."

The nurse gives Ethel a loving pat on the back of her hand.

"You are going to be fine, honey. I will be here all night, and if you need something, push that little button," the nurse says, pointing to the "call nurse" device fastened in a handy position on the side of her bed.

"Call me if you need anything," the nurse says as she leaves the room, turning off the lights and gently closing the door.

In the quiet darkness, Ethel mulls over everything that happened today. The trip to the hospital bothers her. She frowns, disappointed that she has to spend the night here and misses the chance to ride home with Sgt. Steinmeier. Despite everything, she can't help but think that riding in a police car might be fun, especially if you're not wearing handcuffs.

Whatever the nurse gives her with that shot in the arm and the two pills quiet the pain. She slips off into a restful sleep.

Morning comes, and a beam of sunlight streams into her room through a window that could use someone with a brush and water spending a little time washing it. Ethel stretches out in her bed. Oh boy! Is she ever stiff and sore? Every bone and muscle in her body screams, "Ouch!"

Thoughts of escape from this hospital prison run through her mind, but they are interrupted when a gentleman dressed in a suit that looks like it has seen better days walks into her room. Indeed, Ethel thinks, this cannot be the daytime doctor.

No, it is not the doctor. Showing her his badge, the gentleman introduces himself as Detective Kennedy.

"Mrs. Harper, I am working on the theft report at your condo. I'm sorry to bother you here at the hospital. I know you are going through a difficult time, and I hope you don't mind if I ask you a few questions."

"No," Ethel responds, curiosity evident in her voice. *What could a detective want from me? It's supposed to be the other way around. I need his help to find Hershel. This feels all backward.*

"Mrs. Harper, yesterday I talked with your husband and Mr. Morales. They were both very cooperative," Kennedy tells her.

"I was informed of Mr. Harper's disappearance following the theft and want to ask you a question or two. Perhaps you can provide me with some information that may be helpful," Kennedy says.

"Okay, are you working on finding Hershel?" Ethel asks.

"I will not search for him personally, ma'am, but the information I gather has been and will continue to be passed along to the other detectives and officers in our department. We have also passed out bulletins to the news media. We also contacted other law enforcement here in Santa Ana and Orange County," Kennedy tells her.

Ethel feels this is good news and relaxes a bit. She is sitting up in her bed, and the detective has sat in the combination chair-recliner in the corner of the room. Kennedy has his notepad on the arm of the chair, making it easy for him to write.

"Ma'am are you and Mr. Harper having any marital difficulties or problems of any kind?" asks Kennedy.

"No," Ethel answers quickly and emphatically. "We have never had any problems, detective. I resent that question!"

"Sorry, Mrs. Harper. I am just looking for any reason Mr. Harper might be missing. Are you facing any financial issues, borrowing money you can't pay back, or that sort of thing?" Kennedy asks.

Again, a firm "no" is Ethel's indignant response.

And the questions continue for another 45 minutes. By the time Kennedy concludes questioning her, she is thinking to herself; I wonder when he will get around to asking me about my days in Sunday school and the crush I had on Jimmy Brown!

Kennedy tells her he interviewed Carlos before coming to the hospital. He also posted a BOLO (Be On the Look Out) announcement on Herschel's car. Kennedy hopes someone will spot it very soon and report its whereabouts, which would help solve a portion of the case. He does not explain what that portion of the case might be.

"Mrs. Harper, thank you for your time," Kennedy says as he gets out of the chair. "I will be contacting you later."

Ethel has a look of disbelief on her face. A sense of dubiousness overwhelms her thoughts.

"You have a good day," Kennedy says as he walks toward the door.

Before he gets to the door, Ethel asks, "Would you please give me Carlos's contact information? My husband keeps all that information in his little contacts book. I have no reason to contact Carlos directly, so I don't have his phone number."

Kennedy pauses for a moment. The information gathered in an interview is confidential and only to be shared with other police officers assigned to the specific case. However, his nearly twenty years of police instinct tells him this could lead to a theory developing in his mind. Carlos might reveal something to her that he had not mentioned during his interview.

His meeting with Carlos had made him consider that Carlos might be the thief. Another possibility was whether there was a deal between Hershel and Carlos, as they were the only two with a key to the office.

Kennedy thinks for a minute and then says, "Here is Mr. Morales's telephone number." He scribbles it on a page of his notepad and tears it out, handing it to Ethel. "Mr. Morales said this was the number for his new-fangled portable telephone he used for work."

When he stops by to see her again, probably tomorrow, he will ask her about the contents of her visit with Mr. Morales.

As Detective Kennedy turns to leave, he and the doctor run head-on into each other in the hospital room's doorway. Kennedy excuses himself and continues down the hallway. His thinking is centered on who he will talk to and what he will do next. He has another idea he wants to explore.

Doctor Miller introduced himself and told Ethel she was discharged and could leave the hospital when she had transportation. He then gives her several recommendations for caring for her injuries at home, excuses himself, and leaves the hospital room.

Ethel immediately hits the call button by her bed. "Where are my clothes?" she asks when the nurse answers on the intercom.

Alright, I'm getting out of this place, Ethel thinks, as she breathes a sigh of relief, grabs the hospital phone by her bed, and calls a neighbor who lives in condo unit #104. Ethel knows she has a car and will come get her.

It's a new day, Ethel thinks. With a slight grin on her face, *I guess Sergeant Steinmeier's offer to take me home has expired.*

She feels a little disappointed as she thinks Steinmeier is a pretty nice guy, and she wants to ask him for help finding Hershel.

Less than forty-five minutes after Ethel finishes her call, the door to her room opens, and her neighbor steps in. "Hi, Ethel. What in the world are you doing here?"

Ethel explains her situation and shows the neighbor her swollen knee. "They thought I had a concussion, and they wanted me to stay here overnight. I guess that was to see if I would go crazy." She says with a little laugh. "Now, let's get out of here!"

"Well, I am more than happy I came here to take you home. Is what you are wearing the only clothes you have?" the neighbor asks as she looks at her torn dress.

"Yes," Ethel replies quickly. "Now, let's get out of here."

On their way home, they have a serious discussion about Hershel's disappearance. Ethel's neighbor finds the story difficult to believe. Things like this do not happen to good people, she thinks.

Thirty-two minutes after leaving the hospital, Ethel opens her condo door. The faint smell of fried chicken and other good smells lingers, reminding her of the special supper she had prepared for her dear Hershel.

For a moment, she stands looking out their big glass window. She can see people enjoying themselves at the swimming pool. A few birds are feeding in the yard. It is a beautiful, peaceful scene. However, the tranquil scene is blurred by the tears in her eyes. *Oh, Herschel, where are you? I love you so very, very much.*

Her hands tremble as she digs in the pockets of her dress, trying to find a tissue she thinks is there. It isn't. Almost in a daze, Ethel shuffles into the kitchen, where she finds a box of Kleenex on the counter.

And then, Ethel's mind turns to the events of the past 72 hours. There are many questions to be answered. She wants answers to them. Step one is to dig the paper out of her purse on which Detective Kennedy had written Carlos's portable telephone number. She finds the paper buried under her compact and lipstick. Number in hand, her fingers fly as she punches in the numbers on their landline house phone.

Carlos answers on the second ring. He just finished repairing a clothes dryer for Mrs. Carlyle in unit #417.

"Carlos," she asks hurriedly, "would you meet me somewhere? We need to talk."

"Si, Sra. Harper. Be glad to meet you anywhere," comes Carlos' response. "Where you want meet?"

They decided the best place was by the swimming pool. It is a beautiful day, and the large pool has several alcoves with chairs and tables under big umbrellas, providing privacy for their conversation.

Ten minutes later, they meet at the pool. Few people are there at this time of day. They find an empty nook away from everyone and sit in two chairs on opposite sides of the round glass-top table under the umbrella. Each one can watch for anyone approaching from either direction.

The theft of the money is the prime topic of discussion.

"What happened at the office, Carlos?" Ethel asks. "All Herschel told me before he left to meet with you was that someone had gotten in the office and taken all the money."

"Si, the money was stolen," Carlos says. "Big mystery, the office was not broken into. Everything fine." Carlos continues providing Ethel with all the details about the police and Detective Kennedy. He knows Hershel wants to discuss this with her over that wonderful dinner she had thrown away.

"Señor Harper, he was very curious how they got in office and desk without a key," Carlos tells Ethel. "No scratches on desk or door."

"What do you think, Carlos? Do you have an idea who would do this?" Ethel inquires.

"No. No, I have no idea. I never handle money," Carlos answers.

"Why did you meet with Hershel at the maintenance shed?" Ethel asks with great interest.

"Señor Harper, he wanted to talk about theft. He wanted to know if I had an idea who might have a key and robbed the money. He was very worried that someone at the condo was the burglar. We never had a chance to talk when the police were there. He thought the burglar was someone at the condo watching him, knowing he deposited money after everyone paid."

"Do you know where Hershel went after you had your meeting?" Ethel finally asks.

"No, he did not say he was going anywhere."

"Was he going to the mall to pick something up on the way home?" Ethel wants to know.

"No, he no say he want see if anything beside money stolen."

Carlos adds. "He said you be waiting for him when it time for supper, he need to get home."

Carlos is quickly thanked for his time, and then Ethel is gone. Walking back to #102, her mind is running 100 MPH. She has some detective work to do of her own.

CHAPTER EIGHT

With newfound determination, Ethel springs into action, donning her detective hat and drawing on the many skills she has honed while raising her children, especially during their rebellious teenage years.

What's going on here? Ethel wonders as she sits at the small table in the kitchen. The aroma of freshly brewed coffee adding a little comfort to the room. Ethel rests her finger on the handle of her second cup of coffee, which sits before her. As she gazes out the window with her mind racing far above the speed limit, she keeps turning the cup back and forth in its saucer. A light, cool breeze wafts in through the open window, seeming to provide comfort to Ethel as her thoughts swirl around a few central ideas.

Is Carlos involved in this burglary? The question keeps running back and forth in her mind. Hershel always says good things about him, and he trusts him.

She leans back in her chair and takes a big drink of coffee. Looking into the cup, she sees it is almost empty. *Do I really want cup number three? Why not!*

As she gets up from the table and walks over to the coffee maker, she keeps running one question through her mind, *Why do I have this feeling in my gut that Carlos has something to do with that darn theft? He doesn't seem like the kind of person who would do that.*

Ethel puts another pod of the new blend of Brazilian coffee

she bought at the grocery store in the Keurig coffee maker. She closes the lid, and the machine starts making its unique brewing noises. Ethel leans on the counter with both elbows, waiting for the coffee maker to do its magic. *Why would Carlos rob the money? He makes a reasonable salary for the work he is responsible for. The condo residents occasionally tip him after he fixes something for them.*

The coffee machine finishes brewing with its distinctive final gurgle, and the aroma of the new Brazilian blend fills the kitchen. She takes her fresh cup of coffee back to her chair at the table, holding it where she gets that beautiful aroma as she walks. *What does he need extra money for? Maybe that new red Chevy he gets every year? Hmm, how can he afford a new Chevy every year?*

Ethel takes a sip of her newly brewed coffee. She rolls the new coffee around in her mouth, enjoying its wonderful taste. *It has to be that car. We can hardly keep our old car running! But how does he afford it with the size of his family? They live in a nice home, and the kids are in a private Catholic school, and none of that is cheap.*

Ethel ponders this thought for a few minutes more as she takes two or three more drinks from her coffee. *I like Carlos. He has always been honest with me. No, it can't be him… But he has a key to the office, and he does have that very nice car… He sure could have done it.*

Ethel finishes her coffee and then sits quietly at the table. As she idly turns the empty coffee cup in her hand, her thoughts shift from Carlos to Hershel. Tears well up in her eyes. *Oh, Hershel. I love you so very much. Where are you? Please come home. I won't be mad. I love you!* Ethel breaks into a torrent of tears as she lays her head in her arms on the table. She sobs uncontrollably for nearly an hour.

Finally, the tears stop. Wiping the remaining moisture away and attempts to call Carlos at least every ten minutes. *Maybe Hershel has contacted him.* All her calls continue to go straight to his voicemail. She calls all his golfing buddies and anyone she can think of who interacts with Hershel. All have the same response: they have not heard from him and have no idea why he would run away or where he would go.

Ethel, now sick with worry, cannot eat and constantly fights her upset stomach by drowning it in cups of black coffee. It is not working, but the caffeine helps her keep thinking. She needs all the brainpower she can get. Hershel has to be found soon. Each minute without hearing from him drives her frustration and desperation higher.

Where are you, Hershel? keeps running through Ethel's mind. *I love you, and my heart is breaking, sweetheart. Please come home, sweetheart,* she thinks as she, once again, breaks into tears.

Another night passes without Hershel. At least she is home rather than at the hospital like the previous night. Sadly, being in comfortable and familiar surroundings does not have a soothing effect on Ethel. Everything she sees or touches reminds her of her precious Hershel. She lays down on the couch, hides her face in the pillow, and sobs uncontrollably.

It is nearing dawn on the second day since Hershel disappeared. Ethel is still lying on the couch when she finally falls into an exhausted sleep. It will not last long. Ethel is about to face something she will find more complex than anything she has ever experienced in her life.

CHAPTER NINE

Officer Hunt turns into the alley on the 17000 block of Cowan, his eyes scanning the surroundings as he quietly rolls up beside the rundown carport next to a loading dock. He checks it every night because it is a sleeping spot several habituals use as their bedroom. The area is quiet tonight and emits its familiar odor of rotting wood, wet cardboard, and the droppings of various nocturnal creatures that live hidden in the old cardboard boxes. The smell of human urine is also quite strong, along with the lingering scent from a rain shower that just ended a few minutes ago.

He aims his spotlight at the center of the junk under the old, sagging roof. Hunt flips the switch, the light comes on, and a couple of rats scramble out of the place. He can hear other critters scampering around in the boxes and debris. There are fewer wild creatures tonight than usual when he turns on his spotlight.

Officer Hunt swings his light over to the ordinarily empty parking place where the habituals typically sleep. "Well, what do we have here?" he says into the empty night. Tonight, something new is sitting in the parking space: an older Chevy Impala. Hunt has never seen a car there, so he quickly picks up his two-way radio mike, "Adam Four."

"Go ahead, Four," comes the rather crackly response of the dispatcher.

"Adam Four, in the alley of 17000 Cowan, and have an unknown vehicle. I need to run a license check on it."

"I'm ready to copy Four. Go ahead."

Officer Hunt transmits the vehicle license plate number to the dispatcher, who checks the stolen and missing car list he keeps close at hand.

He finds a match: Herschel Harper.

Officer Hunt vividly remembers his call from Mrs. Harper when she was in the parking lot behind the Sunshine Casitas Condo Complex.

Officer Hunt presses the button on his patrol car's two-way radio microphone again. "Adam Four."

"Go ahead, Four," comes the answer from central dispatch.

"Its twenty (location) is a lean-to parking spot behind 17501 Cowan."

"Roger, Adam Four," the dispatcher answers. "Anyone around it?"

"No," says Officer Hunt. "Detective Kennedy was working the case a couple of days ago."

"10-4," responds the dispatcher. "I'll check and see if Kennedy is on tonight."

"I'll be out at this address," Hunt tells the dispatcher as he opens the door and exits his patrol car.

Flashlight in hand, Hunt walks over to the back side of the car and shines his flashlight through the back window. Nothing of interest or out of the ordinary is there. He walks to the front window on the driver's side.

Nothing is out of order here. Whoa! Wait a minute. There are keys in the ignition switch. People do not park in a deserted place like this and leave their keys in the car.

Hunt does not want to touch the door handle to test whether the car is unlocked, as doing so could destroy evidence. He backs off from the door. The Crime Unit will handle entering the vehicle. Hunt walks around the front of the vehicle; seeing nothing, he turns to walk up to the passenger side. Nothing seems out of place. Hearing tires rolling over old asphalt, he looks up and sees the lights from a vehicle coming down the alley.

It is Detective Dewey West. Law enforcement has always been West's dream, starting as a nine-year-old child. He admires the police officer who patrols the block where he lives with his mother and older sister. His father passed away when he was only six years old.

Young Dewey always makes it a point to be outside when he knows an officer will be coming past. He waves at the police car, and the officer waves back. One day, the patrol car stops, and the officer invites Dewey to sit beside him in the passenger seat. As he slides into the seat, his eyes grow as big as silver dollars—their chat sends the young man floating back into the house. He has to tell his mom the story!

He knows he will be a police officer when he grows up, and his dream continues to grow. During his grade school and high school years, he read anything he could get his hands on regarding police work and how it functions. Yes, in his mind, he will become a police officer when he grows up.

However, there is something he has to do before following his dream. The Korean War is raging. Young men are being drafted into the military. Their mission is to support the South Koreans in the war for their country.

Following the conclusion of World War II in 1945, the 620-mile-long Korean peninsula in East Asia was divided into two political factions, separated by the 38th parallel. Both factions claimed authority over the entire peninsula. 1950, a war erupted to resolve the dispute, and it did not cease until 1953. Like many young men in the 1950s, West was drafted into the military. The US is supporting South Korea.

When he returns home from his tour of duty in the US Army, West immediately applies for a job with the Santa Ana Police Department. Fortunately, a new class of recruits is scheduled to start in three weeks. West completes the training and emerges as the top rookie in his class.

On graduation day, rookie Officer Dewey West is 24 years old. Today, a seasoned senior Lieutenant Detective West is 45. He pulls his unmarked car to a stop behind Officer Hunt's patrol car in the alley.

Hunt greets him with a warm smile. "Hey, partner," West says, extending a hand for a handshake. Their familiarity is rooted in years of working together on cases and building trust. Over the years, the two officers have consumed together a few cups of coffee and a donut or two during the graveyard shift break. After exchanging warm greetings, Officer Hunt briefs Detective West on his actions after arriving at the scene.

"The thing that caught my attention is the key in the ignition," Hunt tells West. "When I first saw the car, I thought it could be someone working in one of these businesses along this alley parked here. Then I saw the key in the ignition and knew that wasn't right."

"Yeah, I agree," says West. "People don't park cars in places like this and leave the key in the car. At least those folks who expect the car to be here when they get back."

"When I saw the key, I called dispatch, and they found the plate," Hunt tells his friend West. "As the old saying goes, the rest is history."

The two men enjoy a chuckle.

"Someone as savvy as Hershel Harper would not leave a car in a place like this if he intended to return later and expect the car to be here," Detective West remarks to Officer Hunt, "Maybe Harper dumps the car here and has taken off for someplace by himself."

"I don't know about that, Dewey. When I answered that call the other night when his wife fell running across that parking lot in the dark, she didn't indicate any problems. She is pretty desperate to find him," Hunt injects.

"You never know the secrets in people's relationships," Dewey answers as he dips his chin to better see in the car window.

Officer Hunt briefly chuckles, "Hey man, you are the detective. I'm just the lowly patrol officer driving around in the dark trying to find burglars, but you have someone to talk to and ask all those probing questions you learned in detective school."

They share a good-natured laugh.

Detective West reaches into his trousers back pocket, pulls out, and dons a pair of blue rubber surgeon's gloves. He slips them on his hands, opens the car's driver's door, reaches in, and removes the keys. Several scenarios are circulating in his mind. *Has the car been stolen from Hershel and ditched here?* He crosses that idea off, as it does not explain Hershel's disappearance. *No, it is something else.*

Another possibility is the one he has related to Officer Hunt: *Hershel wants to disappear, leaving no indication of his whereabouts. By not taking the keys to the car, perhaps Hershel hopes someone will steal it. This will help obliterate his trail of departure even further.* West ponders several other possibilities.

The two law enforcement officers move to the back of the car. Detective West places the car key in the trunk lock and turns it clockwise until he hears a click, and the trunk latch is released. The trunk lid pops open a couple of inches. An intense smell floods out, and the two officers gag. The veteran officers are taken aback as the trunk lid swings upward and open. What greets them is something neither expects.

CHAPTER TEN

The mystery surrounding Hershel Harper's disappearance is about to unravel. As Officer Hunt and Detective West open the Impala's trunk parked in the crumbling carport, they are confronted with a gruesome sight. Hershel Harper's body lies curled in a fetal position, a large pool of coagulated blood spreading from the base of his skull. Pieces of deteriorating brain tissue are also visible. The head is nearly destroyed by whatever caused the wound at the base of the skull. Add the pungent stench of death and the sickly-sweet odor of decaying blood and human tissue indicates Mr. Harper died a violent death.

Detective West, careful not to disturb any potential evidence, meticulously examines the body. Every detail, from the position of the limbs to the blood patterns, is scrutinized with a practiced eye.

"He was executed, gang-style," West says.

"There are two bullet holes in the back of his head. He never had a chance."

"Do you think he was shot here?" asks Officer Hunt, his voice tinged with curiosity and concern.

"Hard to say," Detective West replies, his brow furrowing. "He might have been executed elsewhere and then dumped here. Our homicide team will have to piece it together."

Officer Hunt watches as Detective West finishes examining

the trunk area around Hershel's lifeless body. He finds nothing unusual.

The new Motorola Cell Phones were too expensive for the city. They still relied on the two-way radio for communications.

Hunt goes to his car and reports the homicide over his crackling radio to the police dispatcher, requesting the Crime Investigation Unit, the coroner, and a detective from the homicide division to come to the scene. As he waits, his thoughts drift to his own family. He pictures them safe at home, nestled in their cozy living room, munching on popcorn and sharing laughter. The stark contrast between that warm, joyful image and the cold, grim reality before him is jarring.

He knows it will be hours before the scene is worked and the body removed. It is shaping up to be a long, arduous night.

Despite the late hour, with the clock ticking past 2:00 a.m., the flurry of police activity has drawn a small crowd of curious onlookers, their faces illuminated by the flashing blue and red lights.

"Alright, move over here," Hunt commands, his voice uncharacteristically harsh. He recognizes the group as the usual drug and alcohol abusers who frequent the alleys and vacant buildings. These habituals are familiar faces from Hunt's graveyard patrol.

Habituals is the name given to those living on skid row. For the most part, their brains have been fried from the overuse of alcohol and drugs. Most of them are only recognizable by a first name. The name habitual immediately identifies them to any member of the police department.

"Stay over here," Hunt instructs, pointing to a spot about 1,000 feet away across the alley. "Got it? If you leave, I'm calling the paddy wagon. It's a nice night, and you don't want to spend it in jail. Just stay put or go back to your usual spot. Understand? Otherwise, it's three hots and a cot for you."

Hunt returns down the dimly lit alley to the crime scene just as the sergeant and another officer from the neighboring Adam-Three district arrive. Together, they work to secure the area and keep an eye on the habituals, eyes wide with morbid curiosity, who have gathered. Let me rephrase that sentence. Those who are capable have eyes wide. Most are watching through a hazy stare. The coroner's vehicle rolls in, adding to the chaos around the crime scene.

An unmarked police car coasts down the alley and stops behind Detective West's vehicle. The driver's side door swings open with a creak, and Detective George Kennedy steps out, his silhouette illuminated by the car's interior light. He walks over to the back of the Impala, where Officer Hunt and Detective West stand, their faces etched with concern.

"I heard you found Mr. Harper's car on the radio," he says. "I'm the lead investigator on the theft at the condo complex where Harper lived. What did you find here?"

Detective West replies. "Officer Hunt spots the vehicle," as he points to the Impala, "during his routine patrol down this alley. We find the keys in the ignition, open the trunk, and discover Harper's body. It appears he was executed with two shots to the back of the head. We've questioned the onlookers, but none of them claim to have seen or heard anything. That's the gist of it."

"Did you uncover anything of interest?" Kennedy inquires.

"No," West replies. "It appears the car has been wiped down. Maybe the lab crew will find something, but it looks as clean as a freshly washed baby's butt."

Kennedy fills West in on the theft story and explains in some detail how clean the scene at the condo office was.

"Interesting," His voice filled with sarcasm. West adds. "Whoever commits the theft, and possibly Mr. Harper's, murder sure likes to keep their workspace sterile."

"It appears entry is gained using a key. The only two people with keys are Mr. Harper and the Maintenance Superintendent, Carlos Morales," Kennedy tells West as Hunt listens in.

"Their interviews provide little value," Kennedy says. "I think the only thing that might be of value is that both men have keys to the office and access 24 hours a day."

As their conversation continues, the coroner's van, the Forensic Unit truck, and another unmarked car roll onto the scene. The unmarked car contains Detective Charlie Soper, a homicide detective with 15 years of experience. Detective Soper is known as one of the best in the business. He is an old-school police officer, tireless in his pursuit of answers to the cases on which he works. Like a dog with a good bone, he wouldn't let anyone else have it and wouldn't give up until completely eaten. He solves 99.9% of his cases.

West has worked well with Detective Soper in the past.

"Hey, Charlie. It's been a while," West greets Soper, extending his hand for a shake.

"Hey West, good to see you. What's the situation here?" Soper asks.

West gives Soper a short briefing describing what he finds and doesn't find. Maybe the forensic team will find something.

The added lights, the arrival of more police officers, and the general commotion attract even more spectators. Detective West and Officer Hunt corral them over to join the other habituals, many of whom are now sprawled on the alley floor, either passed out, sound asleep, or somewhere in between.

A forensic lab technician meticulously dusts the entire vehicle for fingerprints. "Whoever was driving wiped everything down before they left," she remarks, her voice tinged with frustration. "This thing is as clean as a freshly bathed baby's butt." West grins and thinks where did I hear that before? "Whoever stole this car doesn't want to be found."

The coroner's team carefully lifts Harper's body from the trunk of the car. The three detectives immediately step forward, peering into the now empty trunk, searching for clues that might have been left behind.

A forensic technician taking pictures of the body and the trunk area asks them to step back for him to do the proper exam of the scene before it gets disturbed.

While waiting for the tech to finish his picture-taking, the detectives indulge in idle speculation. They piece together the story, starting with the theft at the condo, Herschel Harper's disappearance, and now the discovery of his body in a vehicle that has been wiped totally clean of fingerprints.

Carlos Morales has not been given an in-depth interview. They think he could possibly provide potential clues. Or perhaps he plays a role in the execution of Mr. Harper. He tells Detective Kennedy in his brief interview that he owns a Glock pistol he keeps for personal protection.

Detective Soper's instincts tell him he needs to interview Mr. Morales immediately. Does he have a motive to commit the burglary? He certainly has the opportunity.

Their discussion is interrupted by a lab technician working the car's trunk.

"I've got a promising piece of evidence," he announces, holding up a small plastic bag. Through the clear plastic, the detectives can see a cartridge case from a .45 caliber handgun.

"I think it's from a Glock," the tech adds. The unique elliptical mark left by a Glock firing pin is unmistakable to anyone in law enforcement. Smith and Wesson is the only other manufacturer using a firing pin with an elliptical shape.

The three detectives conclude Herschel has been executed, standing next to the vehicle with the trunk open. A single cartridge case ejected into the trunk unnoticed, and Herschel's body fell or was dropped on top of it. Unknowingly, the perpetrator or perpetrators of the crime left a brass fingerprint.

Now, the officers know it is up to the firearms examiner in the forensic lab to see if he can match the expended cartridge case to a known firearm and its owner.

The distinct microscopic scratches left on an ejected brass cartridge case are caused by tiny imperfections in a gun's chamber. These imperfections are created by machine tools that chatter during firearm manufacturing. As a result of the minute imperfections, every weapon has its unique signature. Those microscopic marks are what the firearms examiner will search for. The tracks in the brass.

Firearms examiners use powerful microscopes to observe and compare the markings on a cartridge case recovered from a crime scene with a cartridge case from a known firearm. If they find matching marks on the two cartridge cases, they can identify the gun that fired the bullet.

The bullets removed from Herschel's skull by the Coroner during his autopsy, if not too damaged, will provide additional evidence to identify the firearm used in the homicide. With the two bullets and the cartridge case, the firearms examiner has a high probability of making a match and identifying the weapon that fired them. The major challenge is finding that gun. There is a good chance the weapon has been used in another crime. Get a match, and the mystery murderer can be identified quickly.

Detective Soper is confident that a microscopic examination of the expended cartridge case and the bullets recovered from Hershel Harper's body will lead to a positive tie to Mr. Morales, his gun, and the murder.

Detective Soper tells the little group, "It's time to see if the laboratory can identify where these tracks in the brass will lead."

Once that information is turned over to the Orange County District Attorney, the trial date will be quickly set. It will then be followed by a jury trial to decide whether the evidence presented is strong enough to convict and send Mr. Morales to prison.

It does not happen.

CHAPTER ELEVEN

It had been a difficult day at the Sunshine Casita Condo Complex. When Carlos Morales arrives home, his first destination is a nice, hot shower. Carlos's wife, Maria, prepares supper in the kitchen. The wonderful aromas floating through the house put a smile on Carlos's face. Carlos thinks *this is a great way to end a tough day* and heads for the bathroom.

When Carlos finishes his shower, he plops down in his La-Z-Boy recliner and turns on the TV to watch the 6:00 PM evening news. His time for relaxation is about to be destroyed.

No sooner does he watch the weather forecast than the doorbell rings. *Who can that be?* Carlos thinks. He expects no one to come by his house that evening. It could be someone with a serious problem from the condo complex. That is the last thing he wants tonight! Grudgingly, he exits his comfortable, soft chair and walks to the door. When he opens it, Carlos does not recognize the man standing there.

"Hola, Señor," Carlos says. "You have a problem?"

The unexpected visitor displays a police badge from the Santa Ana Police Department. "I am Detective Charlie Soper. I would like to ask you a few questions about what you might know regarding Herschel Harper's disappearance. You were among the last to see him before he disappeared." Carlos is taken aback by the detective's presence and his request. Hesitantly, he invites Soper in and offers him a seat on the couch across from his comfortable La-Z-Boy chair.

Soper pulls his well-used notebook from his suit jacket pocket and comfortably places it on his leg. He needs a place to write. Anyone at the Santa Ana Police Department would tell you Soper's handwriting is terrible and hard to read, even when he has a suitable desk to write on. Notes written when Soper has no place to lay his notebook, such as taking notes while standing and questioning someone while he holds his little book in his hand, are more challenging to read than the prescriptions his doctor writes for the pharmacy.

Well aware of his terrible handwriting, he often jokes that he always wanted to be a doctor, but the handwriting school is as far as he got.

Detective Soper opens the conversation with a few general questions. His softball questions are to relax Carlos and make him more receptive to the hardball questions he will throw later in the interview.

Speaking in a relaxed, conversational voice, Soper asks, "Did your parents immigrate here from Mexico?"

"No, Señor, I came here alone," Carlos answers. "I heard about the American Dream; it made me want to come to America. I wanted to have a family and provide for them, you know. That is much harder in Mexico."

Soper's questioning turns from professional to more personal. "How did you hear about the American dream? What appealed to you most?" Soper asks.

"Oh, Señor," Carlos responds with a smile. "My amigo's padres go to work in the US in the summer. They send money home to their family and talk about how wonderful life is in America. I wanted to have a big family and be able to provide for them. I wanted my children to attend good schools, learn about being good citizens, and get special jobs that pay good money."

Detective Soper smiles silently to himself. Carlos continues in an excited voice before he can ask his next question.

"Some of my amigos' padres... uh... friends' fathers work in America. Each spring, they leave, go to a place called Iowa, work in nursery fields all summer, and come home in the fall. They like America very much. They send home money all summer long. Their family here lives much better than their neighbors."

Anxious to tell his story, Carlos continues with more excitement in his voice. "When I am a niño mayor, uh... older boy, I work in a restaurante, cleaning floors, washing dishes, and hauling out trash. One day, uh... I find a book a tourist drops and leaves on the floor—a book about George Washington, uh... Thomas Jefferson, Ben, uh... Franklin, and the American Constitution.

"I try to catch the tourist, but they uh... have already left. I keep the book and take it home to read—it is in English. I don't know English. The only English I hear is on TV and from tourists talking in the restaurante. I try to read the book. I can't read it. I decide to try to learn English."

Carlos explains to Soper that he watches a Mexican children's TV show in Spanish, which displays the English translation as a subtitle on the screen. He thinks he can learn English by watching children's TV programs, the news, and anything else with English subtitles. He lives in a popular tourist area for Americans, so many English subtitle programs exist.

"Hear an English word on TV, see the Spanish word written on the TV. Learn to say uh… the English word. Find the word in the book. It takes uh… a long time to read the book," Carlos explains.

"Learned much about America, how it got started. More excited with each word I read," exclaims Carlos. He enjoys telling Detective Soper his story about why he came to America.

"How did you get here?" Detective Soper asks.

Carlos's mind suddenly shifts to a cautious gear, wondering if the detective suspects him of being in the country illegally. Does this man think I am here illegally, and he wants to send me back to Mexico, flashes through Carlos's mind.

"Crossed the border at Tijuana," comes the response in a firm voice. "All legal, Señor. Went through American customs. All legal. No sneaking here!"

"Studied hard, took the prueba… uh… test, raised my right hand, and promised to be a good American. They told me… uh… now I am a US Citizen. It is a feliz day! A happy day!" Carlos adds in a proud, happy voice.

Detective Soper enjoys the story. What Soper observes from the appearance of Carlos's home is that Mr. Morales is a hard worker and a good provider. He scribbles roughly legibly, writing the essential points in his notebook.

Soper's next goal is to determine Mr. Morales's honesty level, which is essential to any interview. Soper also wants to establish Carlos's relationship with Herschel Harper, the only other person with a key to the office.

"How did you know Mr. Harper?" Soper asks.

"He is my boss at Sunshine Casita," Carlos answers.

"How long did you work for Mr. Harper?" is the next question from Soper.

"I work at the condo for five years before Señor Harper becomes the manager," Carlos explains. "I am the Maintenance Superintendent the whole time Señor Harper is there. Uh… almost four years. Señor Harper disappears uh… before… uh… four years end."

Soper wonders if there might be something more in Mr. Morales's background that could have given him a motive to rob the money. There is only one way to find out; ask more questions.

"What did you do before you went to work as the Maintenance Superintendent at Sunshine Casita?" Soper asks.

Carlos explains that he worked at Burns Chevrolet, one of the largest car dealerships in Santa Ana. His job is running the car wash rack. As a courtesy and subtle way to keep customers returning, the dealership offers their customers free car washes. Carlos says one customer, Mr. Black, takes advantage of the free car wash and vacuums his car every Saturday morning. Over time, they become friendly.

Sensing Black is the person who hires Carlos to work at Sunshine Casita, he asks, "Is this Mr. Black the person who hires you away from the dealership?"

"Si," answers Carlos. He tells Soper that one day, when his car is in the shop for a minor repair, Arnold Black, the Sunshine Casita Condo Complex manager at the time, casually mentions to his favorite mechanic that he needs a good maintenance superintendent. The mechanic immediately thinks of Carlos.

"Why you?" Soper asks.

"Oh, Señor Miller tells Señor Black he thinks I am a buen hombre… uh… good man for the job. Señor Miller says I help him do mechanic work. He… Carlos helps me do plumbing and electric work in the hogar… uh… home.

Carlos is a buen hombre for the job. Uh… good man for the job."

Carlos tells Soper that one Saturday, during his routine car wash at the dealership, Mr. Black asks Carlos if he is interested in a new job. He explains that this role will offer a higher salary and more favorable hours. Mr. Black proposes that Carlos take on the position of Maintenance Manager for the Sunshine Casita Condo Complex.

"I think about job for a week," Carlos says. "Señor Black comes for his Saturday wash. He asks me what I decide. I tell him si. We are both very happy."

Carlos says he asks Mr. Black why he has chosen him for the job, and he tells him one of the dealership's mechanics has recommended him.

Soper makes the appropriate notes in his terrible handwriting.

In multiple interviews immediately following the theft and disappearance of Hershel Harper, with people living in the Sunshine Casita Condo Complex, Detective Soper discovers that Mr. Morales buys a new red Chevy every year, equipped with lots of chrome and all the latest gadgets. Detective Soper thinks, Where does he get the money? This could be the motive behind the burglary.

Soper probes further. He asks Carlos how much he earns as Maintenance Superintendent. Do any residents pay him extra when he fixes something for them? Is there another source of income he has not revealed?

Detective Soper is convinced Mr. Morales has a motive to steal the money to pay for his new car. Smelling blood, Soper digs deeper. The answers to those questions raise Soper's suspicions even higher.

"Carlos," Soper asks, "How do you pay for a new car every year? You don't make that kind of money."

Carlos's answer surprises Soper, who shifts his position on the sofa and wonders what other weird turn this investigation will take. The investigation is starting to feel like a night drive in heavy rain down a dirt mountain road filled with curves and sharp drop-offs into dark canyons.

Carlos shares that working at the car dealership is his first real job after becoming a US citizen. As he explained to Soper earlier, Carlos also operates the dealership's car wash. He performs some minor mechanical tasks while managing the wash. Carlos works a second job at a popular restaurant.

Carlos tells Soper that during the slow times at the wash, he assists some mechanics with simple car jobs, such as changing air filters, replacing burned-out light bulbs, and other minor repairs.

Detective Soper presses forward. "Carlos, how much do you make?" The response he receives is far from what he anticipates.

"I don't get paid," Carlos responds.

"You don't get paid?" Soper asks in surprise.

"Señor Burns owns the dealership. He is a very bonito hombre… uh… good man," Carlos goes on. "He pays me with a car instead of money."

This comment holds Soper's attention better than superglue! He has never heard of such an arrangement, and if Carlos is getting paid with a vehicle instead of money, how is he buying food to eat and a place to sleep?

Soper asks, "If you aren't getting paid, where do you get the money to eat?"

Carlos responds, "I am not married when washing cars. I don't like to party, and I have a second job. Cuando… uh… when I need a car, Mr. Burns, who owns the concesionario… uh… uh… dealership, loans me a used car. The price is minimo, and he takes a pequeño amount from my paycheck every week. I buy food with the money from cleaning the restaurant."

With a prideful look, Carlos says, "Entonces, one day, I have idea. I ask Mr. Burns if he pays me with a car instead of money. We discuss it for long time, and he says si."

"I start working without pay. I live off second job. End of year, Mr. Burns... uh... how do you say... adds up how much I earn. He tells me pick cheap car when new model comes in. The car price has to match my salary. I buy red Chevy Impala. Red favorite color."

Okay, Soper thinks as he scribbles more totally unreadable notes in his notebook. Carlos's answers raise several questions in Detective Soper's mind. Could he be a burglary suspect because he needs money? His financial situation has changed since he left Burn's Chevrolet dealership. This leads Soper to ask another question.

"You do not work at the Chevy place anymore but still drive a new car every year. Your salary from the condo complex doesn't seem to be enough to allow you to buy a new car, live in this nice home, and enjoy the lifestyle you are living.

"Where do you get the money for the new car?" Soper asks.

"Oh," Carlos responds. "I still work at the car dealership. Mr. Burns lets me work evenings and weekends. He gives me good trade-in value each year. I take a pequeño amount from my paycheck here buy extras to put on car."

Soper thinks that could blow my motive theory, but I need to check it out with the car dealership. He continues questioning Carlos about his relationship with the people at the complex. Soper thinks that Mr. Morales gets along very well with the people. They like and trust him.

Carlos tells Soper that when condo residents have a problem, they give him a key to their condo when they leave or go to work. This allows Carlos to enter the condo unit, be alone during his repair work, lock the unit when he is finished, and return the key to the owner when they return home.

Soper jots a note in his book to re-canvas residents and confirm or deny Carlos's story.

Then come questions about the office door and desk drawer keys. Carlos explains that Mr. Harper often tapes his worksheet to the office door's glass. It is faster for him to grab the sheet and go to work rather than waste time using his key to open the office, go inside, and pick up his list of jobs for the day.

"Carlos," Soper asks. "Do you have a key to the cash box?"

"No, I have no key; only Señor Harper has key to cashbox. I never touch money. That is Señor Harper's job, not mine."

Soper asks a few more questions. He decides that Mr. Morales has given him all the information he is going to. He feels Carlos has been honest with him. Closing his notebook and placing it in his suit pocket, Soper gets up from the couch, shakes Carlos's hand, thanks him for his time, excuses himself, and goes out the door.

As Soper walks to his car, he thinks, *Nothing, absolutely nothing, do I get from an hour and a half interviewing Carlos Morales! Besides getting paid with a car rather than cash,* which Soper thinks is a wild story, the most interesting revelation is about how Mr. Morales learns to speak English and become a citizen. It is apparent that Mr. Morales is very proud to be an American.

Soper tells himself that he still has the possibility of having a motive. *He also is one of the last people to see Mr. Harper. I will keep him on my list of suspects and people to keep an eye on.*

Detective Soper pulls away from the curb and starts his drive home; he silently continues to roll the word "nothing" over in his brain. *Absolutely nothing*, he thinks as he enters the ramp for the freeway. *Where do we go from here?* A question that will not leave his mind and might lead him down a road he does not want to go.

There is one very crucial question he does not ask.

CHAPTER TWELVE

Mother and daughter stood far from Santa Ana, CA, in the small farming community of Farragut, with a population of 400—assuming everyone was home. Hershel Harper had served many years as President of The Fifth National Bank in this tiny town, nestled in Fremont County, Iowa. The Loess Hills, resembling massive snowdrifts draped in greenery, paralleled the Missouri River along the county's western edge.

It was March, and they stood by Hershel's casket before it was lowered into the ground at the small cemetery less than a mile from the farm where Hershel was raised. The temperature was 12 degrees. Ethel pulled her coat tightly around herself to protect against the cold north wind. She wiped a tear from her eye as Betty, her long-time friend from high school, put an arm around her, attempting to comfort her.

Hershel would now watch over his beloved farm for eternity.

Hershel's incredible lifelong adventure started when he was born in the Florence Crittenden Home for Unwed Mothers in Sioux City, IA. His mother, only 19, knew she could not care for her baby. As a result, she went to the home to give birth to a child she would put up for adoption. She did not want to live the rest of her life haunted by two mistakes: accidentally getting pregnant and killing her baby through abortion.

It was a bittersweet day when Hershel was born. His mother

was only allowed to hold him for a few minutes before he was taken away. A few weeks later, Hershel was transferred to a home specializing in helping parents adopt children. He was about to bring immense joy to a farm couple who could not have children, and he was on the brink of enjoying a wonderful life.

This place of final rest was at Hershel's request, as he specified in his Last Will and Testament.

Hershel had told Ethel, "When the day comes for me to go to the Pearly Gates, I want to be planted in the Farragut cemetery where I can watch over the whole farm for eternity." Ethel honored his wishes.

Ironically, the small cemetery was only half a dozen miles from where hundreds of acres of nursery fields once thrived. Carlos Morales's friends' fathers came from Mexico every summer to work in these fields. Two major seed and nursery companies chose this area in the far corner of Southwest Iowa for its fertile soil and excellent growing conditions. The mail-order business for their garden seeds, flower plants, shrubs, and trees was enormous.

Thousands of the nursery's flowers, though currently dormant and out of sight during the winter, would return in spring and bloom in their beautiful colors.

The funeral director walked slowly up to Ethel on the frozen grass. He spoke in a low, comforting tone, "Mrs. Harper. It is time to lower the casket. If you want to do anything else, now is the time."

Ethel was prepared to say her last goodbye. She held a single rose in her nervous hand, gently placing it on the casket. She leaned over and kissed it, stepped back, and stood silently. Another tear ran down her cheek. She watched as Hershel was lowered into his final resting place.

"Let's go to the car and get out of the cold," Ethel's friend said quietly as she gently took her by the arm and led her a few feet to the waiting vehicle.

The young man from the funeral home driving the car opened the door for Ethel to sit in the backseat with her friend. The car's interior was nice and warm, as it had been idling with the heater running. Getting out of the cold north wind and into the vehicle was a welcome comfort. However, Ethel did not notice. Her mind reflected on the beautiful years she and Hershel had been married. Now, it was over, and all she would have were those precious memories made on the farm she could see from Hershel's final resting place.

The car started to roll slowly forward, its tires crunching on the gravel as it moved toward the highway. As they exited the cemetery and turned onto the asphalt roadway, Ethel carefully turned around in her seat to look back. *Oh, no. Hershel, my love. I must leave you here in this cold north wind to watch over the farm now. I love you,* occupied Ethel's mind. She hid her face in a handkerchief as tears streamed down her cheeks.

Much of the negative feelings adding to Ethel's tears stemmed from the consideration that, given her age, this could be the last time she visited his grave. That thought only deepened her sadness. She knew that one day, she would return and spend eternity beside the man she loved so very much.

While Ethel was burying her husband in Iowa, Detective Soper continued his probe into Hershel's death. The coroner recovered two .45 caliber slugs from Hershel's skull. Both were damaged, but not beyond the point that the Santa Ana Police Department's firearms examiner could not view marks the gun that killed Hershel left on the bullets.

Soper had not ruled Carlos Morales out as the chief suspect in the theft and possibly Hershel's murder. His interview and follow-up discussions with Mr. Morales left him feeling he was the only person with a motive for robbing the money. Detective Soper thought he only stole the money. Soper rolled the case over in his mind. Why would he kill Mr. Harper, put him in the trunk of his car, and drive it to the obscure location where it was found?

But Mr. Harper disappeared the night he met Mr. Morales to discuss the theft. Mr. Harper never returned from that meeting. Mr. Harper's body was found in the trunk of his car parked in an alley seven blocks away.

Had Mr. Morales murdered Hershel Harper? If so, why? The one fact that kept Mr. Morales as the potential murderer in Detective Soper's mind was Morales owned a Glock pistol of the same caliber as the recovered shell casing and the bullets used to kill Mr. Harper.

Soper was aware of the Glock from a follow-up interview with Mr. Morales when he voluntarily offered the information that he owned the Glock. Mr. Morales told the detective that he purchased the gun to protect his wife and small family. There had been gang activity near their neighborhood, and he felt unsafe.

Detective Soper asked Mr. Morales where he purchased the handgun. Mr. Morales gave him the name of a local sporting goods store and showed Soper his Firearm Safety Certificate (FSC), certifying that he had completed a firearm safety course, as California law required.

Mr. Morales informed the detective that he stored the firearm in a high cabinet drawer in their bedroom. This ensured the gun was out of reach of his children but still accessible to him at night to protect his family from a prowler.

Mr. Morales's comment caused Soper to reflect on the importance of securely storing firearms. He believed that those who owned guns for home protection should keep them locked away from children while still ensuring they were accessible in case an emergency arose. Yes, Soper reflected that Mr. Morales truly valued his education about being a responsible American.

Mr. Morales's comments provided another twist to Soper's thinking; the typical criminal would not exhibit this level of responsibility.

However, Mr. Morales was the only person with both motive and opportunity.

Soper's thinking was leaning more and more in the direction that Mr. Morales was the prime suspect in the theft and murder. Through his exhaustive legwork and talking with dozens of people, he could not come up with anyone other than Mr. Morales, having both opportunity and motive.

I want ballistics to look at that Glock, Detective Soper told himself.

Detective Soper took the information he had gathered and sought a warrant to search Mr. Morales's house and confiscate his firearm. Soper was convinced that once the firearms examiner in the lab test-fired Mr. Morales's Glock pistol and compared that with the spent cartridge case from the scene and the two bullets removed from Hershel's head, he would have solid evidence that Mr. Morales was the perpetrator. That would be quickly followed by the arrest of Mr. Morales and the beginning of legal proceedings against him to place him in prison.

Soper sat in his office reviewing his notes, looking for something he missed. Nothing. Two hours later, after going through his notes a second time, the result was the same: nothing.

While Soper labored over his notes, Carlos enjoyed a relatively easy day at Sunshine Casitas Condo Complex. Not many issues required his attention, and he had gone home a little earlier than usual. This allowed him to do a few small chores around the house before Carlos relaxed in his La-Z-Boy chair to watch the 6:00 p.m. news just before supper.

Once again, shortly after the announcer finished the weather forecast and the TV station started playing a commercial, Carlos heard a knock at his door. However, it was not a knock but a thunderous pounding as the doorbell rang incessantly.

Carlos exited his chair, walked across the room, and opened the door. He recognized Detective Soper but did not know the officers with him.

"Mr. Morales," Soper said gruffly as he handed Carlos a folded-up paper. "This is a warrant to search your house." With that, Soper and his entourage entered the house and began searching.

The following hour was exceptionally uncomfortable for Carlos and his wife, Maria. Luckily, their children were away at a church youth function.

Near the end of their search, Soper asked Carlos where his Glock pistol was stored. Carlos led him into the bedroom, removed a key from his pocket, and opened a small door located high in a cabinet near the bed.

Carlos reached through the open door and carefully removed the pistol, holding it by the hand grips. He was careful not to point it at anyone in the room, following the safety motto, "Never point a weapon at something you do not intend to shoot." He clicked the button release, holding the magazine in the gun, and let it drop into his hand.

Carlos then laid the magazine down on the top of the dresser. He very carefully checked to see that there was no bullet in the chamber and that the gun was unloaded. With the slide pulled all the way back and locked open, he handed his weapon to Detective Soper.

Soper noted Carlos's proper handling of the weapon. He thought, *Hmm, the average person would just have handed the gun to me, loaded*

Carlos believed Soper would only examine the gun and then hand it back. Instead, he watched the detective remove a plastic bag from his pocket and drop the Glock inside. Soper closed the package, marked it, and handed it to one of the technicians who had accompanied him on the search.

Carlos was bewildered that Detective Soper had taken his firearm. *He had not attempted to hide the fact from the detective that he owned the Glock. He had volunteered the information. Now, why would he do this?*

"Detective, what will you do with my gun? When will I get my gun back?" Carlos asked.

Soper had long abandoned his friendly persona when talking with Carlos. He was now a tough investigative detective and had become gruff.

"You may never see this gun again," Soper responded gruffly.

Carlos wondered what that meant. Soper brushed past him and left the house without further acknowledgment. The other officers and lab technicians followed him out the door without saying a word.

Carlos and Maria grabbed each other's hands. They looked at each other with confusion and fear. Maria broke the silence.

"What is happening, Carlos?"

Carlos dropped her hand and wrapped his arms around Maria, pulling her close. In a skeptical yet as reassuring a voice as he could muster, he said, "I don't know."

They stood in the doorway and watched the police vehicles speed away.

Soper ensured that the lab technician and Morales's Glock accompanied him to the police station in his vehicle. He aimed to guarantee proper handling of the situation. He recalled instances where simple errors led to cases being dismissed by judges. That would not happen this time.

Once they arrived at the Police Station, with the gun in hand, Soper headed down the hallway leading to the back portion of the building and the crime laboratory.

Soper knew in his heart that he now had the linchpin

connecting Mr. Carlos Morales to the theft and gangster-style execution of Hershel Harper. But first, the firearms examiner had to do a test fire from Morales's pistol and then compare the cartridge case and bullets with those recovered from the crime scene.

The exam was conducted under a comparison microscope. This procedure became the standard required throughout law enforcement and the court system following the St. Valentine's Day Massacre on February 14, 1929, in Chicago, IL. Al Capone's gang, dressed as Chicago policemen, murdered members of Bugsy Moran's gang in an attempt to take over all the crime and illegal booze business in the city.

As he handed the pistol to Santa Ana PD's head, Firearms Examiner Shawn O'Neill, Soper told himself that if they all matched, Carlos Morales would be charged with murder, and this case would be closed.

It didn't happen.

CHAPTER THIRTEEN

The airplane flight from Iowa back to California was long and sad for Ethel. She had left her beloved husband in a grave in the cold ground and was now heading back to a life filled with uncertainty. At least the grandkids would be there. They had stayed home with their dad while their mother, Marlene, accompanied Ethel to Iowa. Marlene wanted to be there to support her mother and attend her father's funeral.

Ethel sat gazing out the airplane window, her eyes unfocused despite the clear skies and unlimited visibility. Her mind was lost in memories. They played before her eyes as if she were in a comfortable theatre watching a first-class movie. She thought deeply about all the wonderful things that had happened in her and Hershel's life together: *how they had met at the local A&W Root Beer stand, the weekly trips to the movie theater, and the occasions they had taken a lonely country road home. On those country roads, they had turned off all the car's lights and spent a good bit of time kissing, or as it was called in those days, necking.*

She remembered their wedding day. She had been so nervous and afraid something would go wrong. The wedding went as planned, and the beautiful memories that remained were some of her most cherished. She thought about their first house and how Hershel had taken a teller job at the bank. A smile crossed her face as she recalled how terribly proud she was of Hershel after his first promotion at the bank. She never imagined that someday he would become the bank's president.

The birth of their first child, a boy they named Roy, was a glorious time. All the family came to see him and showered him with gifts. She recalled his high school years and his graduation with honors. She and Hershel were so proud of him. The following year, he was accepted into medical school.

And then that tragic winter night. Roy was on the way home from a date when another car, in a big hurry to pass a truck, even though blinded by the flying snow in the car's headlights, pulled out to pass the truck and hit Roy squarely head-on. When they hit, the two vehicles were crushed like a couple of beer cans. Neither Roy nor the other driver survived the crash.

The Harpers' home was filled with great sadness. Why had this happened to their son, a young man with so much promise? Why? And the tears flowed and flowed. Ethel remembered how she and Hershel had leaned on each other to make it through this difficult time. They were each other's anchor.

Baby number two came along—a beautiful blue-eyed child. Marlene quickly became the object of all their love and attention, bringing so much happiness into their lives. As Marlene grew up, she was a lot like Roy; she excelled in everything she did. Marlene had a large circle of friends; no one she ever met did not immediately become a friend. However, Marlene was quite different from Roy regarding her career. There were no dreams of becoming a doctor, nurse, lawyer, teacher, beautician, or a professional job. She wanted to meet a nice young man, marry him, and have a house full of kids. Period.

Through volunteer work she was doing for her church, a bright young man came into her life. They met while helping a young family find a home and the husband find work. They were successful in their efforts.

The young man she was working with asked her for a date.

She accepted, and Cupid invited himself as well. Her date's father owned a pharmacy in a nearby community and was well-known and respected. Troy graduated from pharmacy school and worked in his father's store. Cupid fired a few arrows, and a beautiful relationship was born.

After a year of dating, Marlene and Troy got married. Troy continued to work in his father's store while Marlene was a stay-at-home mom. Over the next ten years, three daughters and a son were born into their home. The four bundles of joy were the treasure of their parents' lives. Grandma and Grandpa Harper thought there were no children as precious as their four grandchildren in the world. Many wonderful memories of the children warmed Ethel's heart.

The movie continued to roll in Ethel's mind. This was a full-length feature film.

Everything had not been wine and roses, Ethel remembered. Hershel had been given a two-way heart bypass following an episode with his heart. He had taken good care of himself following the surgery and had no reoccurrences of his heart issues. Ethel had faced a serious challenge to her health as well. A routine medical checkup discovered cancer in her colon. Swift action from her doctor resulted in surgery that removed the tumor. Both were doing well.

These and many other positive and negative thoughts floated past as Ethel continued her blind stare out of the airplane window. The movie ended, and her daydreaming shifted when she noticed the airplane starting to fly over mountains. The flat land of Nebraska was left behind as her flight continued westward.

Ethel's thoughts turned to Troy. She did not think there was a finer son-in-law in the entire USA. When Troy was tired of working in his father's store, he landed a job with a pharmaceutical company that would allow him to leave the store and work on developing new drugs. This was an exciting opportunity, but the only drawback was that he would have to pack up the family and move to California. The kids and Marlene were excited about the move.

Hershel and Ethel were happy for Troy. In private, they shared their mutual sadness about the family moving so many miles away. All the joy they had shared spoiling the grandkids would be gone—no more weekend picnics or trips to the park. They kept these feelings to themselves. They were happy that Troy had such a fantastic opportunity to do something he was 100% dedicated to. Marlene was excited that the children continued their lives in a new environment. Hershel and Ethel were determined not to rain on that parade.

As their airplane started its journey over the Rocky Mountains, Ethel slowly stopped her daydreaming. No, she told herself, you can remember the wonderful things in your life and learn lessons from your mistakes, but you cannot live there. That time is gone and can't be changed. It is time to quit looking in the rearview mirror and place my eyes out the front windshield. She would always have wonderful memories; no one could ever take that away. You can only change the future; the past will always be what it will be.

They moved to California. That was a result of looking through the windshield. Things were going so well, and then Hershel was murdered.

Ethel told herself it was time to start looking back through the windshield. There was too much pain in the present and the rearview mirror. Yes, it was time to look ahead. Remember the past but look ahead. She realized she was the only one who could make today and tomorrow better in her life.

Look out the windshield. That is where the future lies. Yes, Ethel thought, *only I can make tomorrow better. Hershel and I did that when the kids moved to California. That is where they are today, and this airplane is headed west.*

Ethel smiled silently to herself, turned away from the

airplane window, leaned back in her seat, and almost immediately fell into a deep, peaceful sleep.

Riding in the center seat, Marlene noticed her mother turning away from the window for the first time since takeoff. She reached over and took her mother's hand in hers. Leaning back in her seat and putting her head near Ethel's, she whispered quietly, "Rest, mama, tomorrow is a new day."

CHAPTER FOURTEEN

Marlene and Ethel, two exhausted travelers, stepped off the plane. The familiar warmth of California embraced them, but the sight of Troy and the grandkids truly made them feel at home. They walked out of their exit gate, and hugs, kisses, and the children's chatter breathed new life into the weary travelers. Ethel felt terrific seeing the kids and Troy. It was good to be home.

After picking up the bags and getting into Troy and Marlene's station wagon, there was much happy chatter on the way to Ethel's condo. They all went inside with her to ensure everything was in order.

Troy carried Ethel's bag into her condo. A quick look around assured them everything was just fine. They all gathered by the door.

Following more hugs and kisses, Troy, Marlene, and the kids headed out the door to continue their journey home. Ethel stood in her doorway and waved at them until they were out of sight.

Suddenly, dead silence. All the laughter and friendly chatter were gone. Ethel was alone. Like a sharp sword, loneliness sank deep into her heart. The quietness of the moment was deafening. She had not been alone since Hershel was murdered, as Marlene and her family made sure she was not left by herself. That was a difficult time. But now that Hershel was, as he would say, "planted" near the farm where he grew up, where he and Ethel had spent many happy hours together with his parents, she heard a silence that she knew would still be there the following day. And the morning after, and the morning after that.

Ethel sank onto the couch, placed her head between her hands, and sobbed harder than she had at any time since Hershel's death. She cried huge tears that ran down her cheeks and onto her blouse. Her sobbing became uncontrollable. She almost screamed, *Hershel, I love you, why were you taken away from me?* She kept crying until she could cry no more.

All the sadness she had been harboring and concealing from others now lay spilled on the floor. Completely drained, she stretched out on the couch and tucked her legs and feet into a semi-fetal position. Ethel mused; I believe I'm now prepared to focus on the windshield instead of the rearview mirror. She knew she would grieve Hershel for many days into the future. However, doing what Hershel expected of her was one way to turn the negative grief into a positive.

Laying there on the familiar couch, where she and Hershel had spent many hours watching "The Boyfriend," the memories continued to pour into her exhausted mind.

Ethel remembered the day Hershel surprised her with a picnic at their favorite spot in Waubonsie Park. They spent the afternoon laughing, sharing stories, and dreaming about their future together. That memory now felt like a distant dream, a stark contrast to the emptiness she felt in her heart.

With a clear image of Hershel's kind face in her mind, she whispered, *I love you* and then fell into a deep sleep—the most relaxed and comforting sleep she had felt since Hershel's murder. Perhaps there will be some answers tomorrow.

****

Firearms Examiner O'Neill set his alarm clock to wake him a little earlier than usual. Even though he had left the lab late last night, he knew the urgency of attempting to make a match in the Morales case. Detective Soper had made that point very clear.

O'Neill, a quiet, knowledgeable, and friendly man, knew Soper was an intense detective. Soper was like a dog with a delicious newfound bone when he got on a case. He chewed on the bone until it was gone. Although patience, persistence, and dedication are the keystones to good detective work, for which Soper was known, patience was not one of his hallmarks. When there was something he wanted done, he wanted it done now.

When O'Neill arrived at the lab, Detective Soper was leaning against the wall by the door, sipping from a large paper cup filled with delicious-smelling coffee.

"Here," said Soper as he extended O'Neill a hot cup of McDonald's coffee he held in his other hand.

"What did you find last night?"

As he turned the lock on the door, O'Neill responded, "Nothing. Absolutely nothing. I worked until a little after 3:00 a.m.. A couple of striations on the bullets showed promise; however, on further examination, there were enough differences that I could not, in good conscience, say I had a match."

"I am going to work on the cartridge cases today. Lots of hours ahead. I hope you have more of this coffee," O'Neill said as he flipped on the lights and headed for his workstation.

Soper pulled up a chair beside the bench holding the comparison microscope. He set his cup of coffee in front of him and, in his haste, spilled a little on the bench. "Sorry, Shawn," Soper said as he pulled a McDonald's napkin from his pocket and cleaned up his mess.

Soper watched as O'Neill repeated the procedure he did

with the bullets. The only difference in his activity was that this time, it was cartridge cases, not bullets. With the light on the examples properly adjusted, O'Neill leaned over the comparison microscope and began the tedious task of finding identifiable marks and tracks in the brass, confirming the cases matched.

"You know, detective, this is your last chance," O'Neill told Soper. "I couldn't get a match on the bullets last night, and quite frankly I thought they would be our best chance. If I don't find a match on these cartridge cases, it's game over for hooking Mr. Morales to the Harper murder. At least with what I can do with ballistic examination."

O'Neill had three more questions to ask before he went to work, "How have you tied Mr. Morales to Harper being shot? What's his motive? Why would he do it?"

Soper gave a little growl, then, "Shawn, these have to match. Morales is the only one with both opportunity and motive. He owns the Glock you test-fired. Harper was killed with a Glock. The office hadn't been broken into. Morales has a key. He also knew about the monthly money. These cartridge cases have to match."

Soper took a big drink of coffee, became very quiet, and sat staring at his McDonald's paper coffee cup. "I don't know," came the relatively quiet answer. "Once we get this gun identified as the murder weapon, I will pressure him to get the answers. I will stay on him until he confesses. He ain't gonna like it."

O'Neill turned back to the microscope, and Soper took another drink of coffee. About forty-five minutes later, Soper excused himself to leave. "I'll be back in a minute, O'Neill. I just have to go pay the rent on that last cup of coffee. You know you never own that darn stuff." Soper headed for the men's room.

When he returned and retook his seat, he watched O'Neill

continue to work. Approximately twenty minutes later, O'Neill took his eyes off of the eyepiece and turned to Soper, "There's nothing there. Not even close. I will work on it another hour or two to be sure I am correct, but nothing there indicates I will find anything."

Soper took a long pause before asking, "Are you sure?"

"Yes," O'Neill answered. "Nothing on either the bullets or the cartridge cases that even indicate the slightest match. The cartridge case found in the trunk of Mr. Harper's car and the bullet the coroner removed from his head are definitely from a Glock, but not Mr. Morales's Glock."

Soper sank in his chair. This couldn't be right! I know O'Neill is the best in the business. He must have missed something. These thoughts drove Soper to ask, "Shawn, are you 110% sure?"

"Yes, there is absolutely nothing here I could go to court or tell you in good conscience they matched. Sorry. I gave it my best try. Even fudged a little bit, but still, nothing came up. Sorry. You need to find the Glock that actually killed Harper. You find that one, I guarantee we will make the match."

Soper leaned forward in his chair in deep thought. Finally, he pulled himself up. Stood looking at the floor in silent contemplation, and then abruptly headed for the door to leave. "See ya, O'Neill."

****

Ethel decided staying busy was the best way to keep her eyes looking out the windshield, not the rearview mirror. She had to put her life together without her beloved Hershel, an emotional mountain to climb. However, she was determined to do it.

All the recollections that kept popping into her mind made putting many of her wonderful memories of Hershel away extremely difficult. She decided to donate Hershel's wardrobe to a local charity, benefiting many men who needed clothing. This is looking out the windshield, Ethel told herself as she carefully placed two of Hershel's suits in a box. This is a challenging but necessary task for me to move forward, she continued the conversation with herself.

Surprisingly, this process was more comforting than disturbing as she had first thought it would be. Even in death, Hershel would still pursue one of his passions: helping others. After a couple of cups of freshly brewed coffee in the kitchen, Ethel moved to the living room and settled down on the couch with her "boyfriend"—the name Hershel had given the large flat-screen TV hanging on the wall.

Ethel made a mental note to call Detective Soper and see if there was any progress being made in solving her husband's murder.

****

Detective Soper was sitting in his office when the telephone on his desk rang.

"Soper," was the stern response as he raised the receiver to his ear.

"Detective, this is Examiner O'Neill over at the lab."

"You found something that matched after all?" Soper asked expectantly.

O'Neill answered in a level voice, "I rechecked the cartridge case as I wanted to be sure I had not missed anything."

After taking a beat, O'Neill continued, "I don't have any good news for you, detective. There is absolutely nothing I could take to court and testify that there is a match. Nothing on the cartridge cases and nothing on the bullets matched. These examples were not fired from the Morales pistol. The bullets and cartridge case came from another gun. I can be no more certain than the sun will come up tomorrow. I did the second check because I know how important this case is to you. I don't want to be the one that messes it up for you."

There was a long pause on the line. Then Detective Soper uttered an expletive or two and almost shouted into the telephone, "Are you sure, O'Neill? Did you maybe miss something?"

"No," came the answer, any friendliness removed from his voice. "I did a triple check—more than I do for a court trial—and these examples the lab guys brought me from the crime scene, appropriately marked for chain of evidence, definitely are not a match. I can assure you they came from a Glock, but not the one you took from Mr. Morales for investigation. Sorry, detective. You have some more work to do."

With a short "Thanks," Soper hung up, or more precisely, slammed down the telephone receiver.

What is going to happen now, Soper thought as he replayed the last few days in his mind. The evidence from the interviews he had conducted locked Mr. Morales up 100% as the perp who killed Hershel Harper. The missing piece of the puzzle was proving Mr. Morales was the person who pulled the trigger. Mr. Morales owned a Glock, but it did not match the evidence collected at the crime scene and from the coroner's office. Did Mr. Morales switch guns? If he did, where is the one used in the execution? Does he have a second pistol? If so, where can I find it?" Detective Soper slammed his fist down on his desk in frustration. "Damn," he said to no one in particular.

Soper settled down a little as his mind started to analyze what he knew for a fact. The same things repeated themselves over and over in Soper's mind. Mr. Morales had "opportunity." He knew Mr. Harper's routine, had the key to the office, and was often alone with Hershel in the office. He had Mr. Harper's trust and friendship.

Mr. Morales had "motive." He always had a flashy new car that his salary couldn't afford, considering he owned a pleasant home and enjoyed a good lifestyle. His children attended a private, church-operated school.

Soper thought Mr. Morales satisfied the two primary elements of establishing a person as a solid suspect in a crime, motive, and opportunity. Now, he had to prove it, but a few other things weighed against Mr. Morales being the perp. Soper took another sip of his McDonald's coffee. It was getting cold.

The interviews he conducted regarding Mr. Morales with the residents of the condo complex were primarily positive. However, some people said they never trusted Mr. Morales and always felt uncomfortable around him. They would never let him work alone in their condo unit.

Mr. Morales owned a Glock pistol, the same brand as had fired the two bullets removed from Hershel's skull and the cartridge case found under Hershel's body in the trunk of the car.

Detective Soper leaned back in his chair, took a sip of his now lukewarm coffee, and cursed to himself. This couldn't be right! O'Neill was one of the best firearms examiners in the country. Still, even the best made an occasional mistake, he thought as he replayed what he knew in his mind.

There is something out there I have missed, Detective Soper pondered. *What is it, what is it?*

CHAPTER FIFTEEN

Ethel worked hard to keep her eyes on the windshield rather than the rearview mirror. This practice helped her work through the grief of losing Hershel and gave her hope for the future. Yes, she kept telling herself, *I am going to make it! Those grandchildren are not spoiled enough yet!*

After cleaning the condo from top to bottom for the fifth time, Ethel stood looking out the glass patio door. She saw a couple walking hand in hand, headed for the swimming pool. *I miss you, Hershel*, she thought. Then, her thought process changed. This place is clean enough to conduct surgery in! I need to get busy doing something new and productive. *Yes, today, I am moving forward. It is time to get a life."* She reached for the telephone and called her church's Director of Volunteer Service.

Ethel volunteered for several projects sponsored by her church. Additionally, she was elected to serve on the local Board of Directors for the condo complex. She greatly enjoyed this work and fulfilled one of Hershel's dreams: painting the complex.

"Our house needs to be painted. It hasn't had a coat of paint in 15 years," Ethel told the residents of Sunshine Casitas gathered for their monthly meeting. Remembering the comment made by Sharon, the realtor, This old girl needs a new coat of lipstick! The meeting attendants all had a good laugh. "I have figured out a way we can pay for it without any kind of assessment."

The project received total support from the Board, and they were delighted that there would not be an additional assessment to cover the project's cost. This would make it easy to sell to the residents.

"There is enough in the cash reserve from our monthly payments of condo fees to pay for the painting. I know Hershel is looking down from Heaven and will be so happy to see this project accomplished. Do you think we should change the color or stick with the one we have?" Ethel asked the group. A friendly, happy discussion followed until everyone agreed to stay with the current color and add a little bright trim.

Even though she kept very busy with the grandkids and all their projects, the questions in the back of her mind would not go away. She wanted to know who killed Hershel in such a violent manner and why. There certainly was not enough money in the cashbox to warrant a murder.

Why had Hershel been killed? He did not have any enemies; everyone loved him. *Where did the murderers capture Hershel after he met with Carlos? How did they know they were meeting and where? Why did they stuff Hershel's body in the trunk of his car and then abandon it where they did?* These questions constantly haunted her. She could not help but look back at them.

Another question that haunted her was, *did Carlos have something to do with it?* The detective's many questions following the murder convinced enough people in the complex to go to the condo's corporate headquarters and get Carlos fired. Ethel was uneasy about this action. She liked Carlos and believed he was a good, honest, hardworking man with a beautiful family. He had shared pictures of his wife and children with Ethel. She thought they were a lovely family and admired them greatly. *I just can't believe Carlos did anything wrong. He is a good man,* she thought.

Every Monday, Ethel routinely called Detective Soper to ask if anyone had been arrested for Hershel's murder. He always responded, "No, but I'm still searching." Soper never revealed that Carlos was his main suspect.

This particular Monday morning, Detective Soper was sitting in his office, mulling over the Harper murder case. A picture of his father hung on the wall. The senior, Mr. Soper, was a top-notch detective well-known in the law enforcement community. He had taught his son well. Soper stared at the picture, wondering what his dad would do. *Am I following in his footsteps or doing something wrong?* Soper thought to himself. Even though his father was gone, Soper wanted to make him proud. *Dad, what do I do next?*

Detective Soper was as frustrated as, if not more than, Mrs. Harper. Their frustrations were similar yet different in significant ways. Ethel only wanted to know who did it and why. She wanted closure. Detective Soper also wanted to know who did it and why. Still, he wanted to put the guilty party or parties in jail to punish them for taking an innocent man's life.

Regardless of how slight or misleading, every lead he followed up on with the determination of a good hunting dog trying to flush a pheasant from a field of tall grass for a hunter to shoot. He diligently searched for the actual murder weapon. He would look for something to tie it to Mr. Morales if he found it. His instincts, honed over nearly 30 years in law enforcement, told him Mr. Morales was the shooter. Now, all he had to do was find the Glock used in the murder.

"Hey, O'Neill, anything show up in those matches?" Soper asked O'Neill two or three times a week. He knew O'Neill checked with and exchanged information with several other labs in the area.

Each week, he expected and took Ethel's phone calls. Each Monday, he had to give her his no-progress answer. That answer bothered him for several reasons. First, he was a good detective and should have found something by now; second, he began to feel the pain in Ethel's voice. At one time, he had a good wife and knew how distressed she would have been if he were the murder victim. It hurt. This case had become personal.

What made the hurt deeper was that Soper's wife had passed away from cancer a few years back. She was a kind lady with a great sense of humor. She could defuse a spiteful conversation with a few words that made everyone laugh. She had the unique ability to put up with Soper's erratic schedule and his mood swings when working on a serious case. Yes, Detective Soper loved and missed his wife very much. He kept a picture of her on his desk, sitting squarely in front of him while working. His fellow detectives often saw him talking to her picture as he worked out a difficult question in his mind. A deep sense of sadness had settled into Soper since his life partner died. He could not hide it from those around him. His personality had changed.

Days without results turned into weeks. New cases came in almost daily, putting more demands on his time. Time was becoming an issue, and the new cases had to take precedence. However, Soper used every spare minute to work on the Harper Case. Many nights, you could see the midnight oil burning through the living room window of his house.

As weeks stretched into months, the Harper case turned cold. The standard investigative procedure was to move unsolved cases into the "cold case" file. Yet, Soper found it challenging to do so. He left the file on his desk instead.

That Glock is out there somewhere, and I am going to find it was a constant challenge in his mind. He was determined to find it, as the months turned into years.

Finally, during these years, Ethel gave up on her calls to Detective Soper. Although she felt he was doing his best, he could not solve the case. Keeping her eyes looking out of the windshield, she continued her volunteer work and spent time with the grandkids. Overall, things were pretty good in her world, with only an occasional glance in the rearview mirror. Hershel was back there, and she missed him.

Other changes were occurring in Ethel's life. As the years slipped by, the children grew, and their activities increasingly took up more of their time. This shift left Ethel with fewer opportunities to spend quality moments with them. Ethel primarily saw her grandchildren at their baseball or basketball games, as their circle of friends and extracurricular activities occupied most of their spare time. In their busy young lives, the enchantment of spending time with Grandma no longer held the same allure it once did.

Another, rather hurtful, change came in Ethel's life. Due to a prolonged disagreement with a fellow church member, Ethel decided to step down from her volunteer role. Consequently, her volunteer hours diminished. Additionally, her term on the local Condo Board concluded, and she was not re-elected.

Ethel found herself with increasing idle time; she noticed she was gazing into the rearview mirror more often. *Oh, Hershel, I wish you were here to help me find answers and help me through this troubling time. Maybe we could go to the park and have one of our wonderful talks. You always made me feel loved, needed, and safe.* She cherished her memories of Hershel, which occasionally brought her to tears; she struggled to comprehend why the police had yet to uncover the truth behind her husband's murder, her anchor in life.

Ethel replayed in her mind what she knew over and over. She was missing sleep and began to feel unwell. Marlene told her she was worrying too much and convinced Ethel to let her take her to the doctor to see if he could prescribe something to help her sleep.

Following much discussion, Ethel finally gave in to

Marlene's request.

At the doctor's office, Ethel sat nervously, her hands trembling. She didn't like doctors or anything medical. After sitting in the waiting room for what felt like hours, a nurse took them to an exam room. The nurse measured Ethel's blood pressure, and it was fine.

"Mrs. Harper, I am going to take a blood sample. We have our own lab, so we should have the results back tomorrow," the nurse said as she removed the sanitary plastic from a syringe to gather the sample. Ethel was not happy with the stick in her arm!

Finally! Ethel thought as the nurse placed a bandage over the stick location on her arm. "Let's get out of here, Marlene. I've had all I want for one day. Take me home. Please!"

And home they went, not even stopping at the Dairy Queen for Ethel's favorite treat, a strawberry sundae with extra strawberries.

The following morning, the telephone rang. "Hello," Ethel answered the phone. "This is Dr. Silverman's office. Is this Mrs. Harper?"

"Yes."

"I have the results of your blood test, Mrs. Harper and Dr. Silverman wants you to take a couple of tests."

Startled, Ethel asked the obvious question, "Why?"

The nurse took a beat, "The doctor wants to do a pelvic exam and possibly other tests. When can you come in the first of next week? We have an opening at 10:00 on Monday or several times on Tuesday?"

"Why?" Ethel asked again, this time indignantly!

"Part of your bloodwork included the CA-125 test that detects the presence of cancer. Your test came back positive."

Ethel was shocked and flabbergasted. "Cancer! How can I have cancer? Cancer."

"Are you sure?" was the frightened response to the nurse.

"Are you sure I have cancer?"

"That's why we want you to come in for more tests. The CA-125 test is preliminary, and we need further definitive tests."

After much discussion, Ethel finally made an appointment, finished the call, and immediately dialed Marlene.

Over the next couple of weeks, Ethel underwent a series of exams, including CT scans and an MRI.

The tests were completed, and Ethel and Marlene were in the doctor's office to receive the results. The doctor entered the exam room with a somber expression.

The doctor got directly to the topic. "I'm afraid you have developed ovarian cancer. It's in the latter stage. You have had it for several years. Unfortunately, it has metastasized and spread to your liver and several other organs. You need treatment immediately."

Ethel felt the room spin around her. Marlene squeezed her hand, her eyes filled with tears. "We'll get through this, Mom. We'll fight it together."

Marlene and Ethel agreed they were going to try whatever it took to kill the cancer.

Several weeks of heavy cancer treatment, including chemotherapy and radiation, followed the doctor's visit. It was a grueling, tough time for everyone. Marlene spent most of her time with her mother. The grandkids visited as much as school activities would allow, and Troy made it a point to drop in and visit every day after work. Ethel received maximum love from her family.

It was a valiant fight. The doctors and nurses gave 100% to the effort. In the end, the treatment was not capable of killing the widespread cancer.

Ethel traveled and walked through the Pearly Gates a month and three weeks later to join her beloved Hershel in Heaven.

Troy, Marlene and the family honored her last wish to be buried next to Hershel in Iowa so they could hold hands and, for eternity, look at the farm that brought them so much joy.

Arrangements were made to transport Ethel's body to Iowa. The entire family flew back to attend Ethel's funeral.

Following the funeral, which was lightly attended as most of Hershel and Ethel's friends and family had preceded them in death, Troy, Marlene, and the kids took a few moments to drive past the farmstead. When they drew even with the front of the house, Troy pulled the car to the side of the road and stopped.

The people living there now had changed the place very little. For the most part, the old house, garage, and garden spot looked just as they had for nearly 100 years.

"She still looks pretty much the same," Troy said, a hint of nostalgia in his voice.

"Yes," Marlene answered, her eyes scanning the familiar landscape. She pointed towards the back of the house. "That old fence that used to run across the back of the house past the garden is gone."

"Yeah," Troy injected, nodding. "The barn has been torn down and replaced with that metal building. I guess they needed something big enough to put their farm equipment in. I bet there's a shop over at that end of the building," he said, pointing. "You can see the windows."

With some sadness, Troy said, "You remember the barn, don't you?"

Marlene shook her head in the affirmative.

"Remember inside where the main beams that held it up were held together with wooden pins?" Troy continued. "I think that old barn was close to a hundred years old. You know, I found one of the old pins they apparently didn't use. It's lying on my desk at home."

Marlene was looking at what Troy was pointing at. "Yes, I

really used to enjoy going in that old barn. I remember those old main beams held together with the wooden pegs you are talking about. My favorite memory is climbing up in the haymow and watching the pigeons on that track that went the length of the barn."

"And how about where the old scale house used to be? It's gone. Grandpa used to weigh cattle and hogs in there. I remember he always had a bet with the truck driver who came to haul the animals to market. They bet on the final weight of the truck. The prize was a chocolate malt, and I don't think Grandpa ever paid for any!" Marlene said, a smile tugging at her lips.

Troy chuckled, "Yes, I remember that. Grandpa Harper used to brag about that a bit."

"Look in the yard," Marlene said, pointing toward the big tree in the front yard. "The old swing is still there." The swing was just a rope hanging from a tree limb that had an old car tire tied to the bottom as a place to sit down and ride in the swing.

"Grandma used to bring out some of her baked cookies when I was in the swing," Marlene said. "They were always so good!"

They sat in the car and reminisced about everything they had done there, all the things they had enjoyed, and all they missed about the old place. Troy became very quiet, and Marlene had big tears in her eyes. Even the kids were silent. An indescribable feeling filled the car. It was a combination of joy and sadness.

Finally, reality set in. Troy looked at the clock in the car's dash and realized it was time to head for the airport.

They all waved at the farm as Troy pulled away. He had to drive the 60 miles to Eppley Airfield in Omaha for their flight back to California. Troy knew their connection would be tight since they had taken time to visit the old farmstead, but he thought it was worth it. I can always speed a little when I get over to Interstate 29, he said to himself as they sped away toward the Interstate.

CHAPTER SIXTEEN

The calendar pages kept ripping off. Seventeen years flew by. Despite Detective Soper's hundreds of hours spent investigating the Hershel Harper murder case, he still has not found the gun that killed Hershel Harper. He knows it is out there somewhere. It is the key to connecting Mr. Morales to the gang-style execution of Hershel Harper. He never gives up on his belief that Carlos Morales pulled the trigger on the still-missing Glock pistol that killed Hershel Harper.

Even though the clock is ticking, and retirement is just around the corner, he will never give up until he finds that gun and slaps the handcuffs on Carlos Morales. That is a promise he made to himself.

Much has happened over the years since Detective Soper went to the crime scene, where they found Hershel Harper's body in the trunk of his car with two bullets fired into the back of his head, gang-execution style. Soper's primary suspect, Carlos Morales, is still on his radar seventeen years later.

But for a few moments, let us roll the calendar back seventeen years. We need to know what Soper's prime suspect has been doing all this time. Soper has had Carlos on his radar. Has Morales displayed any behavior that has incriminated him further? Who has he been hanging with? What type of activities does he engage in? Where does he hang out? Are there any changes in his lifestyle or activities that are negative?

Any suspicious activity or friends? The thinking list in Soper's mind is many pages long. Where is that dang Glock is always paramount.

Carlos's interaction with Detective Soper began the day the major theft occurred at the Sunshine Casitas Condo Complex, seventeen years ago. At the time, Carlos was the maintenance superintendent at Sunshine. Soper spent a lot of time interviewing Carlos. The fact he owned a Glock and had a key to the office moved him to the top of Soper's suspect list. Soper's interviews and questioning of residents raised enough distrust in a portion of the resident group that they went to corporate management and had Carlos fired. Here is Carlos's story starting seventeen years ago after he was fired.

Carlos felt devastated after being dismissed as the Maintenance Superintendent for the Sunshine Casita Condo Complex. His performance was outstanding, with only one or two minor complaints during his nine years there. He struggles to comprehend why the condo corporate board of directors let him go, primarily since the complaints stemmed from the murder of Hershel Harper. Carlos could not fathom how the residents he had supported over the years turned against him due only to the distress caused by the police questioning. It simply did not seem fair.

He needs a job quickly. Will Mr. Burns hire me back full-time to work at the wash rack in the Chevrolet Dealership? It will not pay much, but it will fill in while he looks for a better job. He is still moonlighting part-time at the dealership, so it will be easy to talk to Mr. Burns. Burns has always been very friendly to Carlos, and he thinks that might work in his favor.

Carlos goes to the dealership in the morning, arriving just as it opens for business. He finds Mr. Burns in his office. He knocks softly on the door frame. The light tapping sound gets Mr. Burns' attention, and he looks up from the paper he is working on.

"Well, good morning, Carlos," Burns says in a friendly voice. "Come on in and have a seat. I'm tired of working on this crazy paperwork stuff, and it can wait until later. What's on your mind?" he asks Carlos as he directs him to a chair opposite Burn's desk.

"Señor Burns," Carlos says in a shaking voice. "I need help, and I hope you can give it to me."

Over the next 20 minutes, Carlos tells Mr. Burns the entire story about the burglary, finding Hershel Harper's body in the trunk of his car, the session he had with Detective Soper at his home, Soper getting a warrant and coming back and taking his gun, and how he was fired because some of the residents at the condo complex wanted him fired.

Carlos answers all of Burns' questions, and there are quite a few. Burns wants to know everything about what has happened. He had seen the story on the nightly news but had no idea Carlos had been involved in any way.

Carlos finishes his story, then takes a deep breath. "Señor Burns, could I have my job back on the wash rack full-time? Maria and I need money to live on."

Burns momentarily taps his pen on his desk and then looks up at Carlos. "Carlos, you are one of the hardest-working people I have ever hired. I always knew the rack was in good hands when you were on the job. I assume you want to be paid this time rather than get a new car at the end of the year," Burns says with a smile just beginning to come on his face.

"Sí," Carlos quickly responds. *Maybe he will give me the job I need,* Carlos thinks.

Burns leans back in his big leather desk chair. Looking Carlos squarely in the eye, "Carlos, I will make you a better deal than the wash rack. How would you like to be a salesman?"

A salesman thinks Carlos. *They make more money than anyone else in the dealership except Mr. Burns. Salesman, I don't know how to be a salesman.*

Almost as if reading Carlos's mind, Burns continues, "Carlos, I have watched you interact with our customers and the employees in the dealership. You and I made a crazy deal to pay you with a car rather than wages when you first started to work here. You honored your part of the deal without us ever having the slightest problem. That's a pretty darn good record, you know."

"You have a great personality. People automatically like you. You are intelligent, a quick learner, and as honest as the day is long."

"I can teach you what you need to know as a salesman. You are a quick learner, so we won't be in school very long," Burns chuckled as he finishes his sentence and waits for Carlos's reaction.

Carlos sits in his chair with his mouth part-way open. An astonished look is on his face. Carlos is at a loss for words.

Sensing that Carlos is trying to digest everything, Burns says, "Look, Carlos. I don't need an answer today. If you want to go home and discuss it with Maria, that's fine with me. I will be here all day tomorrow. The car auction isn't until Friday this week."

"Oh, by the way, we pay our salespeople a salary plus a bonus based on the dollar amount of the cars they sell. Some dealerships have their salespeople on straight commission."

"I do not like pushy, hard-sell salesmen. That is what straight commission breeds in a sales force. The competition between the salespeople becomes so intense the customer suffers."

Burns leans forward in his chair and becomes very serious.

"I want my salesmen to be our customer's friends, a person they trust and will want to come back and see the next time they need a new vehicle or want to make a trade."

"I have found that paying our people in sales better than a

livable wage and offering them a bonus related to the units they sell eliminates the in-your-face hard-push salesmen. Instead, they become the customer's friend."

"The more customers like and respect our salesmen, the more likely they will remain customers of Burns Chevrolet," Burns concludes his pitch with pride in his voice.

"No," says Carlos. "No wait, Señor Burns. I will take the job right now. When you train me as a salesman?"

The two men shake hands, and Carlos starts on a sales career that pays him far more than he made at the condo complex. Within a year, Carlos is the top-producing salesman in the dealership. He and Burns forge a special relationship that endures for years.

Beyond Carlos becoming a successful salesman and earning enough money to do a remodel job on his house and enrolling his children in prominent schools, some sad things also occurred during these years. The most sorrowful event was the passing of Ethel Harper from cancer.

With the passing of Mrs. Harper, Detective Soper no longer receives her weekly calls. He misses not getting them. Soper uses every free moment he can find looking for the murder weapon. It is an obsession with him. He knows in his mind that Mr. Morales is the perp. All he must do is find the gun, link it to Mr. Morales, and put him away for life.

Another page tears off the calendar. It is the year for Detective Soper to retire. *Retire. Damn,* Soper thinks, *it has been over seventeen years since the Hershel Harper murder. I still have not tied Morales to that murder, and I know in my heart of hearts he is the perp who did it. And now I must retire, and this thing is still not solved. Damn,* Soper says to himself.

Soper decides to attempt something he did not believe could be done. He pleads his case to the Chief of the Santa Ana Police Department.

"Chief, I would like to make a request. You know I have

spent seventeen years working on the Harper case. I know this is a weird request, Chief, but I won't sugarcoat it and just tell you what I would like to do." Soper takes a deep breath and continues. "I would like to have your permission to make a copy of the Harper file to take with me when I leave. Now I'm retired, I have plenty of time to work that case."

The Chief was taken aback. "Well, Soper, that's a noble idea, but regulations will not allow that file to leave this department."

"Chief, I have put hundreds if not thousands of hours into that case. Now I have the time I think I can break it," Soper pleads.

"Detective, I just don't think we can get permission for you to copy and take it." The Chief stands his ground.

Soper continues to plead his case. He is not going to give up.

Following nearly two hours of discussion, phone calls to the District Attorney's office, and a private lawyer that Soper had used for legal work, the Chief agrees to let Soper make the copies. However, he is to store them in his gun cabinet, and he is to only review the papers at home. Nothing is to leave the house for any reason.

Soper agrees to the terms and returns to his office and the copy machine. Some people are startled when they hear him whistling in the copy room; he has never done this before.

Soper is sitting in his office cleaning out the final drawer in his desk. Today the retirement date rolls around. Soper knows the detective who will take over his job. Detective Roger Blair has been with the homicide division for ten years. Soper knows him well and thinks of him as a good detective. He has broken some problematic cases. Soper does not know anyone in the police department who did not respect him and his great work.

A great replacement, Soper tells himself. *I am going to get him interested in the Harper case.*

Detective Roger Blair enters the office and bids Soper a friendly greeting. "Well, how are you doing, Soper? Are you going to go fishing now?"

The two men have known each other for years, and they share a warm handshake.

"No," Soper responds with a bit of laughter in his voice. "I am just not a fisherman. Went once, spent my time rebaiting my hook and fighting mosquitoes. I decided that fishing was not for me."

Blair laughs at his response. "Detective, I think you need to find something to fill your time. People have told me that retirement can be rather boring, and they need something to do."

Soper senses an opening. "I have a project I'm going to work on, and I think you might be interested in it as well," Soper says. Picking up the Harper murder case file, he hands it to Blair. "Detective, I think this is something you will be very interested in. This started seventeen years ago, and it's still unsolved. However, I think I am getting close to a solution. Let me tell you about it."

Soper spends nearly an hour going over the file with Blair. He is surprised to learn that Detective Blair knew quite a bit about the case, as it had started years before Blair was even a beat cop.

Blair surprises Soper with his response. "My grandparents lived at the Sunshine Casita condo when this happened. It became a dinner table discussion for the people that lived there."

When Blair finished the police academy and received his gun and badge, Grandpa had spent an entire Sunday afternoon telling him about the case. Every time he saw him, up to the time of his death, Grandpa always wanted to know if he had made any progress working on the case.

Now, Blair is a detective and can work on the case, even if

it is cold. Soper handed Blair the official Harper Case file, which he placed on his desk.

Soper smiles to himself after wishing Blair luck in his new job. The two men share another friendly handshake, and Soper leaves the office for the last time. *Yes, this will work out,* he thinks as he walks down the hallway toward the station's front door. An unidentifiable tune is being whistled as he walks along.

CHAPTER SEVENTEEN

The telephone rang, shattering the silence and jolting Detective Soper from his troubled sleep. He fumbled for the phone and lifted the receiver. Before he could say "hello," a voice came on the line.

"Detective Soper," the voice said, sounding tired but still professional.

"Hi, Charlie. It's me, Detective Blair. I know it's late, but I couldn't help but notice that you've been working on this Harper case for years. I was hoping to get some insight from you about it."

There was a pause, and Blair wondered if Soper didn't want to talk. He was relieved when Soper finally responded.

"What do you know about the Harper murder? I can't tell you what you want to know unless I know what you know," Soper asked, his voice slurred and tired.

"Well, I've been going over the case files," Blair said, "it's a fascinating cold case, but a few things have me stumped."

"Go on," Soper said, his voice rough from his troubled sleep. Years of exhaustive work had caught up with him, and now that he was retired, he thought he could finally rest.

"Do you have any idea why the gun wasn't found at the crime scene?" Blair asked, his curiosity piqued. "It's one of the biggest mysteries in this case, and I'd like your take on it."

There was another pause, and Blair, unaware he had woken

Soper from his troubled sleep, thought for a moment he probably should not have called him at this early hour.

"The gun was never found because we couldn't match it to any other crimes," Soper said finally. "The killer took it with him when he left Sunshine Casita Condo Complex that night, which isn't unusual, but then never committed another shooting. O'Neill checked all the guns in the evidence room but wasn't finished when I left."

"Did you ever find any leads on who might have been responsible?" Blair asked, absentmindedly scanning the Harper file on his desk. "Did you ever establish the location where Mr. Harper was killed?"

Soper sighed, and Blair could almost hear the weight of years of frustration.

"No, we never found any proof Harper was killed at the office, and we didn't determine any other location."

"There were plenty of suspects," Soper said. "But we never had enough evidence to tie anyone to the crime. We had Morales as our prime suspect, but even that was tenuous at best."

"I heard you are convinced Mr. Morales is the perp," Blair states.

"Yeah," Soper responds wearily. "Mr. Morales was my prime suspect from the start. I still think he's the triggerman, but we need more evidence for a warrant. He had motive and opportunity, but I could never prove it. One positive thing about Mr. Morales is that no one spoke against him. Some people at the condo forced him out of his job, but they only had positive things to say about him before the money theft and murder. I think his being Mexican influenced their opinions."

"Interesting," Blair said. "I'll talk to him soon. The file says he's working as a salesman at a Chevy dealership. Is that still valid?"

"Yeah," Soper replied. "Interesting situation. Burns Chevrolet is one of the dealers on Dealership Row. Mr. Morales worked there before Sunshine Casita. When he went to Sunshine, he moonlighted at Burns; when things went south at Sunshine, he ended up back at Burns. Instead of the wash rack, Burns hired him as a junior salesman this time. Last I heard, he's doing pretty good."

"What about the fingerprints?" Blair asked, recalling something from the file. "You found prints on Mr. Harper's desk."

"Naw, nothing we can use, mostly Harper and a few unknowns on the front of the desk. The prints indicated that whoever left them was probably facing the desk. My guess is they are from customers leaving their monthly rent. Most were too bad to use anyway," Soper said.

"So, you aren't too keen on making an ID of the shooter from the prints?" Blair asked.

Soper chuckled, a dry, mirthless sound.

"Nowhere near enough," Soper said. "I don't know, Blair. Read the file. We didn't find any sign of a scuffle or anything indicating a homicide in the office. Harper might not have been there but was killed elsewhere. We placed Harper there because he had keys to the door and desk. What would his motive be? I don't know; maybe we're right, maybe wrong."

Blair's mind raced with possibilities.

"I didn't see any mention of blood at the Sunshine office. Do you think whoever killed Harper took him somewhere else before they shot him, or did they do it outside and then just push Harper's body in the trunk of the car?"

"That one is a bit of a puzzle," Soper responded. "I'll have to admit that one has eaten up a couple of cups of coffee. Did the killer drop him on a blanket or something and then drag his body out and throw it in the car? Was he standing up or sitting in his chair when he was shot? He was shot in the back of the head. The lab guys found heavy gunshot residue on Harper's neck, so whoever did it was standing right behind him. They didn't find any residue anywhere in the office. I don't have the answer to that one."

"What about the car?" Blair asked. "According to a report, a patrol officer spotted it parked in a lean-to carport behind a commercial building." He hesitated, re-checking his facts. "Yes, Patrolman Hunt found the vehicle."

Soper sighed again, and Blair wondered if he had worn him down.

"That was one of the biggest disappointments," Soper said finally. "We had leads that went nowhere. We had the cartridge case and the bullets in Mr. Harper's head, but the firearms lab couldn't match them to another gun. All we know is they came from a Glock, which leaves a distinct firing pin impression."

Blair sat silently, thinking about everything Soper had told him.

"Thanks for your time, Charlie," Blair said finally. "I appreciate it. I'm sorry I ruined your sleep."

Soper's voice was tired but professional.

"No problem, kid," he said. "Just be careful. This case is not like any other. It's got a life of its own. There's something strange out there we have not found. We have to keep looking."

As Blair hung up and stood to leave his office, he couldn't shake the feeling he had just scratched the surface of something deeper—something beyond solving a murder case.

Blair thought that technologies exist today that weren't around in Soper's days. Maybe Soper was so hung up on solving the crime the old gumshoe way that he ignored new technologies. Or maybe, Blair thought, Soper was an old-style detective uninterested in new gadgets.

Well, Blair thought, it is time to see if a little up-to-date technology will unlock this thing.

He sat at his desk, mulling over the idea, and made a mental note to contact the firearms lab first thing in the morning. He rose, reached over, pulled the little chain that turned off the green desk lamp, and finally exited the office door. Blair hoped his wife would be excited to hear about his first day on the new job. He glances at his wristwatch—3:14 a.m. On second thought, she probably does not even want to wake up this time in the morning.

CHAPTER EIGHTEEN

Detective Blair nudged open the door to the Santa Ana Police Department Crime Laboratory, using his butt instead of his hands. The door creaked slightly, echoing in the eerily quiet lab. In his grasp were two large paper cups of steaming hot McDonald's coffee, each crowned with a fresh glazed Dunkin Donut. The rich aroma of coffee mingled with the sweet scent of the donuts, creating a comforting contrast to the sterile environment. As he entered, his eyes roamed the room, searching for Firearms Examiner O'Neill. The lab was eerily quiet, the usual hum of activity replaced by an unsettling stillness. Blair scanned the dimly lit room, the flickering fluorescent light casting ominous shadows on the walls.

He found O'Neill working, his head down, peering into a microscope on a small table. "Morning, O'Neill! Thought I'd bring a little breakfast cheer," Blair said, forcing a smile as he carefully set the cups down next to O'Neill. The lab was filled with the sharp scent of chemicals and the persistent buzz of a flickering fluorescent light added to the sterile atmosphere.

O'Neill looked up from the microscope, his eyes widening at the sight of the coffee and donuts. A big smile lit up his face as he leaned back in his chair. "Ah, Detective Blair, always a pleasure. And I must say, I'm impressed by your...generosity." O'Neill's voice was laced with amusement, but Blair knew better than to be fooled. He had been doing this for years, and

O'Neill was no stranger to the coffee-donut bribe.

Blair pulled up a chair and sat beside O'Neill, trying to appear nonchalant despite his excitement. "So, O'Neill, I need your help with something." The rich, hot coffee smell made both men feel better about attacking the issues of the day. The donuts were a sound reinforcement as well. O'Neill raised an eyebrow, his eyes never leaving Blair. "Oh? What might that be?"

Blair hesitated for a moment, then leaned in closer, his voice dropping to a near whisper, "I need you to take another look at the bullets and cartridge case from the Harper murder. See if you can match them to any guns in your evidence database. Maybe one of the guns from a case long after Harper was shot." O'Neill's expression did not change, but Blair knew he had piqued his interest. O'Neill took a sip of his hot coffee and a bite from the donut. Then he took another.

"I think I can do that," O'Neill said, his voice neutral. "But it won't be easy and might take some time. That is an ancient cold case, and as you can see," he said, pointing to the large stack of case files sitting on his desk, "many current cases should be worked on first." Blair nodded, knowing what he was up against. Everyone in the Santa Ana Detective Bureau knew of Soper's obsession with the Harper case. Blair had read the file and was drawn to the case. Even though he might not have realized it at the time, it was now Blair's obsession to find the elusive Glock pistol used in the Harper homicide. Now, he needed all the help he could get.

"I know," Blair said, trying to sound nonchalant. "But I need your expertise, O'Neill. You're one of the best in the business."

O'Neill smiled, a small, knowing smile. "Blow my ego up as much as you want, but we both know why you came here today, Blair."

"I need your help, O'Neill. And I'm willing to do whatever

it takes to get it." O'Neill's smile grew more expansive, and he nodded slowly. "Alright, Blair. I'll take another look at the evidence. But don't get your hopes up; I worked on this years ago when it came in. I have worked on it for Detective Soper several times since then. Finding something new is akin to me winning the lottery and splitting it with you."

Blair grinned, feeling a sense of satisfaction wash over him. He had gotten what he wanted, and now all he had to do was wait for O'Neill's results. There had to be a clue to the whereabouts of the murder weapon. O'Neill had not found it before. Blair had a feeling that this time, he would get a hit. O'Neill had a new tool to work with. As he left the laboratory, Blair couldn't help but feel a sense of pride. He was one step closer to solving the Harper murder case – and proving himself as the better detective.

O'Neill took the last sip of his coffee and tossed the empty McDonald's cup into the waste basket by the microscope table. A sly smile crossed his face as he finished the last bite of his donut and wiped the crumbs off the IBIS desktop. One of his favorite phrases, which he loved to use with colleagues and others seeking help on a complex case, he smiled and uttered to an empty room: I know a trick.

What is that trick?

A glimpse of the history behind the ballistic forensics curtain may provide a clue.

The Comparison Microscope came into use for doing forensic ballistics following the February 19, 1929, St. Valentine Massacre in Chicago. Al Capone's gang members dressed as Chicago cops savagely murdered seven members of the North Side Gang. The bloody event is part of the gang rivalry between Al Capone's Chicago Outfit and Bugs Moran's North Side Gang over who controlled Chicago's bootleg booze business during the Prohibition era.

There is a desperate need for a way to prove the shooters

are not members of the Chicago Police Department. The best system they can find is the Comparison Microscope. Its use proves that the bullets that kill Moran's thugs did not come from a Chicago PD firearm.

The Comparison Microscope establishes itself as the nationwide benchmark for ballistic forensics. When a skilled firearms examiner performs the analysis, the results can be trusted for judicial proceedings. Nonetheless, this process is highly labor-intensive, demanding several hours to determine a single possible match.

Today, the comparison microscope is still the only ballistic identification process recognized by the court. The system is slow and very labor-intensive. O'Neill knows a modern, accurate, high-speed system is waiting in the wings. It has an unlikely connection.

This connection brings us to "The question of the day. What do brake shoes and bullets have in common?"

The answer may surprise you.

It all starts when a bright, engaging, freshly minted engineer walks out the door of McDill University in Montreal, Canada. Robert Walsh knows what he wants to do. He aims to specialize in applying automation and cutting-edge technology to manufacturers, helping them decrease waste and improve company profits.

Process Control was born in 1969. The engineering company developed a successful new procedure used in several manufacturing quality control systems. "Artificial Vision" incorporates high-definition cameras that take high-speed, hi-resolution photos of products as they pass by on an assembly line. An algorithm produced from the camera image is compared with a standard algorithm stored in a computer. If the algorithms match, the product continues down the line for packaging and shipping. If they do not, the faulty item is automatically sent to a "mistakes bin." In some operations, instead of a "mistakes bin," the entire assembly process shuts down.

The automation process saves the company thousands of dollars in wasted material and downtime and increases its reputation for providing the customer with a superior product.

Process Control becomes a very successful company and the word about its artificial vision technology spreads.

One day in the main office at Process Control, the telephone rings. The call is for Bob Walsh, owner and CEO of the company. The call is from a company in Georgia.

After the usual short exchange at the start of the call, the smooth southern voice begins to tell Bob his story in a rather excited but desperate tone. The caller is with a company in Georgia that receives used brake shoes from its customers and refurbishes them to make them as good as new. The shoes are then shipped back to the customer for resale or use.

Handling the old shoes being received is a very, very dirty process.

"I'm telling you, Bob, it's a mess down here," says the plant manager. "We've got twenty-four people sorting these brake shoes by hand into bins. It's a filthy nightmare."

The reason for the filth is the old, worn shoes are shipped to the plant in barrels. Upon arrival, twenty-four people work by hand to remove and sort the shoes in preparation for the refurbishing process. Years of fine, black brake dust has accumulated on each shoe. When a worker picks a shoe out of the barrel it arrives in, a cloud of fine, black dust fills the air. The additional movement needed to sort the shoes creates more floating dust, making this a horrible job.

Once sorted by brand and size, the old shoes undergo refurbishing. The old, worn, remaining lining is removed, the shoe is cleaned, and a new lining is placed on it. Then, it is shipped back to the customer as good as new.

The plant manager wants to get his workers out of the filth

and save time on the production line by improving the sorting process. Being familiar with custom-designed systems for other companies built by Process Control, he desires a system that automatically sorts incoming shoes into the correct bin. When full, the bins will be moved out of the receiving area and into the proper position on the production line for refurbishing.

Bob Walsh, never one to shy away from a new challenge, accepts the brake shoe project. Walsh does not realize that Walsh Process Control, while addressing the Georgia brake shoe "nightmare," will also start a historical connection between brake shoes and bullets.

The system devised to solve the problem eliminated the hand-sorting process. Instead, when the old shoes arrive in the barrels, they are simply dumped onto a conveyor belt: no more hand sorting and all of its associated filth and dust.

The old shoes then ride the conveyor belt, passing under a machine designed by Walsh Process Control. That is where the magic happens.

In Mr. Walsh's own words: "We take two images. One is taken from the top to determine the width of the brake shoe, which immediately eliminates about 100 different shoes. Then, the following image of the profile is taken.

"Those two together would tell us what model the brake shoe is. As the conveyor kept going, there were all these bins, and it would kick the shoe into the proper bin.

"So long story short, we did that system, and they were very happy, and it worked, it worked very well," concludes Walsh.

The connection between brake shoes and bullets is about to begin when a civilian employee of the Royal Canadian Mounted Police calls Bob Walsh.

He has read an article about Walsh Process Control's artificial vision. The story describes artificial vision in some detail. He makes the connection between recognizing the size and kind of brake shoes and the process used in the crime laboratory to identify, and match spent bullets. Could this technology be used to improve ballistic forensics?

In addition to identifying a gun used in a specific crime, a significant concern is that every law enforcement agency across the U.S. and Canada have evidence rooms filled with firearms taken from crime scenes. These weapons have yet to be test-fired. It is just too time-consuming to fire and test them all. What mysteries might they conceal?

Bob Walsh is intrigued by the prospect of uncovering those mysteries and assisting law enforcement in identifying firearms used in crimes. Bob learns that every gun manufactured has its own "signature" due to the unique chattering of the tools employed during production. These tools leave random, tiny flaws in the rifling of the gun's barrel, which the bullet picks up as it passes through.

Walsh puts his crack staff of engineers to work on the project to determine if their artificial vision could "see" and match the microscopic marks left on a bullet by the rifling in a gun's barrel.

When Forensic Technology, Inc. (FTI) begins in 1991, a new company and a ballistic forensic legend are born. FTI's parent company, Walsh Automation Inc., combines automation, optics, and hardware to help law enforcement quickly identify firearm evidence at crime scenes. The creation of the Integrated Ballistics Identification System, or IBIS, revolutionizes ballistic forensics, bringing it into the modern world.

Firearms examiner O'Neill has just been informed that the Orange County Crime Laboratory will be receiving an IBIS machine, one of the first the Bureau of Alcohol, Tobacco, Firearms and Explosives (ATF) installs as it starts to build its National Integrated Ballistic Information Network (NIBIN) system.

Tracks in the Brass

Yes, it appears O'Neill does know a trick.

CHAPTER NINETEEN

The arrival of the Integrated Ballistics Identification System (IBIS) at the Orange County Crime Laboratory marked a groundbreaking moment in forensic science, promising to revolutionize the analysis of spent bullets. As a firearms examiner, O'Neill had examined countless bullet evidence in the lab. He knew traditional methods for identifying matches between bullets and guns were time-consuming and labor-intensive, so he was thrilled to see the IBIS machine in action.

Robert Walsh, owner and President of Forensic Technology, Inc. (FTI) based in Montreal, Canada, was the man who connected brake shoes and bullets. Walsh, an engineer with a background in quality control systems for manufacturers, applied his expertise to develop IBIS for ballistic forensics. Using the same principles employed in brake shoe operations, he created a system that could revolutionize how forensic scientists analyze bullet evidence, potentially solving more cases and reducing the backlog of untested firearms.

Mr. Walsh stood beside O'Neill, explaining how the system worked. "The IBIS machine uses advanced imaging technology to examine the tiny marks left on bullets by the grooves inside a gun barrel. These marks are unique to each firearm, making it possible to identify matches with guns in evidence rooms," he said.

"Absolutely, those are the same markings we've been painstakingly identifying with our old comparison microscope for years," O'Neill responded, squirming in his chair. "As you know, Bob, it sometimes took many hours to match two bullets, especially if the crime scene samples were heavily damaged at the time of impact."

O'Neill watched intently as Walsh carefully attached a spent bullet to the IBIS machine. The machine swiftly used its high-resolution camera and computer system to generate an algorithm unique to the bullet in just over 16 minutes. "This is it," O'Neill nearly hollered to Walsh, his eyes excitedly shining. "This is the future of ballistic forensics science."

Walsh smiled, his eyes sparkling with pride. "With IBIS, you can analyze several bullets per hour, solving more cases than you ever could with your comparison microscope." With a broad grin, Bob patted O'Neill on the shoulder. "Who knows, the Chief might even notice and give you a raise," Walsh said with a reassuring chuckle. "Every police department in the country has an evidence room filled with untested guns. IBIS can break that logjam."

"Thanks for letting the Chief know I need a raise," O'Neill chuckled. "What really excites me is the potential to go through the thousands of guns in evidence rooms across the country. What kind of secrets have been locked up there for years because we had no way to do the test-firing and then comparisons using the old microscope? It is just too slow."

"I can't disagree with that," Walsh responded.

"I wonder how many firearms trafficking and cold cases we can solve?" O'Neill pondered. "I bet it will be significant, especially when we are all tied into the nationwide ATF NIBIN system. I can match my hits with guns all over California, not to mention Arizona and the rest of the states. At the risk of sounding childish, I'm as happy as a kid with a brand-new toy."

With a sense of urgency, O'Neill rushed to the Santa Ana Police Department Evidence Room, eager to test-fire the guns and uncover the secrets they held.

"Bob," he said. "You know some examiners are going to see IBIS as some new-fangled machine that will take their job, and they will push back against it." He paused for a beat and then continued, "The smart ones will figure out really quick that they can start making more matches and increase their production considerably. I guess they are the ones the Chief will give a raise to."

The two men shared a good laugh, and an understanding of what progress would be quickly made. Any way you looked at it, firearms examiner O'Neill knew a huge trick.

As the sun began to set on another busy day at the lab, O'Neill turned to Walsh with a question. "How soon can we expect this technology to be adopted by law enforcement agencies across North America?"

Walsh's expression turned thoughtful. "We're already in talks with several major agencies," he answered. "But I think the technology will take some time to become widely available. We will continue to refine our algorithms and ensure the system is reliable and accurate. However, the bigger issue is negotiating with the proper government agencies. Dealing with the US Government is always a long and complicated experience."

O'Neill nodded, his mind racing with possibilities. He knew that IBIS was just the beginning. A new era in forensic science had dawned, and he couldn't wait to see what the future held. Now, if the bureaucrats and government agency fiefdom builders would get the heck out of the way and allow the technology to move forward at the speed it was capable of achieving.

O'Neill felt proud and excited as he sat at his desk that evening. He knew he was part of something special—a team of scientists and engineers pushing the boundaries of what was possible in forensic science. With IBIS now a reality, he couldn't help but wonder what other breakthroughs lay ahead.

Yes, the old firearms examiner knew a trick or two. Now, he needed to find the gun that fired the fatal rounds into the back of Hershel Harper's head. He knew it was a Glock based on the markings on the spent shell casing found under Harper's body in the trunk of the car.

O'Neill glanced at his watch. It was a little after 7:00 p.m. Oh well, he thought. I don't care who wins the Monday Night Football Game on TV. He took the last sip of coffee from his well-worn cup, placed it on his desk, and headed for the evidence room. He had a few Glock pistols to fire and recover their bullets from the firing tank.

Would the new IBIS machine provide a link to the Harper murder?

CHAPTER TWENTY

The flickering streetlight cast eerie shadows on the walls of Soper's dimly lit room. He sat hunched over the Harper murder file, his mind racing with unanswered questions. Retirement had not brought peace; it had only intensified his obsession. Once celebrated for his keen investigative skills, Detective Soper had retired with a heavy heart. The Harper case, his last unsolved mystery, haunted him. The death of his beloved wife, who had been his pillar of support, made the nights unbearably lonely, amplifying his obsession with the case.

With his days stretching endlessly before him, Soper found solace in the worn pages of the Harper murder file. He poured over each detail, his eyes scanning the familiar words with a desperate hope of uncovering a hidden clue. His nights became increasingly restless. He tossed and turned for hours before grabbing his copy of the Harper file from his nightstand. It held a special place, just as it had on his desk when he was Chief of Detectives.

Most nights, the neighbors could see the light in his window at any hour. Soper lay in bed, reading through the Harper Murder file repeatedly. *What had he missed? There had to be something that connected Carlos Morales to the firearm that killed Mr. Harper. What was that connection? Where could he find it?* These questions circled in his mind, preventing him from sleeping.

Soper muttered under his breath, his voice tinged with frustration and determination. *I just can't shake this feeling, Carlos. You're hiding something from me, and I won't rest until I uncover the truth.*

The questions surrounding Mr. Morales and his inability to connect him to the murder weapon had become the dominant force in Soper's life. Memories of his wife flooded Soper's mind, each one a painful reminder of his loss. He felt a lump in his throat as tears streamed down his face, his sobs echoing in the empty room. The grief was a constant companion, driving him to the brink of despair.

Soper's grief and obsession with the Harper case led him to seek solace in alcohol. The whiskey haze clouded his judgment, but he continued searching for answers, driven by a relentless need for closure. He had always been a light drinker, but now he tried to hide his pain behind a haze created by alcohol. A haze he fueled with a bottle or more of Jim Beam per day. Jim Beam was his new friend.

Even though his thinking had become clouded by excessive alcohol consumption, he continued to ponder the case almost constantly. It was all-consuming. *What have I overlooked?* is the constant drumbeat in his mind. Soper had read the file so many times that he could recite it verbatim to anyone who asked. No one asked. He was always alone, and he never left the house. A neighborhood grocery store delivered to him and left the groceries on the porch, rang the doorbell and then the delivery boy walked away.

There was never a doubt in his mind that Mr. Morales had pulled the trigger on the Glock that killed Herschel Harper before his body was shoved into the trunk of his car. Where was that Glock? Did Mr. Morales throw it in the ocean, or was he hiding it somewhere?

Despite his years of experience, Soper had become so convinced of Mr. Morales's guilt that he neglected to ask obvious, probing questions about why Mr. Morales would even own two Glock pistols.

Why does Mr. Morales have two Glocks? I know where he bought one of them. Why can't I find where Morales got the second one? I don't think he stole it from any condo residents, as no one mentioned a stolen gun when I did the interviews.

Yeah, Mr. Morales purchased that second Glock to confront Hershel Harper and steal the money from the condo. Soper took another drink of whiskey, the last one in the Jim Beam bottle, and sank into a troubled sleep.

At the Santa Ana Police Department building, Detective Blair sat at his desk with a cup of hot McDonald's coffee he had picked up on his way to the station. He was searching for the answer to what he felt was a key question. The Harper file showed that Mr. Morales was very forthcoming when asked if he owned a firearm. There were no indications in the file that Mr. Morales had tried to obfuscate his answers. He was straightforward during his interviews.

Blair decided he wanted to talk to Mr. Morales. He reached up, pulled the little chain that turned off his green desk lamp, grabbed his car keys from the desk drawer, and headed to the PD parking lot. He was going to visit Burns Chevrolet, but not to buy a car.

Obtaining an answer to his ownership of a firearm was one of the reasons Blair stopped by the car dealership to visit Mr. Morales. Even though many years had passed, he wanted to ask Carlos Morales that question again and gauge his response.

Another issue that bothered him from reading the file was Mr. Morales's motive to commit such a crime. Why had he shot a man he knew and appeared to like in the back of the head, put him in the trunk of his car, and driven the vehicle into the back alley in a very rough neighborhood?

Reaching Burns Chevrolet from the PD parking lot did not take long. When he pulled onto the lot and up by the building to an area that appeared to be a parking place for guests, he parked beside a flashy red Chevrolet all decked out with the latest accessories.

Blair walked into the dealership and located Mr. Morales's office. It was evident Mr. Morales was extremely busy. Blair thought it best to ask only a few questions about the case's potential motive.

Blair knocked on Mr. Morales's office door and announced his presence with a firm tone. "Mr. Morales, Detective Blair. I hope I'm not interrupting anything important."

Mr. Morales looked up from the paperwork in front of him, a hint of annoyance flashing across his face before he composed himself. "Not at all, detective. Can you please make it quick? I have a lot to do today."

Blair sat across from Mr. Morales's desk, his eyes watching for any signs of nervousness or distraction. "I appreciate your time, Mr. Morales. I will make this as quick as possible. I can see you are very busy. I will just put it up front, plain and simple: I ask you again: do you own a firearm?"

Mr. Morales hesitated slightly before responding, "Sí, detective. I do own a firearm. I think I told those detectives who interviewed me after Señor Harper was...was shot. That I owned a gun. It is a Glock."

Blair leaned forward, his expression serious. "It's just something we're trying to clarify in the case."

"You said you owned a firearm," Blair asked, his tone direct. "Was it with you on the night of the murder?"

Mr. Morales looked down, and for a moment, Blair thought he saw a flash of something - guilt, maybe? – Mr. Morales quickly regained his composure. "I did not use my gun that night, detective. I swear to you. Señor Harper was my amigo. He was a good friend."

Several more probing questions were asked, but nothing suspicious or new resulted from them.

Blair noted Mr. Morales had been very cooperative and agreed to set aside time for the detective to return for a more extended conversation.

Blair made a mental note to investigate further, but he knew this was just the tip of the iceberg. He thanked Mr. Morales for his time and left the dealership with more questions than answers. And that was what weighed on his mind as Blair opened his car door, paused for a minute to study the pretty red Chevrolet he had parked beside and then drove away from Burn's Chevrolet. Blair had something else that needed to be checked out. He pushed the accelerator toward the floor.

CHAPTER TWENTY-ONE

The Santa Ana Crime Laboratory buzzed with anticipation. The new IBIS technology, a game-changer in forensic science, had just been installed. O'Neill could not shake the feeling that this was the beginning of something big. It required novel thinking to find a place to fit it in. O'Neill had to keep the comparison microscope he had employed for years, as the courts would only allow matches made on the old, outmoded comparison microscope in their courtrooms.

O'Neill was an excellent examiner, known for his meticulous attention to detail and unwavering dedication to justice. His talents extended beyond bullets and cartridge cases. One notable case he solved involved the sabotage of a high-tension powerline that people did not like being near and, in some cases, through their property. Eminent Domain had been used to secure some of the land for the line's pathway, and people were angry. All their complaints to officials were ignored.

One night, the electricity in the line went out. Power company employees discovered the cause was several of the tall wooden poles had broken off about five feet above the ground and fallen, taking the power lines with them. Upon close examination, it was clear that explosives had been used to sever the poles about five feet above the ground.

O'Neill was selected to go to the site and determine if any

evidence would lead to the perpetrators of the crime. Arriving on the scene, one of the first things he noticed was wood shavings on the ground by each pole. The shavings resulted from someone boring a hole in the wooden pole. Based on residue on the poles, O'Neill decided someone had drilled holes, then inserted a stick of dynamite and rigged a system to cause all the dynamite to explode simultaneously. The weight of the wires pulled the line down for several miles.

Upon closer examination of the wood shavings, O'Neill detected a distinctive scratch line in each shaving. He believed the line was caused by a nick in the drill bit that bored the holes. O'Neill determined the approximate height of the person using the drill to bore the holes was approximately six feet based on the distance of the holes above the ground. Find the drill bit with a nick and a six-foot-tall person who used it to drill the holes, and you have your person who destroyed the power line.

This information was passed on to the investigators, and a few days later, the drill bit was found. It was in the garage of a six-foot-tall man, angry about the power line. He was arrested and later found guilty in a court trial.

O'Neill had been tracking scratches and other imperfections in almost anything you could imagine for years. His expertise led him to his favorite task, performing firearms ballistic examinations. O'Neill was known for his ability to find the needle in a haystack. Now, he had the latest technology in the business sitting in his laboratory. O'Neill had the equipment to back up his "I know a trick" comment to Detective Blair.

The IBIS unit was larger than Firearms Examiner O'Neill had expected. Some of his already cramped lab equipment had to be moved to make space. The IBIS system was composed of a desk-like structure about ten feet long. The microscope and image acquisition station were placed on one end, standing about three feet tall with viewing eyepieces on the front.

A shelf the length of the desk, about a foot and a half above the desk, provided space for two large computer monitors and a printer sitting on it. Beneath the shelf were the computer keyboards and screens associated with the large monitors above. The two monitors on top projected the images captured by the microscope and allowed for manipulation by the examiner.

This morning, Firearms Examiner O'Neill sat studying the image on the screen of one of the bullets recovered from Hershel Harper's head. As he manipulated the IBIS image, he felt something was missing. Not in the image, which was sharp and clear, exposing markings that were nearly impossible to see when using only the microscope. O'Neill was seeing marks he had missed on the comparison microscope. No, something was missing in this case. He wondered if this new technology would find that needle in a haystack.

Just then, his phone rang. It was Dr. Lee, O'Neill's supervisor. "O'Neill, how's the IBIS unit doing?" she asked.

"It's doing great. I am seeing markings I never saw on the comparison microscope. Now, we must find the gun that fired the bullets that killed Harper. We don't have a match in our files. As soon as I can, I will share my image with the other labs in the area and see what we can come up with," O'Neill replied. Some frustration crept into his voice. "I've sent the image to ATF, but so far, no match with anything in their database, but it's still pretty small."

Dr. Lee's tone was sympathetic. "Don't worry, O'Neill. It's still the early days for IBIS and ATF's NIBIN. We need to keep pushing forward."

"Yes, you are right. NIBIN doesn't have much in its database yet. I will sure be happy when they get the nationwide setup they want," exclaimed O'Neill.

"That will certainly make a big difference," responded Dr.

Lee. "When we can enter images from here and find out what they have in LA nearly instantly, that will be one super tool for us. At least that's what your friend, Mr. Walsh, promised you, didn't he?" Dr. Lee asked.

"Yes," answered O'Neill. "I have known Bob for many years, and he has always been a man of his word. Anybody that converts brake shoe quality technology into the IBIS machine and NIBIN is one smart man to trust."

"Can you imagine the thousands of firearms gathering dust in evidence rooms across the country that have never been processed due to the long time the comparison microscope takes? Now, IBIS can do what used to take hours in minutes. As you know, we have close to two hundred firearms in our evidence room. What kind of clues to cold cases are hidden there?"

"Yes, it is quite a leap for our work," Dr. Lee added. "It might even make us look better to the Chief," she chuckled.

"Yeah," O'Neill replied. "But what fascinates me the most is how many secrets may be gathering dust in those evidence rooms. If we can start to roll these old weapons out, test fire them, run the bullets through IBIS, and compare them to all the IBIS results, I can't help but feel we will see a lot of cold cases cracked. At least, that's what I hope."

"Well, I better get back to work and let you do the same. Talk to you later," Dr. Lee said as she hung up.

O'Neill sighed, knowing she was right. It was time for a fresh cup of coffee, O'Neill thought. He pushed back his chair and headed for the breakroom.

A few minutes later, with a hot cup of coffee in his right hand and a big, glazed donut from the box someone had left in the breakroom in his left hand, O'Neill returned to his chair at the IBIS machine. Leaning back in his chair, he sat staring at the image of the bullet removed from Hershel Harper's head.

O'Neill picked up his phone and dialed a number displayed on the computer screen on the IBIS desk. When that call was completed, he dialed another one. He had pulled up on the computer, the telephone numbers of crime laboratories in the area.

He continued dialing numbers, working on the case, and contacting all the police departments with crime labs in a 300-mile radius of Santa Ana. His mission was to find any match that would crack this old cold case open.

The elusive Glock might be residing in an evidence room somewhere around the Santa Ana area. He had been asking his counterparts in the labs he called, now equipped with IBIS, to go through any Glocks they had and share the images with him. O'Neill knew a trick.

While O'Neill pondered his thoughts and plans in the crime lab, down the hallway and up a half flight of stairs resided the Detective Bureau. The sign on the door said Chief of Detectives. Inside sat Detective Blair, his little green desk lamp lit, a nearly fresh cup of what was now fairly hot McDonald's coffee sitting on his desk, and a look of deep concentration on his brow.

Blair sat in his customary posture, leaning back in his chair, with the transcript of the Morales interviews conducted immediately following the tragic events at the Sunshine Casitas Condo Complex in his lap. He slowly reread the words he had already read a half dozen times. Leaning on his years of varied and sometimes complicated detective work, he could not shake off the feeling that he had missed something with Morales' response to the interview questions he had been asked.

Chief on his mind, Blair wondered if Mr. Morales had been telling the truth about his Glock and if he had a second one he kept hidden or perhaps threw away after shooting Mr. Harper. And what about his alibi for the night of the murder? Also, the new car each year was a troubling question. His story made sense on the surface. Mr. Burns confirmed Mr. Morales's story, but it sounded a little fishy. *Is there something in that situation I am missing,* Blair thought?

Blair had many questions, so he decided to revisit Mr. Morales, this time with a different perspective. He wanted to ask more questions about Mr. Morales' background, his relationship with Harper, and anything else that might shed some light on the case.

Yes, Blair thought to himself, *that may be where the answers to this case lay.* He threw his now cold and only about an eighth-full McDonald's coffee cup into the trash, pulled the little chain that turned off his green desk lamp and headed for the PD Garage. Blair picked up his car. It roared to life, and he pointed it toward Burns Chevrolet.

When Blair arrived at the car dealership, he found a parking spot directly in front of the building. Entering the showroom, he was met by a young salesman. After he assured the young man he was not there to buy a car, he went down the side hallway to Mr. Morales's office. Blair noticed that Mr. Morales was still busy. He tapped lightly on the doorjamb and entered the office.

Morales looked up from his paperwork and was surprised to see Detective Blair back in his office again. After exchanging greetings, Blair told Mr. Morales he realized he was busy and asked for a few minutes of his time anyway. Morales offered him a chair.

"Mr. Morales," Blair said, sitting across from him, "I am so sorry to bother you again so soon, but I want to ask you something again. I think I may have missed some of your answers when we talked the other day. Can you tell me more about your background? Where did you grow up?"

Morales hesitated and looked around the room nervously before responding. "I grew up in Mexico, but when I come to

US I first live in Temecula, California. I still have family there, a couple of cousins. My parents...my mom passed away when I was young. My two sisters live in Colorado, and my brother is here in Santa Ana. My dad... he's still alive."

Before Blair could follow up on Mr. Morales's response, they were interrupted by a tapping on the open door to Morales's office; a uniformed officer stood at the door, eyes scanning the room, typical of his training, before locking onto Blair. "Detective Blair?" he asked.

"Yes," Blair responded, and the officer handed Blair a file folder. "Firearms Examiner O'Neill asked me to bring this to you wherever I could find you. He said it was crucial, and you needed it as soon as possible."

Blair thanked the officer and then excused himself to open the file. Morales returned to a contract he was working on for a customer who was scheduled to come to the dealership later in the day.

There was only one sheet of paper in the file folder: a copy of the computer message O'Neill had received from ATF. ATF had found a match for the bullets O'Neill had submitted. The match was to a Glock pistol stolen from a pawn shop in Phoenix, AZ, four days before Hershel Harper was shot and killed. This was a home run for the case and ATF at this early stage of developing a database of ballistic images.

Blair's eyes widened as he read the message a second time. This could be the break they needed!

Blair stared at the message, pondering possible scenarios. His thoughts were interrupted when Morales spoke up, his voice laced with concern: "Senór Blair, I think there's something you should know—something that might change everything."

Morales's eyes darted back and forth between Blair and the paper on his desk as if searching for the right words to say. "I didn't kill Harper," he said finally, his voice shaking slightly.

"But I think I know who did."

Whoa, Blair thought, *maybe the dam is breaking on this thing.* O'Neill's news was a big crack in the dam. Was Mr. Morales going to blow it the rest of the way open?

Blair was excited but cautious. He had heard it all before the "I didn't do it" confession, which often led nowhere.

"How do you know that?" Blair asked, trying to keep an open mind.

Morales took a deep breath before speaking. "It's about my family, my past. I've been keeping secrets from you."

Blair leaned forward ; his eyes locked on Morales. "What are you trying to tell me?"

Morales glanced around the room nervously before focusing on Blair. "My father...he was involved in some shady dealings. He's been in prison several times for smuggling and trafficking."

Blair's ears perked up at this new information. This could be a significant lead.

"What does your father have to do with Harper's murder?" Blair asked his voice firm but controlled and showing neutral emotion.

Morales hesitated before responding. "My father was in debt to some... unsavory characters. They were threatening to hurt my family if he didn't pay up. I think they're the ones who killed Mr. Harper."

"Why would they kill Harper when your father was the one who owed them money?" Blair asked.

"They knew I worked at the condo complex. I spotted a man riding the garbage truck who I knew was part of a gang my father hung around with. He had seen the people paying each month. I think he stole the money and killed Mr. Harper. They wanted to blame me for stealing the money and put more pressure on my father," Carlos said.

Blair's eyes narrowed as he considered this new

information. It was a long shot, but it was worth exploring.

Blair had an impulse. Mr. Morales was talking. If I could get him in front of his father, I could question them together. This situation should keep both honest, and I could apply more pressure on them.

"Can you take us to your father?" Blair asked, his voice firm.

"Sí," responded Carlos. "I can take some time off tomorrow."

"No, I mean right now," Blair said firmly. "We need to go right now."

Morales nodded reluctantly before standing up. "I'll need some time to gather my thoughts," he said, his eyes welling up with tears. Following several moments of silence, Morales looked Blair in the eye. "I... I can take you to him."

Blair did not want to miss the moment.

Reluctantly, Morales laid his pen on the desk, quickly called the receptionist at the front desk, informing her he would be out of the dealership for a short time, and led Blair out the door of his office.

Blair pointed to his car when the two men reached the front of the showroom and stepped outside into a beautiful southern California day. Morales entered the passenger door as Blair got in the driver's side, and they drove out of the dealership. Blair could not shake the feeling that he was on the right track. This could be the break Blair needed to crack the case wide open. But he did not want to jump to conclusions too soon.

Following Mr. Morales's directions, not far from the dealership, they turned into the clean, well-kept Mexican neighborhood where Morales lived. A few blocks later, as they turned a corner to follow a different street, the houses turned from neat with nice yards to rundown buildings with tall grass, trash, and weeds in the yard. Old cars were parked in several driveways and on the street. Some were sitting on concrete blocks with missing tires and open hoods. This was a poor and very rough neighborhood. Blair was familiar with some of the addresses they drove past. The people living at those addresses had been involved with the police department in the past.

Morales finally pointed to a house. It was an old, rundown place with trash in the yard and a rusty, old Ford parked in the driveway. At least the tires on the car were all inflated.

"This is it," he said, embarrassed, his voice barely above a whisper. "This is where my father lives."

Blair glanced at Morales before getting out of the car, signaling him to proceed carefully. Blair was aware of the danger that lurked behind many doors in this part of the city. They approached the house cautiously, Morales in the lead; Blair followed, his hand under his suit jacket, resting on his gun.

CHAPTER TWENTY-TWO

Mr. Morales knocks on the door, and a gruff voice bellows from inside. "¿Quién es?"

Morales hesitates before responding. "Soy yo, Ángel." Ángel is the name his family called him rather than Carlos.

The door creaks open, revealing a burly man with a thick beard, a menacing scowl, and hair that hangs in unkempt, shaggy strands. Blair thinks his overall appearance reminds him of Hollywood actor George Lopez. A good bath and some clean clothes would help his appearance.

"¿Qué quieres, niño?," he growls.

Blair has his badge attached to his belt and makes sure the man in the door sees it. He determines the man is not armed and then steps forward; his eyes locked on him. "We're here to talk about your involvement in Hershel Harper's murder," Blair says firmly.

The man's reaction tells Blair that the rough-looking man in the doorway does not speak English and can only understand a little. This situation just became more difficult, Blair thinks.

The man snorts, his expression twisting into a sneer.

"Nunca me derribas," he spat. Carlos translates, "He said, you will never take him down."

Blair nods to Carlos in appreciation. Then, with his voice calm but firm, he says, "We don't need you to come with us, Mr. Morales. We just want to talk."

Carlos says, "No, Detective Blair, his name is not Morales, it is Gallegos. He does not speak any English."

Blair's jaw tightens as he realizes the language barrier will complicate the interview. Gallegos's blank stare confirms his suspicion. A translator is the only good answer. *Blair ponders whether he should wait for a department translator to travel from the office. No,* Blair thinks. *I need to strike while there is an element of surprise.*

The situation and the look on Blair's face tell Carlos there is a big problem. *Maybe I can help,* he thinks. "Detective, I can translate if that helps," Carlos says to Blair.

Even though he is investigating Carlos, Blair trusts him. Carlos is here, and he can start asking questions right now. He turns to Carlos, "Well, thank you, Carlos. I was getting ready to ask you if you could translate for me. It will save much time, and your father might be more comfortable answering my questions, but I caution you, there might be uncomfortable questions I want to ask Mr. Gallegos."

"Si, Senór. I will do it. You have been nice to me; tough questions, no problem."

Blair asks, "Where were you on the night of Hershel Harper's murder?" He watches Gallegos's body language as Carlos translates.

Carlos repeats the question to Gallegos in Spanish.

The man shrugs, a smirk still playing on his lips. "Who is Hershel Harper?" he asks. Carlos translates for Blair.

Blair has Carlos tell him the date of the murder and then ask where he was and what he was doing.

Gallegos responds, "I was at home, watching TV. You can ask my wife; she'll vouch for me," comes the translation.

Blair raises an eyebrow, skeptical of this alibi. He makes a mental note to speak with Harper's family and see if they know Gallegos or can confirm or deny his story that he does not know them.

As Blair, with Carlos's assistance, continues questioning

Gallegos, he notices that the man is evasive and nervous. Gallegos keeps glancing at Morales, his eyes filled with fear, resentment, and hatred. Blair decides there is more hatred than anything else.

Is he uncomfortable with Carlos translating, or is he afraid Carlos will reveal something he wants to keep secret? Carlos is his son, but Blair senses Gallegos does not trust or even like him.

Blair shifts gears for a moment. "Ángel, why did you tell me you had something to confess?" Blair asks, trying to keep his tone neutral.

Morales's eyes drop, his voice barely above a whisper. "I am scared. I didn't know what else to do."

Blair's expression softens slightly as he looks at Morales. He can understand the fear and desperation in his eyes.

"Tell me more?" Blair asks gently. "What did you learn about your father's dealings?"

Morales takes a deep breath before speaking, his words spilling out in a rush. "My father was involved with some shady characters, like I said. But it went deeper than that. He was in debt to a man named Victor Vex. I think he said Vex worked for a Mr. Petrov."

Blair's ears perk up at this new information. Vex is a name he is very familiar with - a notorious gang leader with a reputation for ruthlessness.

"What did your father do to get in debt to Vex?" Blair asks, his eyes locked on Morales.

Morales hesitates, his eyes darting back and forth between Gallegos and Blair. "He...he stole from some people. People he owed money to. People connected to Vex. He thought he could outrun it but Vex found out."

Blair's expression darkens as he listens to Morales' story. The situation grows more complex by the minute, but the new information is invaluable.

"Did your father admit to stealing the condo money to pay his debt and then admitting to Harper's murder?" Blair asks, his voice firm.

Morales shakes his head vigorously. "No, I not tell you that. I just tell you it Vex who want my family dead. My father no steal condo money or kill anyone. He still owe Vex."

Blair notices that Carlos is very nervous and has lapsed into his broken English. Is he involved in this money business? Or is the threat against his family real? What else is Carlos not telling me?

Blair's mind is racing with possibilities. He knew he had a long way to go before he cracked the case, but he was getting new information, and he felt he was getting closer.

Blair turns his questioning back to Gallegos. He can talk to Carlos later. He continues to probe Gallego's connection with Vex. How much did he owe him? Gallegos, after much probing, says $12,000. What did he borrow the money for? Gallegos said to pay some bills. What kind of bills? Nothing specific. Carlos thought it was gambling debt. How did he plan to pay Vex back? Just the runaround on these questions. Who had he approached to get the money from? Another runaround. Did it bother him that Vex threatened his family if he did not pay up? Carlos received a look from Gallegos that could kill, but no specifics, just BS, Blair thought.

As he continues questioning Gallegos, Blair can't shake off the feeling that there is more to Vex's involvement than meets the eye. He makes a mental note to dig deeper into Vex's activities and see if he can find any connections to Harper's murder. Vex is known for stealing money from people he did not have a beef with or even know. He just stole money when he saw the opportunity, many times being brutal to the victim. Human life did not mean that much to Vex.

The investigation has become much more complicated, but Blair is determined to get his needed answers.

"I don't know what kind of game you're playing, Gallegos," Blair asks Carlos to translate, his voice firm but controlled. "But I'm not buying it. You'll either tell me the truth, or I'm taking you downtown to jail. Maybe a little vacation there will jog your memory." Carlos passes the message along to Gallegos as he has been doing for Detective Blair for the last forty-five minutes.

Even though Blair cannot speak or understand Spanish, he feels Carlos has expressed his statements with emotion and a force equal to his own. Carlos has picked up Blair's feelings and intentions.

Gallegos sneers at them. "You'll never take me down. I've got connections, just like my father did before me. I know how to play the system. You cops are all for sale for a price!"

Carlos translates the nasty answer, and Blair gives him a response to provide Gallegos.

Blair leans forward; his eyes locked on Gallegos's. "We'll see about that."

As Carlos finishes the translation, another idea crosses Blair's mind. "Carlos, can you tell me more about what your father told you about the money?"

Morales nods, his voice barely above a whisper. "He said...he said Vex was going to hurt our family if we didn't pay up. Vex said he'd do whatever it took to keep us quiet."

Blair's expression softens slightly as he looks at Morales. "I'm sorry, Angel. I wish you hadn't gotten involved in this."

Morales shook his head. "I had to protect myself and my family. I couldn't just sit back and let Vex hurt us."

Blair nods sympathetically. "I understand that, Carlos. But now we need your help to take Vex down. Can you tell me where he is?"

"No," Carlos answers. "I will ask Senór Gallegos if you want me to."

Blair shakes his head. "Yes."

"¿Dónde está Vex? ¿Se esconde?"

Gallegos laughs. "You think I'd ever tell you that? You'll never find him. He's too smart for that."

Blair's eyes narrow. "I don't believe you, Gallegos. We'll find Vex, and we'll bring him down. And when we do, you'll be the first one to testify against him."

Once again, Carlos translates for Detective Blair.

Gallegos snorts. "You think I'm afraid of you? You're just a fool playing at being a tough detective. I'll never tell you anything, you big sissy."

This time, Carlos's translation carries much anger that Blair detects.

Blair stands up, his eyes locked on Gallegos's. "We'll take that as a yes, then. We'll book you for obstruction of justice and leave the rest to us."

Carlos translates Blair's statement with a great deal of energy this time. Maybe this load he has been carrying for years would be lifted off his shoulders.

As Blair handcuffs Gallegos and reads him his rights, Blair can't help but feel a sense of unease. He still has a long way to go before he cracks the case, and he knows that Vex will not give up easily.

"Alright, let's get him out of here," Blair says, leading Gallegos out of the house. "I'll drop you off at the dealership on the way to the police station," Blair tells Carlos. "And muchas gracias for your help, Carlos. You have been very cooperative and helpful. Let's hope I can clear you after looking into the Vex issue."

Blair puts Gallegos in the backseat of his police car. Carlos hops into the right front seat. Blair and Carlos chat about Carlos's family on the way back to the car dealership. Blair notes how proud Carlos is of his children and his wife. Carlos Morales is a good man, Blair thinks. I hope what I find will clear him.

Blair pulls into the jail's security parking area. It is not busy this time of day. Booking Gallegos into the Santa Ana Police Department jail did not take long. The heavy activity is at night. Officers working the graveyard shift will tell you with a smile, "Nothing good happens after midnight." The graveyard officers make sure a lot of the "nothing good" lands in jail.

Blair believes he knows how to put some "before midnight bad" in jail. As Firearms Examiner O'Neill would say, "I know a trick." In fact, Blair knows several tricks he plans to use soon.

CHAPTER TWENTY-THREE

After booking Gallegos, Detective Blair and Carlos Morales walked up a hallway. Carlos thought they were headed to Blair's office, but little did he know, they were on their way to an interrogation room where the atmosphere would soon change.

Blair leaned in, a friendly smile on his face. "Carlos, how about a drink? We might chat for a while."

"Sure," replied Carlos. "Do you have Dr Pepper?"

"We sure do," responded Blair cheerfully. "The soft drink machine is right around the corner; I'll pick up a Dr Pepper for you; it's on me. I want a cup of coffee, too."

The coffee machine, perched on a rickety table beside the soft drink dispenser, hissed as Blair poured himself a cup of steaming black coffee. The rich, invigorating aroma filled the air, momentarily cutting through the tension. With drinks in hand, they continued down the hallway. Carlos noticed that many interview rooms were lined up along the hallway. As they passed one with a green light, Blair said, "Let's stop here for a minute or two. It's quieter than my office."

Once they were in the room, Blair closed the door behind them and offered Carlos a chair opposite him across a small table. Unseen by Carlos, Blair touched a concealed button next to the door that activated the camera and recording device in the room. Once they were settled, Blair began.

"Carlos, I want to ask you some questions about the money stolen from the Sunshine Casitas condo complex and your relationship with your father. I am going to be very blunt with you. Did he ask you to steal the money for him?"

The firmness in Blair's voice and the question jarred Carlos a bit. He thought they would only continue the friendly conversation about his family they had in the car. He was thrown off balance a little. Exactly what Blair intended.

Carlos's eyes widened, his breath catching in his throat as he processed Blair's unexpected question. "No, Señor Blair. My father never mentioned the money. I don't think he even knew about it."

"Why do you think that?" asked Blair.

There was no verbal answer; he sat quietly and lightly shrugged his shoulders.

Blair took a sip of his coffee and sat silently for a few seconds as he gathered his thoughts. The pause was also for effect. He wanted Carlos to sit for a minute to think about his situation. "Carlos, how would he have known about the money without some inside contact? I think it was you."

"No, no," came the hurried, almost frightened answer. "He did not think I knew anything about the money. He just thought I worked there doing maintenance work. He knew nothing else, I promise you. We did not talk often, and we are not close. Not even friends. He hates me."

"Because I have a good job, he thinks I must be cheating some way. That's how he always lived," Carlos responded. "He cheated at everything. He did not do honest work. I do not want to be like him!"

Blair sat for a moment, considering his next question. He was starting to believe that Carlos was innocent of wrongdoing. His answers indicated that Blair's hunch was probably correct. But Blair wanted to be sure. Gallegos knew about the money he would steal to pay back Vex what he owed him. Someone had told him about the monthly collection at the condo, and Carlos was the most likely suspect.

Blair's questions grew more intense as the minutes ticked by. Carlos's answers remained consistent, but Blair's instincts told him there was more beneath the surface. After 35 grueling minutes, Blair finally leaned back, convinced but still wary. He decided to let Carlos go, but the nagging doubt lingered.

"Are you ready to go home, Carlos?" Blair asked in a friendly voice. "I will take you back to the car dealership so you can pick up your vehicle. By the way, I assume it is that tricked-out red Chevrolet Impala sitting by the dealership's front door."

"Sí," responded Carlos as the tension of the interview faded away and a big smile came on his face. "I love red Chevrolets. I get a new one every year."

"You want another Dr. Pepper?" Blair asked as they neared the breakroom on their way out the door.

"Thank you, but no, I've had my limit for the day."

The two men walked outside and entered Blair's car. They headed back toward the dealership, and Blair had more questions than before they arrived at the police station. He believed Carlos. Someone else had told Gallegos about the money, and he must find out who that person is.

After dropping Carlos off at the Burns Chevy dealership, Blair decided he needed to go back to the office and catch up on his paperwork for the day.

As he settled into his chair with a fresh, hot cup of McDonald's coffee he stopped to pick up on his way, he reached up and pulled the little chain that turned on the green light on his desk. He started to shuffle through the stack of papers that had accumulated on his desk while he had been out with Carlos and suddenly stopped.

He picked up his phone and punched in Betsy's number. He knew she was already gone for the day, but he wanted to leave her a voicemail. "Betsy, will you please pull me anything we have on Victor Vex and his friend Petrov? Thank you."

Blair dug through the paperwork for nearly two hours. When he was satisfied he had read and signed everything he needed to do for the day, he reached up and pulled the little chain that turned off the green light on his desk, left his office and headed for the PD garage.

On his way home he swung into a handy McDonald's, ordered a McDouble and a large coffee. Blair munched on the hamburger as he drove the rest of the way home. When he arrived in the driveway his house was dark.

Making his way to the front door, holding what little was left of his McDouble in his mouth, the coffee in his left hand, he fished the door key out of his pocket with the right and unlocked the door. Stepping inside he could see there were no lights on in the back of the house either.

"Barb!" he hollered, "Are you here?" No answer. Maybe one of her friends came by and picked her up and they had gone to a movie. This wasn't the first time this happened, and she did not bother to tell him. In fact, it happened several times in the past few weeks. *Oh, well,* Blair told himself. *I'm beat on my butt so I'm going on to bed. Maybe she will tell me where she has been in the morning, even though she didn't do it the last few times.*

Blair was up early, and Barbara was still asleep. Let a sleeping dog lie, went through Blair's mind as he picked up his suit jacket and headed for the police station. When he arrived at his office, he discovered that Betsy had laid the files for Victor Vex and Alexei Petrov on his desk. Although he was familiar with the contents of both, there were details he had never pursued. This might be the time to do so.

With his ever-present friendly cup of coffee in hand, Blair pulled the little chain that turned on the green lamp on his desk and started to pore over the files in earnest. He reviewed the familiar parts first, wondering if there was something he had missed.

After finding nothing, he started digging deeper into the minutiae of the information. There was much to dig through. These two men had quite a history. Vex was openly known as the boss of the biggest gang in the city. Violence was just a part of his nature. He mainly operated out of a dingy bar in a rough part of the city.

Petrov was his opposite. He worked from an impressive office in the city's best office building. He circulated with the money crowd and was known as a very shrewd businessman. However, there was a side of him that most people did not see. He was associated with organized crime. Some of his business deals were highly questionable.

A couple of hours into his workday, Betsy entered the room. "Do you want another cup of coffee, boss?" she asked.

"I don't mind if I do," responded Blair as he stretched his arms. "I think I'll take a little break while you're gone. You know you never own a cup of coffee; all you do is rent it for a short period of time."

They both chuckled and headed out the door to do their respective chores.

Blair decided it was essential to know the relationship between Gallegos, Petrov and Vex. Were they business partners or just casual acquaintances? Which one of them was doing the dirty work? What exactly was the criminal activity they were involved in? Blair had many more questions than answers.

Back at his desk with the new cup of coffee steaming away, he asked Betsy, "Is there anything else we have on these two characters that you haven't brought me?"

"No, this is everything we have in our file. I checked before I pulled the main file, and every detective who has worked on a case associated with these two thugs and written a note or report is right there on your desk."

With that comment, Blair thanked her for her conscientious work. As she left his office, he took a sip of that delicious hot coffee, grabbed another paper from the file, leaned back in his chair, and started to read again. He knew he had a long way to go, but the information he needed to crack this cold case was somewhere.

A small beam of sunlight was shining through his office window. It was focused like a spotlight on the Harper cold case file laying on Blair's desk. Blair stared at the file and then ran the case through his mind for the thousandth time.

Seventeen years had passed since Hershel Harper's body was discovered in the trunk of his car, which was parked under a lean-to in a rough part of town. Ethel, Harper's wife, had passed away and was now buried with him in Iowa. She never knew what happened to her husband. Their daughter Marlene, her husband Troy, and the grandkids still lacked answers and had no closure. One detective, Charlie Soper, had become so obsessed with the case that he took it home after retiring. He could not solve it and had turned into a severe alcoholic, spending very few days sober enough to even know what the weather was like. Every lead had been a dead end except for a couple that seemed to hold little promise. There is a good chance some of the work that needs to be done will have to be done undercover, Blair tells himself.. I will cross that bridge when I come to it.

The case is now mine, Detective Blair told himself. It was time to solve this, and Blair was determined to do it. There were a couple of interesting people he wanted to talk with as he pulled the little chain that turned off the green light on his desk and left his office.

CHAPTER TWENTY-FOUR

Petrov and Vex, Petrov and Vex—those names haunted Detective Blair's thoughts, a relentless reminder of the dark secrets he was determined to uncover. Add in Gallegos, and you had a threesome you would never want to play golf with, Blair thought with a smile on his face.

No, these three men had something to do with the murder of Herschel Harper. What is that secret? he asks himself. A secret that remained buried all these years. Where is the Glock pistol used in the murder?

His first stop is to grab a cup of coffee at McDonald's. His wife keeps telling him the caffeine is going to fry his brain. He just laughs it off. Without his coffee, he is no good. It is an addiction, almost like cocaine.

Turning down a street into a rougher part of the city, he looks for the "Happy Time" Bar and Grill. He has been here before. This is the hangout and headquarters for Mr. Vex. Usually, Vex is in the bar, and that is what Blair is hoping.

This time, he left the McDonald's coffee in his car's cup holder. He did not think walking into a bar with a cup of coffee would be very impressive. Being impressive is necessary when he met Mr. Vex. Detective Blair had some serious questions to ask the thug and well-known gangster.

Pushing through the door into the "Happy Time," Blair is greeted with the acrid smell of cigarette smoke that stings his lungs, the sour scent of stale beer, and the grime of a building that hadn't seen a mop in years. The jukebox blares an old blues tune, its melancholic notes weaving through the thick haze of cigarette smoke, and the place is very noisy. It is filled with men dressed in worn Levis and old shirts, some with motorcycle club vests. There is also a sizable complement of females with blouses unbuttoned to a "Hey, look at me!" level.

Blair, dressed in his worn suit, caught everyone's attention. A dozen pairs of eyes turn to him, their gazes sharp and unwelcoming. The air grew thick with tension, and the low murmur of conversation ceased. He is a stranger from a different world, and the people in the bar are not necessarily happy to see him. They almost instantly pegged him as a cop.

"Where is Vex?" Blair asks in a demanding voice.

He is answered with nearly total silence other than a growl or two. Then a scruffy little guy about 5 foot 10, with hair that had not been cut in months or maybe a year, nor had it been washed in the same amount of time, pushed through the crowd and addressed Blair as he held a beer in his hand.

His voice, harsh from many years of heavy smoking, demanded, "What the hell do you want to know it for?"

"Mr. Vex doesn't have any use for a lawman like you. Dick Tracy, why don't you just turn around and go out that little door you came in through?"

Killer's retort drew laughter from the thugs in the bar, their amusement echoing off the grimy walls. Then, everything fell silent for a moment.

Blair broke the impasse with, "Mr. Vex and I need to have a serious conversation. He might want to stay in business."

The place became quiet again, and before anyone else could say anything, a big man about 6 foot 2 pushed through the crowd. "What do you want, Barney Fife?" came the question from Vex. A former boxer with a broken nose and a scar running down his cheek, had a reputation for being both ruthless and cunning. "This is my place, and we don't allow coppers to hang out here. You guys don't understand what it's like to have to work to make a living like we do."

Blair summed up the group in his mind as the typical gang. As a group, they were big, strong, and vicious. However, they usually proved to be cowards if you pulled one off by themselves. Blair thought it is the old "strength in numbers" theory.

"Vex, we need to talk. And I don't mean out here, but in private," Blair said sternly. "Do you have an office in this delightful little place?" Blair asks.

Vex took a drag from the cigarette in his hand and then dropped it on the floor. Aggravation in his voice, he says, "Come on, copper," as he turns and starts toward the back of the room.

Blair follows him to a small, dingy office, even more decrepit than the bar. The walls are adorned with pictures of naked girls, while the desk is a chaotic mess of papers, girly magazines, and whiskey bottles of various brands. Blair thought to himself, it's obvious Vex isn't into much high-level literature.

Vex points to the one empty chair in the room. It has seen better days as it appears to be an old chrome kitchen chair, and its plastic covering is worn, ripped, and has holes in several places. Blair takes a seat, wondering if the rickety old chair will hold his weight.

Vex plops down in his well-worn old office chair, puts his feet on the desk, extracts a cigarette from his pocket, and lights it. After inhaling deeply and blowing the smoke in Blair's direction, he asks, "What do you want?"

In a nonconfrontational voice, Blair says, "Nothing. I only want to talk about your relationship with Mr. Gallegos."

"And why do you want to know that? I very seldom see him, and he is not part of my social circle," Vex says with a wave of his hand, indicating his social circle is the people out in the bar.

"I'm not going to beat around the bush with you," Blair states. "I'm working on a cold case. It's nearly 17 years old, and I believe you can help me solve it. I'm not implicating you or any of your people. I only want some information."

Blair is thinking, if I come at him from a non-confrontational point it will be something he is not accustomed to from a police officer. This might be enough just to throw him off and gain some information he wouldn't otherwise share.

Vex sits quietly, contemplating Blair for a minute or two. It is apparent several questions are rolling around in his mind. The strongest amongst them is, *Should I talk to this clown?*

Finally, Vex asks, "What do you want to know?"

"Do you remember the money theft at Sunshine Casitas Condo Complex about 16 or 17 years ago and the murder of Herschel Harper, the manager of the property?" Blair asks.

Vex takes a couple more drags off his cigarette that he lit after throwing his other one on the bar floor and contemplates the question. Dropping his feet off the desk, he leans forward, places his elbows on the desktop, and looking firmly at Blair, he answers, "Yeah, I sorta' remember it. Don't think there is much money, as I recall. I think they found some guy named Harper in the trunk of his car, I think. You guys with all your fancy equipment never caught anybody. That's about all I remember."

Blair is not taking notes in a notebook in his conventional fashion. Before entering the bar, he decided that asking, talking, listening, and then committing the information to memory are much more effective methods for conducting this type of interview. He thinks Vex will be more likely to give him information if the interview is more like a conversation than the usual formal interview.

"Did you ever hear of anyone involved in the money theft?"

185

Blair asks, as he leaned back in the old kitchen chair the best he can. The chair cracked and popped but did not let him down.

"Do you know a fellow named Gallegos?" Blair asks.

"Gallegos? Yeah, he's a lazy bum. He hangs around and always wants something. He wants to borrow money; he wants to go with us when we make one of our trips downtown," Vex says with a bit of laughter in his voice. "Yeah, I know him, but I would never hire him to clean the toilet."

Blair notes what he interprets as more sincerity in Vex's answers than deception. Blair continues asking questions, "Vex, did he ask to borrow any money from you about the same time as the Sunshine Casitas burglary?"

Vex lets out a bit of laughter, "Detective, I can't remember that far back. In fact, I can't remember what I did the day before yesterday. I just don't have that kind of memory."

"No, I don't believe he asked to borrow any money. He hasn't asked to borrow any money in a long time, and when he does, it's usually, oh maybe a hundred bucks or so. I will admit for a bum, he's good 'bout paying it back." Vex gives a nasty little laugh, "Course he is familiar with the collection agency I use." Another big puff on the cigarette.

"I do my best to stay away from him. He is one of those parasites that can suck all the blood out of you if you're weak. He's lazy. He doesn't work, he doesn't steal much, he just kind of sits around on his butt and bitches about how bad everything is. Naw, I can't see a big steal with him as possible. I doubt he'd even sit in the car and watch one."

Blair believes Vex is being honest with him or at least as honest as he ever gets. His hunch that Gallegos had stolen the money and killed Harper is starting to fade. The man did not seem capable of doing that kind of activity. *Maybe I'm wrong,* Blair thinks. *I will check this out further, but right now, I don't think Gallegos has anything to do with the situation at Sunshine Casitas.* This hunt for answers is becoming more complex.

Blair thanks Vex for his time and heads out the door. Vex says, "Come back again, and I'll buy you a beer the next time." He gave a little laugh but never got up from his desk. "You know the way out, don't you detective?"

As Blair walks out of the bar, he catches a glimpse of the grip of a Glock protruding from the pocket of one of the thugs at the bar. He immediately thinks, is that the gun that killed Harper? This is not the time to pursue the situation. He is alone and surrounded by a group of people who have strength in numbers, and they will take him out in a minute. Perhaps later this would prove to be the gun he is looking for.

Blair leaves The Happy Time Bar and goes to his car. Mr. Petrov is next on his list to question. Blair guessed it would be a little cleaner, fancier place, but he is probably going to make even less progress than he did with Vex.

Blair thought Vex was basically only a street thug, a brute who relied on muscle and intimidation. Petrov, on the other hand, was a slick mob member, a man who navigated the underworld with cunning and charm.

With that, he reaches over, takes a big sip of his coffee that has now turned cold, starts the engine, and heads down the street. Blair glances at his wristwatch. He needs to catch Betsy at the station before she leaves for the day. I have time to get there, park, and grab a fresh cup of coffee. He squeals the tires as he pulls away from the curb.

CHAPTER TWENTY-FIVE

Detective Blair's mind is a storm of troubling thoughts as he stares blankly at the yellow notepad on his desk. He has set up a meeting today with Petrov and is attempting to form the questions he wants to ask him. He is having trouble concentrating. He hopes another sip of hot McDonald's coffee will clear his mind.

He has a yellow paper tablet on his desk for making notes. After 10 minutes, he looks at the pad. It's covered in scribbles and a little stick figure he drew repeatedly—a female figure.

Despite the sunny California day, Blair feels as if storm clouds are gathering over his life, each clap of thunder and bolt of lightning disrupting his concentration.

Throughout his years in law enforcement, starting as a patrolman and eventually moving up to the detective bureau his wife had always been very supportive. However, she had now become distant and no longer engaged in the friendly conversations they used to enjoy at the end of his workday, whether it was in the afternoon or at 2 a.m. Blair had always shared the adventures of his day with her in colorful detail while keeping secret those aspects he needed to safeguard to maintain the integrity of his investigations.

Blair takes another sip of coffee and thinks back to yesterday. Vex was cooperative during the interview. Blair jots down a solid note on his yellow pad: 'Vex didn't put this together.'

He next writes on his pad, "Vex has no use for Gallegos. He is a real loser." Blair reflects on his interview with Vex. He had deliberately left his small notepad in his jacket pocket, aiming for a friendly conversation rather than an interrogation. Blair feels his technique paid off.

Again, his mind is not concentrating on writing down the facts he has gathered. It keeps drifting back to his wife. He takes another sip of coffee and asks himself, *What's wrong with me? I've never had this much trouble concentrating on my work.*

This time, instead of the sip he customarily drank, he took a big drink of his coffee. His wife keeps popping into his mind. *What's going on with her? Things are not right; she has become distant and more aggressive about me not making enough money.* Blair stares out his office window and taps his ballpoint on the yellow tablet for several minutes. He tells himself he has to get back to the Harper case.

He thinks Vex has cooperated and jots that note down on his yellow pad. He pauses momentarily and then writes, "He never mentioned Carlos." During the interview, Blair deliberately did not mention Carlos, wanting to see if Vex would bring up his name. Vex did not. Hmm, he wonders, did Vex not have any dealings with Carlos, or perhaps he did not know him?

Blair's thinking moves back to the relationship between Vex and Gallegos. Since Vex had such a low opinion of Gallegos, Blair feels Vex never had a deep conversation with him. Vex had described him in sharply negative terms. The possibility Gallegos made a deal with Vex seems to be slim and none. Vex had no trust in the man and believed strongly the man was a fraud. Blair writes these observations on the yellow tablet.

Blair is becoming frustrated. He had not asked Vex the proper questions regarding Carlos and Gallegos, and he had not pushed Gallegos as hard as he should have. For the first time in his long history as a detective, he feels a case is getting under his skin. This is not normal, and it troubles him. Perhaps his wife's attitude toward him is to blame. This is the first time his personal life interfered with his thinking.

He resumes scribbling on the pad again. After finishing his last sip of coffee, he craves another cup. Tossing the empty McDonald's cup into the trash, he stood up from his desk and walked down the hallway to the break room. A large coffee pot brews around the clock, as the detectives often worked late into the night and needed their caffeine fix.

As Blair poured his second cup of coffee for the morning, which he did not think was nearly as good as the coffee he purchased at McDonald's daily, his mind continued to be confused. He mixes thoughts about the many different parts of the Harper case with thoughts of his wife. He has more than one case to solve. One is cold, and the other is personal.

Meanwhile, over at the crime laboratory, firearms examiner Shawn O'Neill is trying to tie the bullets and cartridge case recovered from the Harper crime scene to the gun that fired them. He had to find that Glock and find out who owned it. He knew this was essential and would finally break the case. Once the gun is identified, Detective Blair would need to gather evidence that tied the gun to the person who shot and killed Herschel Harper.

O'Neill ran both of the crime scene bullets through the IBIS machine. However, he could not process the cartridge case recovered from the trunk of the car in which Hershel Harper's body was found because IBIS did not handle cartridge cases at this stage in its development. Cartridge case analysis capability would become part of the system later. O'Neill passed his image and algorithm of the crime scene bullets on to the National Integrated Ballistics Information Network, or

NIBIN, in the ATF laboratory in Washington, DC. Hopefully, NIBIN could identify the gun that fired the bullets.

NIBIN is a collection of ballistic image algorithms from firearms laboratories across the United States. The algorithms from the samples sent to NIBIN by different laboratories were compared to the data in the NIBIN computer database. If the submitted algorithm matched one in NIBIN, the laboratory that submitted it would be notified and informed about the firearm it matched. This information is invaluable for investigators.

The old ballistic identification process of the comparison microscope is extremely slow, and the evidence rooms of police departments were full of guns used in crimes. Now, a system is in place to analyze the bullets and make comparisons that ran at a high speed. As a result, more and more guns were being tested for matches with bullets recovered from crime scenes. In addition to helping make active investigations swifter, guns used in a crime lying in evidence rooms for years were being connected to the projectile they fired. Cold cases started to be solved.

The thought in O'Neill's mind is this cold case is seventeen years old. What are the chances of finding a gun that old that will match up with the bullets it had fired? It is an interesting experiment, he thinks, as he places a bullet recovered from a murder last night into the IBIS machine and starts his examination. It is time to catch a current murderer.

In the meantime, Blair continues to wrestle with the cases on his desk and in his mind. Number one, Is my wife messing around with another man? The thought hurts him deeply. I have to get back on the Harper case, he tells himself and drinks nearly half of his fresh cup of coffee.

Today, he is going to interview Petrov. Petrov is known as a prominent businessman and worked from an expensive office, as opposed to Vex and his dirty bar; Blair is curious as to how open he will be to his questions. In addition to being a businessman, he is known to the Santa Ana Police Department as a boss in an organized crime organization. Petrov used his businessman persona to cover up his criminal activities.

Blair glances at his watch and decides it is time to leave to make the appointment on time. This is going to be a very interesting hour, he thinks, as he finishes the cup of coffee and heads out the door. He will stop and pay the rent for his coffee on the way to the car.

CHAPTER TWENTY-SIX

Blair steps off the elevator into Alexei Petrov's opulent penthouse office reception area in Santa Ana. A colossal fish tank, filled with vibrant, darting fish, dominated the room, flanked by exquisite paintings that added splashes of color to the walls. Plush couches and chairs offered a comfortable waiting area, and Blair couldn't help but notice that the furniture was a cut above first-class.

To his right sat the very attractive receptionist. He reported in, and the pretty young lady told him to have a seat. Mr. Petrov would be with him in a moment or two, so Blair used this time to collect his thoughts. He wanted to establish any possible connection between Petrov and Vex. He needed to find out if there was some motivation to hire Carlos Morales, or someone else, to steal money from Sunshine Casitas Condo Complex. And why would someone of Petrov's wealth be interested in the few thousand dollars from a month's condo fees? The $12,000 stolen was chump change for Petrov.

The secretary interrupted his thoughts, "Mr. Petrov is ready for your meeting." Blair rose from the plush sofa, following the secretary through a locked door and down a hallway. When she opened the door at the end, the beauty of the office took his breath away.

Petrov sat behind a colossal maple wood desk. The entire

wall behind him was glass, offering a breathtaking view of the city.

As Blair entered the office, Petrov rose and extended his hand across the desk. They shook hands, and Blair took a seat in the exceptionally comfortable chair that Petrov indicated. Petrov certainly knew how to make his guests feel at ease; Blair mused. It beat that old kitchen chair at Vex's joint!

"And why do I deserve the presence of Santa Anna's top detective?" Petrov stated politely.

Before Blair could answer, Petrov continued, "Detective Blair, would you like a cup of coffee? It's about that time of day, you know."

"Sure, Mr. Petrov, I'd love a cup of coffee," Blair responded.

Petrov punched a couple of buttons on his telephone and asked for two cups of coffee in his office. "Sugar or cream or both?" Petrov asked Blair.

"No, just black, please," responded Blair.

Blair started the conversation warmly, aiming to put Petrov at ease and gain insight into his thinking. This technique often helped interviewees relax and provide more candid answers. By beginning with friendly, easy questions and gradually introducing tougher ones, Blair hoped to elicit crucial information that might otherwise remain hidden. Blair knew getting information from a mobster wouldn't be easy.

"I'm here to ask you a few questions, Mr. Petrov, regarding a cold case I am working on," Blair began. "You may or may not remember this case as it occurred nearly seventeen years ago. We still haven't solved it, but I thought you might know some of the people involved and could give me some background."

Petrov leaned back in his chair, and a small smile came across his face. "Detective, I'll do my best to answer your questions, but I will tell you right up front: I have reached the age where I don't remember what I had for breakfast this morning."

Another cute answer to that question, Blair thought, thinking back to the response he received from Vex when he asked him the same question regarding the Sunshine Casitas incident.

They shared a light chuckle, and Blair continued. "The case I am working on involves a burglary at the Sunshine Casitas Condo Complex. The manager of the property was murdered. His body was found in the trunk of his car parked in an alley several blocks away."

Petrov showed no emotion or signs of recognition of Blair's comment. He sat quietly in his chair for a moment or two and then leaned forward, placing his elbows on the desk and looking at Blair more seriously. "Why would I know anything about something like that?" Petrov leaned back in his chair and opened his arms like a tour guide showing off his office.

"Detective, as you can see, I am a successful businessman. My company owns a chain of restaurants, car washes, and several individual businesses across California, Arizona, and Nevada. Why would you think I know anything about a burglary that happened seventeen years ago at, of all things, a condo?"

Blair placed his notepad on his knee, ready to take notes this time. "Mr. Petrov, with all due respect, we in law enforcement are aware of your hidden business dealings," he said, watching closely for Petrov's reaction.

Petrov did not seem particularly moved by the accusation and, with a neutral look on his face, inquired, "And why, sir, why do you think such a thing?"

Blair became assertive in his manner. "Mr. Petrov let's not waste time dancing around the bush. You know as well as I do that you have connections with organized crime in this town. You have kept your apparent legitimate business open to public view, won several awards, and received significant public exposure. You always step up, donate to worthy causes, and help people suffering from financial crises. And, I assume you have kept it all legal as you have gained quite a reputation as a developer, an entrepreneur, and a philanthropist. All noble things.

"However, in the dark, you have worked with organized crime to assist them. In return, they apply pressure where it is needed to make property available to you."

Blair paused for a moment and pretended to be reading something from his notepad. "You do not do this on your own or in a manner easily detectable by the general public."

"We know you have worked with various members of the underground criminal element in Santa Ana to get what you want." Blair paused a moment to let his statement soak in with Mr. Petrov.

Blair sat up straight in his chair and sternly said, "Mr. Petrov, I want a list of who those people are."

Petrov turned his chair and stared out his window for a moment. Then he swung rapidly back to face Blair, "Detective, I ought to throw you out of here for asking a question like that! You are treading on thin ice. I am not involved with anything illegal in this town, and I certainly do not know any of the thugs you mention who put pressure on people."

Blair made a big deal by writing a note in his little notepad. And then, very sternly, he asked, "Do you know a man named Victor Vex?"

"No," responded Petrov. "Who is Victor Vex, and why should I know him?"

"I believe you know him, Mr. Petrov. He is a first-class thug, known for putting pressure on people and twisting their arms in return for financial remuneration," Blair started applying more pressure.

"Mr. Petrov, we know you used him to pressure Robert

Winger to sell you his property at a very reduced price."

Before Petrov could answer, in as stern a voice as Blair could come up with, "What I'm telling you is not chatter on the street. We have investigated Mr. Winger's situation and have the case on file. The investigation is ongoing at this time."

Petrov became very quiet and stared at his desk for a moment. Finally, he raised his eyes and looked Blair straight in the eye, "Detective, if you are aware of this so-called arrangement I have with a thug on the street, why have you not taken some action? This is the first I have heard anything about your so-called investigation."

"Mr. Petrov, we do not have a practice of telling the people we're investigating what we're doing. You should know that better than anyone else," Blair stated sternly.

"If you know Vex, answering my questions would be to your advantage. Tell me now before this gets in the hands of the DA. I am in a position to offer you some protection from your situation. I assume you would like to remain the professional, successful businessman that people think you are?" Blair offered with conviction.

There were several moments of silence. Petrov looked concerned but also looked like he was considering the deal Blair was offering him.

I've done all the business I intend to do here in Santa Ana; if I give up a couple of second-rate thugs, this could all go away, Petrov thought.

"OK, detective," Petrov said. "What do you want to know about Vex?"

Internally, Blair smiled to himself. The ruse had worked. There was no investigation going on against Petrov. That is one thing about interrogations that police officers are allowed to do: bend the truth just a little bit if it will elicit the answer to a key question in an investigation. Blair deserved an A+ for this little deception.

"Tell me what you know about Vex," was Blair's next

question.

Petrov paused for a minute and then leaned forward at his desk as if he was making a business deal with someone. "He did put pressure on Winger. It isn't that big of a deal. Winger needed to be pushed just a little as he was asking too much for his property and didn't want to sell it. I needed it, so I hired Vex to convince Winger that he ought to sell the place to me for a reduced price."

Blair made the appropriate notes: "During your dealings with Vex, did you ever hear of a Carlos Morales? He worked at the Sunshine Casitas Condo Complex."

Petrov hesitated for only a very brief moment, "No, I've never heard of him."

Blair quickly fired back, "How about Juan Gallegos?"

Petrov gave a little chuckle. "Do you mean that idiot that hangs around Vex trying to borrow money all the time?"

"Yes," responded Blair. "I understand he does some of the dirty work for him."

"Look, detective," Petrov said with a smile on his face. "I don't want to sound disrespectful, but Gallegos is a fifth-class neighborhood snitch and a panhandler. I don't think he has ever done an honest day's work in his life; he certainly doesn't understand Vex's business, and I don't think he's smart enough to ask Vex for a loan. He wants to hang around in the bar with Vex's people. I guess it makes him feel important or something like that."

After a few more questions, Blair was satisfied that he was not going to get any more information from Petrov. Blair thanked him for his time. They shook hands again, and Blair went to the parking garage to pick up his car. The destination was his office.

On the short drive back to the police station, Blair ran the case through his mind one more time. Petrov had been no help and probably had been honest with him. Petrov had much to lose, so giving up a 2-bit punk like Vex was not that big of a deal for him. Even if the word got out of his association with Vex, he had many influential friends around the city. His public image was a very successful businessman, so his chances of deflecting anything like Vex were very high.

Petrov knew that, so he was not reluctant to give him up when Blair asked the right questions. Blair thought if he had pushed on, Petrov would have tried to make a deal with him. Making deals was how he became so successful. It didn't make sense that he dabbled with organized crime. Perhaps that was just a little power trip for him, Blair thought as he turned into the parking lot of the Santa Ana Police Department.

Blair wanted to conduct another investigation. This one was not in the files or on the docket of the Police Department. He wanted to know what was going on with his wife. She had changed so much in the past three or four months that he hardly recognized her.

Once Blair reached his desk, he pulled the little chain that turned on the green desk lamp, then checked for any messages. Finding none, he picked up the telephone receiver and punched in his home number.

After four rings, a very grumpy female voice came on the line, "Hello."

"Barbara, I'm caught up for the day. How about I buy you lunch somewhere?"

"I don't think so," she responded. "We never go out for lunch," she fired back. "What makes you think you can just call me and ask me to drop everything I'm doing and go with you wherever you want to go?"

"I didn't intend to upset you," Blair said. "I just thought it would be nice to have a little private time and enjoy a lunch you won't have to fix."

"No thanks. I don't want to go out with you. Come on home, and I'll fix you a sandwich," she responded irritably.

"OK," Blair responded. "I'll see you in 15 or 20 minutes."

When he arrived home, his reception was about as cold as inside a refrigerator's freezing compartment. Yes, she had tossed him in the ice maker.

Barbara hollered as he walked in the door, "Go to the kitchen. I'll be in there to fix your lunch in a minute."

Blair entered the kitchen and took a seat at the table. Momentarily, Barbara walked in without saying a word and went to the kitchen counter, picked up a paper plate with a baloney sandwich on it.

"Here," she said gruffly as she tossed the plate on the table in front of Blair.

She started for the kitchen door and then abruptly turned around. "Why don't you get a decent job?" she asked in her most disgusted tone. "You messed around and didn't go to college so you could get a degree and a good job or profession. No, you decided to do this dumb cop thing."

Instead of the door, she changed direction and went to the sink, where she rattled a lot of dishes together as if washing them. Blair sat at the table, starting to do a slow burn. She had been putting this story on him for the last four months or so. It was beginning to wear thin.

"It's been good for twenty years. We have a nice house that is nearly paid for, our kids have attended good schools, and we have lived a pretty decent life. What's changed with you? You didn't used to be this way. I thought you were happy with our life," came the statement in a somewhat disgusted voice.

"Well, you may have thought we were happy, but I didn't," she fired back in a nasty manner. "While you were out chasing down the dregs of society, I am here raising the children and running the house alone. We never had any money beyond our basic needs. Going to a movie is nearly impossible. You never made enough money for us," her anger spewing.

"Now, wait a minute; I've never heard you complain about

this before. We've put our kids in good schools. Come on, our house is nearly paid for, we have money in a savings account, and you go play with your girlfriends whenever you want to," Blair fired back.

"You've never complained about money before. And I've also noted you are mysteriously gone in the evenings and at other times. I know your social clubs only meet in the afternoon. So where are you going, and who are you with?"

"None of your damn business. I have my friends, and if you came home at a decent time, I would be here. Besides, I couldn't be doing much because we do not have the money. You need to quit that lousy job and get something that pays better," she nearly yelled at Blair.

Blair took a breath and tried to calm down the anger that was starting to rise in him. "Why would I change jobs? I just got promoted to Chief of Detectives. I'm only 10 years from retirement, and it is a good retirement with a lot of benefits. The city is generous to us," Blair was now having trouble staying relatively cool.

"Well, maybe I should quit my job here as the slave working for peanuts and find me another place where I'm appreciated!" she hollered at Blair, turned around, and stomped out of the kitchen, leaving Blair sitting at the table with his baloney sandwich on the paper plate.

Blair's police training told him he was very angry and needed to blow off steam before making any decisions. It felt like he would have to make some big ones about his life and future. I do not need this mess on my shoulders now, he thought.

After sitting for a moment, he decided that a good place for him to think was back at his office. He stood up, took his hand, knocked the paper plate and baloney sandwich off on the floor, and slammed the door as he left the house. Gravel flew as he pulled away from the curb. His destination was

McDonald's, where he grabbed a big cup of coffee.

Once he returned to his office, he reached over and pulled the little chain that turned on his little green light. He walked around his desk and took a seat. As he took a sip of the fresh, hot coffee, he noticed a sheet of paper on his desk. He thought Betsy might have put it there.

Blair picked the paper up and read what was on it. He paused a moment and then decided to reread the paper. He took a pause and then reread it one more time. *Is this what I have been looking for, he thought? Where will it lead?* He took another sip of coffee, laid the paper back on his desk, leaned back in his chair, and started to think. *Where are we going? Where are we going?*

CHAPTER TWENTY-SEVEN

Blair read the paper on his desk twice, his heart pounding with each word. Its contents wiped the conversation with his wife from his mind, and he immediately grabbed the telephone and dialed, his fingers flying over the keys.

"O'Neill, crime lab," came the quick answer.

"I understand you have some good news for me?" Blair responded, trying to mask the anxiety in his voice.

"Yes, I think this might make your day. I've heard back from ATF, and they have found a match to the bullet images I sent them," O'Neill said.

"They have traced the gun that fired them to its first owner. The first purchaser is Hiram Jones. His address is in Sun City, Arizona.

"Jones later sold the gun to the Easy Money pawnshop in Phoenix."

"Here's the part of the report you won't like. The Glock is stolen from the pawnshop three weeks before Herschel Harper is murdered. Basically, we have found the gun used in the Harper murder, but its whereabouts are still unknown."

"You have a lot of work to do, detective. I guess you're going to Phoenix," O'Neill said.

"Thanks, Shawn, for your great work. Do you know anyone in the Phoenix crime lab?" Blair asked.

"I have the name of a guy I met at one of the annual FTDI

conferences. I think it was about five years ago, but I have his name and number in my contacts list. Hang on while I look on my computer," said O'Neill.

Blair tapped his ballpoint on the desk, impatience growing with each passing second. Finally, after what felt like an hour, O'Neill's voice crackled back on the line, breaking the tense silence.

"Believe it or not, I found it. His name is Charlie Regan. I will text you his telephone number. I have no idea if he is still in the laboratory or not. As I said, it's been a few years ago," O'Neill added.

Blair thanked O'Neill for his good work. As he was about to hang up, O'Neill added, "By the way, Blair, there's something else I just remembered that you should know. Regan has a habit of going missing from time to time when he is on a case. Sometimes, it can be for weeks. He might have some good information to help with the case if you can find him."

Better yet, Blair thought, I will contact the Phoenix Detective Department. Blair believed that if the gun was stolen, they would undoubtedly have a file on it. He turned to his computer and started his search for the Phoenix Police Detective Department.

In a few minutes, he found the telephone number he was looking for. As he reached for his telephone to make his call, it rang just as he touched it.

With a bit of disgust, he answered, "Blair."

"This is Chief Boone, detective. I have some bad news for you," came the solemn voice of the Santa Ana Police Chief. "We have just received word and have a patrol car on the scene to verify the call that Detective Soper has committed suicide. A neighbor has reported they heard a gunshot. When they looked out their window into the backyard of Soper's house, they saw him sitting in a lawn chair slumped over with the gun on the ground by his side," said the Chief in a soft voice.

"I just happened to be in the radio room when the call came in. Word is on the way to your department. Just send your men out to the scene. We have known each other for years; I feel it better to tell you than you get the news from your secretary."

"I'm really sorry, Blair. I know you spent time with him on the Harper cold case and have developed a good friendship. Losing one of our own is always heartbreaking, but it is especially tough when they are a close friend," the Chief continued.

"Trust me, I know. A perp shot my best friend as he was walking into the front door of his home. I made a mistake and took the call. I was a detective at the time. Take my advice, send another officer, don't go yourself," the Chief offered sternly but friendly.

"I know you have seen a lot of murders. Some of them were horrific. But you will never forget seeing your friend's dead images; they will never leave your mind; they will haunt you at night and always be there whenever there is a moment of quiet."

"Obviously, it is your choice to go or stay. But you are in a position to send one of your detectives rather than go yourself."

"Your brothers in the department will support you. They have a love like you will never feel from anyone else."

"I guess what I have been fighting all these years is called PTSD amongst our military veterans. I'm just telling you that you can avoid this by not going to the crime scene. You have good men in your department who can work on the case. Stay in your office, and let the brothers support you through this difficult time," said the Chief as he concluded the call.

Blair sat quietly, his eyes fixed on a picture of Soper and himself at a reception celebrating another officer's retirement. Memories of their laughter and camaraderie flooded his mind, contrasting sharply with the heavy sorrow weighing down his heart.

There was no joy in Detective Roger Blair's office nor in his heart at this moment. He had just lost a person he respected highly. Soper had been his role model as a young detective working his way up through the department. Now, he had replaced him as Chief of Detectives and was sitting at the same desk Soper had used for many years. The Harper murder case had driven Soper to heavy drinking to escape his obsession with the case and the fact he had never broken it in nearly seventeen years.

And now Blair wondered, has it become my obsession?

He pulled the little chain that turned off the green light on his desk. It was time for him to see his friend before the coroner took the body away. *I know Chief said not to go*, ran through his mind, *but Soper is my friend. He taught me so much and brought me along until I replaced him when he retired. Yes, I have to say goodbye.*

As Blair left the office, he carefully closed the door with a soft click. This quiet gesture was his subtle way of saying goodbye to his friend, Detective Soper.

When he reached his car in the parking lot, Blair headed for Soper's home. This was the place where he had spent many hours. Watching Soper decline and slip deeper and deeper into his alcoholism had been heart-rending. Blair was devastated he had been unable to get him to stop. If he had stopped drinking, he probably would be alive today. All of Blair's urging him to attend an AA meeting had been futile. Beyond the sadness of losing his friend, Blair carried a load of guilt along with the unsolved Harper cold case Soper had thrown his heart and soul into solving.

What would happen now, Blair thought? *I am obsessed with this case almost as much as Soper. It is my duty to solve it in Soper's memory.* Blair decided solving it would be his life's goal, no matter how long it took. His friend deserved that. Little did he know, the journey ahead would test his resolve in ways he never imagined.

Blair arrived at Soper's home, noting the police cars and coroner's van parked in the street. With a heavy heart, he made his way to the backyard, bracing himself for the scene ahead.

As Blair walked through the gate into the yard, he paused for a moment to absorb what he was seeing. The officers, technical crew, and the coroner noticed his presence. They ceased their activities to give Blair the opportunity to observe the suicide scene.

Blair walked over to where Soper was sitting in the lawn chair, his heart racing. He looked at him for a moment or two, the silence deafening. Then, with a trembling hand, he reached down and patted him on the shoulder, whispering, "I'm sorry, old friend." He turned away, his mind swirling with unanswered questions, and returned to his car.

Once alone in his vehicle, tears welled in his eyes, his chest tightened, and his heart raced until he finally broke down in a torrent of tears. He leaned forward, rested his head on the steering wheel, and sobbed so intensely that the car almost shook.

It was several minutes before the sobbing subsided, and Blair regained control. He wiped his eyes, blew his nose, looked out the windshield for a few moments, and then decided what to do.

He started the car, put it into drive, stepped on the accelerator, and headed toward the Santa Ana Police Department and his office. O'Neill had come up with something that might lead to the resolution of this cold case. Blair made a vow to himself that he would crack it to honor his friend, Detective Charlie Soper.

Back in the office, Blair reached for the little chain that turned on the green light on his desk. Sitting down, he immediately turned on his computer. Blair pulled up the telephone number of the Phoenix Police Department he had located earlier. He dialed the number and waited for an answer.

After being relayed through a couple of people, he talked with the Chief of Detectives, Jim Daley. There was a little opening chatter between the two men. Once a sense of solid communication was established, Blair started inquiring about the Glock that had been stolen from the pawnshop.

Detective Daley did not have much information beyond the date and approximate time the gun was stolen. The pawnshop owner had described three young men in the store looking around. They did not appear interested in any particular section of firearms he had on display.

Detective Daley told Blair that one of the young men asked to see two or three of the handguns locked away in the display case counter. The owner said he took the guns out and laid them on the display counter for the young man to look at. According to the report filed by the detective on the scene, the other young men came up to the counter to join their friend in looking at the pistols. They handled each one, passing a couple back and forth between themselves.

The store owner said that a long-time customer came in to pick up an item he had purchased the day before. The owner said he knew him and trusted him, so he often let him pick out something he wanted and then pay for it two or three days later. He said he left the young men with the firearms on the counter and went to take care of his customer because he knew it would only take a minute or so to complete the transaction.

While he was talking to his customer, the three young men left the store. He glanced out the window as they left and noticed they were in a car with California license plates. When he walked back to the counter to put the guns away, a Glock pistol was missing.

He quickly called the Phoenix Police Department, which

dispatched a detective to investigate. The detective collected information about the incident, including the serial number of the stolen firearm. After returning to the station, he entered the serial number into the computer. He forwarded it to the ATF in Washington, DC.

Daley said that was all he had in the file.

Blair thanked Daley for the information and concluded the call.

Blair sat and thought for a few minutes. *Hmm, so the Glock turned up at the pawnshop, but it had been stolen from the shop.* Daley's report stated that the pawnshop owner had seen a car with California license plates drive away from his store right after the gun was taken by the group of young men.

Fiddling with his ballpoint pen for a few minutes, Blair wrestled with the idea of driving to Phoenix to interview the pawnshop owner in person. The longer he thought about it, the stronger the urge became to go. Blair reached up, pulled the little chain to turn off his green light, and headed for his car. If he drove all night, he could be in Phoenix when the sun rose and at the pawnshop when it opened.

Blair's planning was nearly perfect. As he pulled into Phoenix, the sun was just breaking over the eastern horizon. His first stop was the Phoenix Police Department and a visit with Detective Daley if he was at work this early in the morning.

As Blair entered the door to the Phoenix PD, he arrived simultaneously with another gentleman wearing a suit. They exchanged the usual good morning greetings, and the man in the suit asked Blair who he was there to see. When Blair said he hoped to catch Detective Daley, the gentleman extended his hand and said, "Glad to meet you. My name is Jim Daley."

Following a stop in the police break room to pick up a cup of coffee each, the two men went to Daley's office. They spent the next hour discussing the report that Daley had given to

Blair over the telephone. Once Blair decided he had all the information he would get, he told Daley, "I think I need to visit the pawnshop. There is always the chance the owner recalls something he didn't tell your detective when he was interviewed the first time."

"Yes, that does happen," Daley agreed. "I think it is the same old man running the store that was there seventeen years ago. I thought he was an old guy back then but when I checked to see who was running the store now, he is still there. I drove by the place, and it looks pretty rough. Time has taken its toll on the old building."

Blair asked for directions to the pawnshop from the police station.

Blair thanked Daley for his cooperation, left the Phoenix Police Department, and headed to the pawnshop. He wanted to get the owner's story directly from the horse's mouth. Hopefully, there would be a forgotten detail that would give him a vital clue that, so far, had been missing.

Blair found the address Daley had given him. Was this the right address?

A dilapidated old building stood baking in the Arizona sun that had bleached out the writing that once had been painted on its sign. What paint might have once been on the building had departed years ago. Blair thought it looked like an old, almost tumble-down building and that Daley had given him the wrong address. Then he spotted the old neon "open" sign hanging by just one chain in the dingy front window.

The sign was turned on. Blair decided he had found the correct address, but what was he going to find inside?

Blair pushed the door open and stepped inside. An old-fashioned bell dinged as the door struck it when opening. The smell that assaulted Blair's nostrils was hard to describe. It consisted of old cloth and paper, musty smelling water from the old swamp-cooler laboring away on the roof, maybe a toilet that should have been cleaned several weeks ago and sundry other aromas Blair could not identify. The place seemed very dark, but Blair thought that was because he had just come in from very bright sunlight. Yes, that was part of it until he looked up and spotted the one lone flickering fluorescent tube in a fixture high on the ceiling.

"Can I help you, stranger?" came the voice of an old gentleman sitting behind a desk at the back of the store.

The gentleman owning the store was now 92 years of age. He could hardly remember and discuss the details from the report. The interview was a bust for Blair. He thanked the old man, left the dingy, rundown old shop, and got in his car for the long 365-mile drive back to Santa Ana.

Was that ever a bust? Blair thought as he pulled away from the shop. The sun was starting to set.

The trip home would take all night. On his way out of Phoenix, Blair stopped at the local McDonald's and purchased two black coffees. He was not looking forward to the seven-hour trip ahead of him. Blair had spent the entire day in Phoenix, and it was nearly night again. The traffic would be light, and he had his badge in his pocket, a "pass go free, collect $200" ticket if a state trooper pulled him over for speeding. Maybe he could cut an hour or more off of his travel time. The biggest challenge might be staying awake.

He hoped there would be a 24-hour McDonald's or two along his route. One positive was that the drive would give him quiet time to think about the case. He quickly calculated his arrival time back in Santa Ana: 6:00 a.m. That would be late, but he might be able to shave that time back closer to 5:00 a.m. by exceeding the speed limit. Hmm, he thought, I have a big day tomorrow as there's much to do with the information from Firearms Examiner O'Neill and Detective Daley.

He took a big swig of his coffee. He pressed the accelerator to the floor as he watched his speedometer race past 80 MPH.

211

When Blair reached Santa Ana, he was on the freeway that would take him to the turnoff that led to the street his house was on. As he started to slow down for the turnoff, his eye caught the clock on the car's dash: 5:05 a.m.

Instead of turning off for home, he continued to the police station and caught a couple of hours sleep in his office. There was an old couch there. He wanted to start making calls as early as possible. He was suspicious his wife Barbra was messing around. Maybe she would return her attention to him if he did not come home tonight.

Blair felt like he had just layed down when his cell phone alarm began to play its annoying little song. Blair awoke, shut off the alarm, and stretched as far as he could; sleeping, or should we say trying to sleep, on the couch had provided him with a few stiff muscles. Sitting up, he looked at the time on his cell phone and decided there was enough time to go to McDonald's for breakfast and a big cup of coffee before he made his calls. There were a couple of questions Blair had thought of on his long drive home. The answers could provide the clues he needed.

CHAPTER TWENTY-EIGHT

Blair, unshaven and with dark circles under his eyes, felt the weight of the past day's events pressing down on him. Each mile he drove home for nearly seven hours felt like a battle against his own fatigue, his mind a whirlwind of unresolved questions and relentless determination.

After sleeping on the couch, he sat at his desk, munching on a breakfast sandwich while sipping coffee he had purchased from McDonald's. As he finished his last bite, Blair reached over to pull the little chain, turning on his green desk lamp.

Glancing at his watch, Blair picked up the telephone and dialed a number. "This is Detective Dailey. May I help you?" came the voice on the other end of the line.

"Morning, Daley. Blair here from Santa Ana. Thanks again for your help yesterday. I couldn't stop thinking about our conversation on the drive home, and a few more questions popped into my head."

"You're in Santa Ana?" exclaimed Daley. "You must have driven all night. I thought you'd spent the night here and would drive home today. Wow, that's quite a journey after the day you had with me and the guy at the pawnshop. I had something to discuss, but I was going to wait an hour until your time changed to give you a call," Daley said, somewhat surprised that Blair had driven home last night.

"Yeah, a couple of armadillos along Interstate 8 still don't have a clue about what went past them. I'm sure glad none of our brothers in the highway patrol were out last night. I have a question for you about your interview with the pawnshop's owner."

"He was old at the time of the money theft, and that was seventeen years ago. I couldn't get much out of him," Blair replied.

"The angels must be with us, Blair. After you left yesterday, I pulled a file for a case another detective asked me to review. He had a hunch that I knew more about some details than he did. When I opened the file drawer and searched for what I needed, I stumbled upon another file that piqued my interest. This file belongs to the detective who conducted the follow-up investigation of the pawnshop theft. Somehow, it got misfiled. There's information in it that might interest you," said Daley.

"What have you got?" asked Blair.

"Yesterday, when Betsy ran the plate and found the car registered to Philip Pierce in Irving, CA, they made another stop before leaving town, and it wasn't for an ice cream cone. They robbed a convenience store just off I-80."

"They must have wanted to try out the Glock," Blair responded sarcastically.

"Nobody got hurt. They just waved a gun in the clerk's face, and she handed over the money. After they left, she called us," Daley said. "She is so scared that all she told the investigating detective is that there were four guys she guessed were around thirty years old."

"Anything else?" Blair asked.

"No. The only thing in this report that might interest you is that the time they robbed the store aligns with the time it would take to drive from the pawnshop. It seems they left the pawnshop and drove straight to the store. Oh, I forgot to mention, they filled their car with gas before entering the store for the robbery." Daley chuckled softly. "They didn't pay for the gas, either."

"Is that it?" Blair asked.

"Yep, just thought you would like to know. Happy hunting. Keep me posted. This looks like an interesting case. Talk to you later."

"Will do, and thanks for the info. I'll let you know where this thing goes. Have a good one," Blair said as he hung up the phone.

Blair took a final sip of his cold McDonald's coffee, deciding he needed a fresh cup. But first, there was something crucial he had to do before leaving his office. Blair clicked on his computer and pulled up the roster of the Santa Ana Police Department. He went to the search engine and typed in 1977, the year of Hershel Harper's murder. He wanted to find anyone working in the department at that time. They might remember something about Mr. Pierce, such as if he had been picked up for something or called the station.

As Blair's brain kicked into high gear, a seemingly insignificant detail from the records room nagged at him. He decided the McDonald's coffee would have to wait; there was something crucial he needed to find, something that could change the course of the investigation. Instead, he grabbed a cup of coffee from the break room coffee pot on his way to the elevator. His destination is the records room; there is something important he needs to find that might be hidden there.

As Blair entered the records room, the musty odor of old paper mingled with the sharp scent of something rotting nearby, assaulting his nostrils. The dim lighting cast eerie shadows on the rows of dusty files from 1977, enhancing the room's air of mystery. He hoped to find information regarding an encounter between a police officer and Philip Pierce. Blair believed this was his best chance to uncover what Pierce might have been involved in during the time of the Harper murder. The officer who spoke with him might remember something significant.

Blair knew finding Pierce was his best shot at cracking the Harper case. But with every lead turning cold, he faced mounting pressure from his superiors, who doubted his methods and the importance of the case. The stakes had never been higher. He might have provided information that could help identify who pulled the trigger on the Glock that killed Harper. This could also lead to finding the last known location of the Glock, which was stolen from a pawnshop in Phoenix. Pierce likely knew the person who stole it and left in a car registered to him. Blair is determined to uncover that clue. It is critical to the case.

As the clock ticked past noon, Blair's frustration grew. He had sifted through several hundred dusty files, each a dead end. The pressure mounted with every passing minute, knowing a crucial piece of evidence could be hidden in the following file. Philip Pierce's name hadn't shown up in any report.

Blair was hungry; worse yet, his coffee cup had been empty for hours. His last cup was from the coffee pot in the break room. He needed real coffee from McDonald's, where he could also grab something to eat. Alright, Blair decided it was time for a break. These files would still be here when he got back.

When Blair pulled up to the drive-thru order window at McDonald's, he felt he deserved a Big Mac as a reward for his dedication to sifting through all those dusty old files that had remained untouched for years. If he had found Philip Pierce's name, Blair told himself, he would have added fries and an apple pie. Well, there's always tomorrow.

On his drive back to the station to spend more hours in the records room, Blair dialed a number on his cell phone. Betsy, his secretary, answered on the third ring.

"I have a special task for you. Drop everything you're doing, as this is priority number one," Blair told her.

He laid out a plan for her to review the roster of all the officers working in the Santa Ana Police Department in 1977. Betsy wrote down the names of half a dozen detectives. Blair instructed her to pull them from whatever they were doing and search the employee records. Once they had the list, Detective James would distribute the names among as many available detectives as possible. Their task is to locate anyone in and around Sunshine Casitas at the time of the theft. At the top of his list, he identified any officer who had contact with or knew the name Phillip Pierce.

"Will do, boss," Betsy replied as they finished discussing her assignment. They hung up as Blair entered the police department parking lot, parked in his designated space, grabbed his food bag and the coffee cup with McDonald's printed on it, and headed for more hours in the records room.

Hours later, Blair finally reached the last file; it was empty. "Empty" perfectly summed up his day. He briefly checked his watch—9:12 p.m.—while signing out of the records room. Blair hadn't been home in three days, shaved or showered in two, and dreaded going home now.

Blair's heart sank as he thought about going home. He could already hear his wife's sharp and insistent voice criticizing his meager earnings and urging him to give up the job he loved. The weight of her words pressed down on him, making each step toward the door feel like a march to his own execution. Oh well, at least there is a guest bedroom with a nice bed. Chuckling to himself, he thought, I smell so bad she probably won't come near me anyway. Blair left the records room and headed straight to his car.

CHAPTER TWENTY-NINE

Blair stepped into his office, but the usual comfort of his surroundings did little to quell the unease gnawing at his gut. Something about the last two days didn't sit right, and he was determined to uncover the truth.

Despite his rested appearance, Blair's step had a newfound spring, and a rare smile tugged at the corners of his mouth as he walked into his office. The crisp scent of his freshly dry-cleaned suit mingled with the rich, earthy aroma of his morning coffee, creating a comforting blend that invigorated his senses. He was surprised at how good he felt after the last two days on the road to Phoenix and back.

One factor contributing to his good mood was the surprise he received when he arrived home last night. He almost considered returning to the office or even checking into a motel. He had no desire to open that front door. Behind it, waiting for him would be a torrent of accusations from his wife about not making enough money. She never gave up. He heard it all the time he was home.

What had happened to the days when she fixed a great meal they enjoyed together? As Blair's mind drifted back to his rookie days, he remembered the adrenaline rush of his first night on duty, the camaraderie with fellow officers, and the pride he felt wearing the badge. Those memories were a stark contrast to the strained relationship he now had with his wife.

Many times, after her great supper, they went to a movie. The timing was perfect: when the movie ended, she went home, and he went straight to work at 11:00 p.m. They used to enjoy camping and having great vacations in Utah. Something had changed with her, Blair thought.

These heavy thoughts weighed on Blair as he finally turned off his car ignition. Slowly making his way to the front door, he inserted and turned his key in the lock.

Barbara heard him come into the house and greeted him cheerfully. He did not sleep in the guest bedroom as he had expected. They enjoyed an excellent breakfast together. She was cheerful and asked about his adventure in Phoenix. What pleased him most was that she never said a word about not making enough money or quitting his job and getting something better. This is quite a shift in mood, Blair thought.

So much for the daydreaming, time to get to work, Blair told himself. Sitting at his desk with his cup of McDonald's coffee, he reached up and pulled the little chain that turned on the green desk lamp on his desk. It was time to start the day's detective activities. The first job was to call his secretary and see how successfully she had implemented the project he gave her yesterday.

"Betsy, how did the project I assigned you yesterday go?" Blair asked, leaning back in his chair, his fingers drumming on the desk.

"Boss, it went better than expected. I located an officer who had been in the neighborhood of Sunshine Casitas when we think the murder occurred. He remembers a couple of things that might help you. I will text you his name, badge number, and telephone number. I have checked, and he is working the morning shift today, so you should be able to reach him through the dispatcher," she told him.

"Great work!" Blair told her. "I need to talk to management and see if they will give you a raise!" Blair exclaimed delightfully. "You're the best in the business. Contact the dispatcher and see if you can locate our officer. By the way, what is his name?"

"Patrol Sergeant Bill Livingston. He is due to retire next year," Betsy answered before they hung up.

Blair decided he would contact the dispatcher, too. Meanwhile, he couldn't shake the feeling that something was off with his wife's sudden change in behavior. "Is she hiding something?"

Without telling him, there is nothing like making the dispatcher realize how important this is. Show, not tell sometimes worked the best. It is not that he did not trust Betsy; he is just anxious to talk to Officer Livingston. And dispatchers tended to listen to officers with more interest than they did to secretaries.

Blair dialed the dispatcher, relayed Betsy's information, and requested Officer Livingston's presence in his office. He also asked for the officer's supervisor's number to ensure Livingston could take a break from patrol duty.

Blair dialed Officer Livingston's commanding officer. "I need Livingston in my office now," he said, cutting straight to the point. Time is of the essence.

"I would like to accommodate you, Detective Blair, but I don't think I can this morning. Officer Livingston has a new rookie officer riding with him, and I have nowhere to put the rookie. All my cars are carrying rookies from that new class that graduated from the academy last week. Sorry, can't do it," said Lieutenant Parker.

"Can't you cut him loose for a half hour or so? The rookie can come with Livingston and learn a little about how our various departments work together," Blair offered.

"No, sorry, detective. I can't pull a car out of that district this time of day. It's too busy," the Lieutenant responded.

Blair did not give up and dug in a little harder. "Look,

Lieutenant, the world won't stop spinning if you loan me Livingston for a half-hour. I don't recall many burglaries in broad daylight."

Following a little livelier negotiation with the Lieutenant, Officer Livingston and Detective Blair nearly simultaneously pulled into the nearest McDonald's parking area in Livingston's patrol district. They went inside and found a booth in the corner for a private conversation.

Following the usual greetings in conversations between three people meeting for the first time, Livingston and Blair took a seat. At the same time, the rookie went to the counter and ordered three large coffees. Blair handed him a twenty-dollar bill before he went to the counter.

"Coffee is on me, gentlemen. I appreciate you agreeing to meet with me."

Following a small amount of friendly chatter, Blair opened the serious discussion.

"I realize it has been a long time ago, but what do you remember about that night at Sunshine Casitas?" Blair asked to start the discussion.

"I have a couple of vivid memories because I never understood why the detectives working the scene never contacted me. There is no follow-up either. At the time, I am a new patrol officer. I'd been out of the academy a little over six months," Livingston stated.

"I was on the street two blocks away when I heard the activity on the radio with the dispatcher regarding the potential theft at the condo. I was parked at a red stop light when a vehicle passed through the intersection at a high rate of speed. There were two cars between me and the red light. I hit my red light and siren, but the two cars were slow to figure out I wanted them to move. By this time, the car is down a couple of blocks," Livingston explained.

"I saw it turn down an alley, and I pursued but lost it,"

Livingston added. "I did get a good look at the vehicle when it cleared the intersection in front of me. I passed that information along to the dispatcher. I thought it might be a getaway car from the money theft."

"Did anyone get back to you?" asked Blair.

"No," came the reply. "Being new on the force, I thought maybe I could solve a theft. You know that first few months when you think you can save the world... Pay attention, rookie," Livingston said as he gently punched his rookie partner on the arm.

"After a few days of not hearing from anyone in the detective bureau," Livingston continued, "I took some of my free time and stopped by the DMV. I knew a guy there I played softball with on our church team," Livingston said.

"I had a clear view of the car as it sped through the intersection. I could identify the make, model, and year, but due to me being at a 90-degree angle to the car, getting a clear view of the license plates was not possible. I did get a partial plate," the officer added.

"My friend and I started to search for the numbers I had. It took us a couple of hours to put together a list of the three numbers," Livingston put a smile on his face. "We emptied a pot of coffee in the process."

Blair joined him with a knowing smile.

"Anyway," Livingston continued, "We started to match up the complete numbers containing the three numbers I picked up with their registration information, looking for a match to the car's description I saw.

"After another pot of coffee," Livingston continued, "Are you paying attention, rookie? We found a match. The car is registered to a Philip Pierce with an Irving address."

Blair is now wide awake. Philip Pierce? That is the car sighted, leaving the pawnshop in Phoenix following the pawnshop theft. "What did you do with that information?"

"I turned it over to a detective I knew; his name is Harry Smith. But I never heard back from him, so I assumed the detective department did not figure it was important. You could ask him about it, but I'm sure you know he got killed in that shoot-out down on the south side last year," Livingston added.

Blair thanked Livingston for his cooperation but, more importantly, his memory. Little did he know, this seemingly minor detail would unravel a web of secrets that would change everything.

"Pay attention to this guy, rookie. He can teach you a thing or two," Blair told the young officer.

"Yes, sir," came the quick answer as he and Sgt. Livingston walked out the door.

As Blair left McDonald's, he purchased another hot coffee.

Returning to his office, Blair told Betsy about his experience with Livingston. He wanted answers from his department about why there had been no follow-up regarding Livingston's information. This had occurred on Soper's watch. He hoped the detective or detectives involved were still on the active roster. He planned to have coffee with them, but it would not be a friendly discussion about the kid's baseball game last weekend. In the meantime, he will find out the situation with Philip Pierce.

Blair fired up his computer and checked to see if Pierce had ever been arrested. After scanning several screens and repeating the process, he found nothing. He then requested that the DMV investigate whether the Pierce vehicle had been involved in a registration transfer or destroyed in an accident and is off the DMV records.

DMV told him Pierce sold the car to a dealership two years after the murder. The dealership sold the vehicle to another individual six months after buying it from Pierce. Blair assumed this was a routine car trade.

The next stop in Blair's computer search is the Orange County Records of Property Titles. Once on the correct computer page, Blair input the address from Pierce's driver's license and auto registration. The property is registered in Pierce's name, leading Blair to conclude that Pierce still resides there. It's time to pay Mr. Pierce a visit.

Blair is unfamiliar with the address of the Pierce home. After a few turns down the wrong street, he finally found the address. As Blair pulled up in front of the Pierce home, he noted that it was a cozy little cottage-style house built in a design popular in the early 1950s. The yard is neatly trimmed, even though the house shows signs of needing a bit of careful and tender care.

The second ring of the doorbell produced an attractive older lady with a pleasant smile. "Hello, may I help you?" came her delightful voice.

Blair introduced himself, his mind racing with questions. "I need to ask you about a car you owned in the 1970s," he said, his voice friendly but tinged with urgency.

"Certainly, detective. Please come in. We can talk in the living room. I am just about to prepare myself a cup of tea. Would you like one?" she asked as she led Blair into the living room and offered him a seat on the couch.

"Thank you for offering the tea, but I am a coffee drinker," Blair responded. It is almost an addiction for me," he said with a slight chuckle.

"Oh, that's fine," she said. "I have a coffee maker I use for guests. I'll pop in a pod and brew you up a cup. How do you take it?"

"Black," Blair responded as he settled into his seat on the couch and noted the many pictures sitting on a small decorative table and an old-fashioned buffet. The walls were covered with professional photos from their wedding, other photos Blair assumed were the graduation of three children, and some small children Blair believed were grandchildren. Philip Pierce is a handsome man of a modest build. The two of them together made a very attractive couple.

Mrs. Pierce returned from the kitchen carrying a small tray with cups of coffee and tea. She had added a few cookies as well.

Once she was settled on the couch and each had their favorite hot drinks in hand, Blair began asking questions. The answers to two questions caught him slightly off-guard but provided vital information.

The first of these two questions is when he inquired if Mr. Pierce could join their conversation.

Mrs. Pierce's voice trembled as she responded, "No, detective, he cannot join us although I wish he could. He crossed the Bridge to Heaven three years ago. I miss him every day," she said, her eyes welling up with tears. "Cancer took him from me, slowly and painfully. It ate up his brain, and his last years were a torment. Cancer is a cruel, unforgiving disease," she concluded, her voice barely above a whisper.

Blair knew it was a moment of opportunity, but he wanted to be gentle. Mrs. Pierce was a gentle lady, and he aimed to extract the information he needed without upsetting her. He regarded her as a nice, friendly lady who likely had many friends.

"Mrs. Pierce, I couldn't help but notice the pictures of your family on the wall. Could you tell me about them?" Blair asked as he picked up his coffee and took a drink. It is quite good, he thought.

This question lit up Mrs. Pierce's face, and she started through the pictures one at a time, telling Blair a small amount about each. Blair noted that she had much to say about her children except for one of the sons. She only mentioned his name, Joel.

"You have a wonderful family," said Blair. "You have every

reason to be proud of them and their accomplishments. I'm impressed by the work your daughter is doing with her company, trying to find a cure for cancer. You didn't say much about your son Joel. What is he doing now?"

Mrs. Pierce became very quiet. She fiddled with a small handkerchief. She dropped her head, looked down, and started to speak sadly. Blair detected a tear running down her cheek. "Joel, my dear Joel, is in jail. He has been there ten years and still has five to go. His life will be over by the time he gets out. He will be an old man," Mrs. Pierce said as she broke down in tears.

"I'm sorry, detective," she said. "He is my pride and joy when he is young. He was doing well in school, and then, during his junior year, he started to run with three other boys that were very bad. They had been in trouble with the police and the school officials. I begged him to quit running around with them, but he always had an answer as to why he wasn't doing anything wrong, just having fun with some friends. He never listened to me or his father."

Mrs. Pierce fell silent. She looked down at her hands, twisting her hanky into a tight little roll. Blair remained silent to allow her a moment of grief. Then she raised her head, smiled, and said, in a much happier voice, "Detective, would you like another cup of coffee? It will only take a second to make it."

"No, thank you," Blair responded, unmistakably examining his wristwatch. "I have used up enough of your time. I have another appointment I need to attend. Thank you very much for your time."

Mrs. Pierce escorted Blair to the door, and they had a pleasant goodbye.

As soon as Blair was in his car, he grabbed his cell phone and punched in Betsy's mobile number. When she answered, "Betsy, find anything you can on a Joel Pierce. I also want to know what prison he is in. I've got some work to do."

CHAPTER THIRTY

Blair, driven by a relentless obsession to solve the case, decided that his next step was to visit the Sunshine Casita Condo Complex, hoping that seeing the place in person might spark an idea. The complex consisted of several large buildings covering nearly a city block. What he knew about the scene of the money theft and murder came from the cold case file. The details haunted his thoughts day and night, driving him to the edge of madness. He also began to understand why his late friend, Detective Soper, had allowed the case to consume him.

Upon arriving at Sunshine Casita Condo Complex, he went to the office. It was locked. He decided to see if he could locate any residents living there at the time of the theft. He noticed a group of people gathered at the pool and headed in that direction.

As Blair turned the corner of the building and followed the sidewalk to the pool, he noticed a gardener trimming a hedge. He decided to stop and ask when someone would be in the office, as he wanted to see what it looked like inside.

The gardener, a weathered man with a kind smile, answered Blair's questions with ease, including his name, Juan Rodrigues. Blair noted that he was an older gentleman, and a hunch urged him to ask, "How long have you worked here?"

His response perked up Blair's ears. "Oh, a long time, Señor. I like it here. Came twenty-two years ago."

This response prompted Blair's next question, "You were here when the money theft happened, and Hershel Harper was killed?"

"Sí, Señor. Very sad day. Señor Harper is a very nice man. He is my boss. I liked him very much."

Blair, sensing a breakthrough, decided to dig deeper. "What do you remember about that day?" he asked.

The gardener told Blair he had been working at the side of the building and did not know anything had happened until the police cars started pulling in. He said he watched the activities of the police who investigated the crime. Blair asked if anyone had talked to him. He told Blair that a detective had asked him questions about what he had seen.

Since he worked around the property eight to sometimes ten hours per day, he was aware of everyone who came on the property and would recognize any unusual activity. Blair asked him if the detective he had talked with had asked if he had seen anyone on the property who he felt might be out of place.

"Sí, Señor. I remember telling the detective three people were around the pool. I didn't know who they were. They seemed happy when the son of the locksmith walked up. They left the pool, walked the same sidewalk you're on, and went to the car parked across from the office."

"How did you know the man is a locksmith's son?" asked Blair.

"Señor McQuire fixed locks for many years. He had his name painted on the truck. His son came with him sometimes. I think he is 17, 18, or 19," Juan answered.

"Do you know the son's name?" asked Blair.

"No, Señor," came the quick response.

Blair, with a sense of urgency, asked a few more questions, thanked Juan for his time, and hurried toward his car, his mind racing with the possibilities of what he might uncover next. A burning question was in his mind: why didn't the original interview with Juan get in the Harper file? I read that thing until I nearly went blind, and I do not recognize one thing Rodrigues told me, Blair thought. *I don't need to spend any more time around here. I need to get to the car,* Blair decided.

Blair had his cell phone in his hand before his butt hit the seat. "Betsy, did you find anything on Joel Pierce?"

She gave Blair an earful, "He has a rap sheet about a mile long. He has been vacationing at the California Institution for Men in Chino. That's all I have been able to dig up so far, boss. I'll keep working."

"As usual, great work, Betsy. Call the warden at Chino and tell him I am on the way to have a sit-down with Mr. Pierce. Thanks."

Blair slid into the driver's seat, started the engine, and drove toward the state prison in Chino. If Juan's memory is correct about the car parked near the condo office, it's the one registered to Philip Pierce. That could place his son Joel at Sunshine Casita. I'll know soon, Blair thought, as he turned on his red and blue flashing lights hidden in his car's grille. The speedometer climbed quickly, well above the speed limit.

Blair navigated the tedious sign-in process at the Chino prison facility, his impatience growing with each passing minute. Finally, he was led to the interrogation room, where the real work would begin. The room had a small table in the center, concrete on three sides, and bars for a wall on the fourth side. The bars allowed a guard to sit several feet down the approaching hallway, keeping an eye on the room yet being far enough away not to hear the conversation in the room clearly.

Blair took a seat in the chair with its back to the wall. Shortly, two guards entered the room with Pierce, dressed in prison coveralls, between them. Pierce was in shackles on his ankles and his hands in handcuffs in front of him.

Pierce sized him up as the guards seated him at the table, unfastened one handcuff from his wrist, and fastened it to a heavy metal ring mounted on the tabletop. Blair noted that Pierce was tall and lean, had his head shaved, and was covered with tattoos, including on his head. To Blair, the tattoos looked like prison tattoos, not the kind you see done by professional tattoo artists on the outside. His persona fit his rap sheet.

"This won't take long, Pierce. Just give me straight answers, and I'll be out of your hair. But if you feed me garbage, I'll make sure we both have a long night ahead. Got it?" Blair said in a firm voice—no cozy warming up in this interview. Pierce knew the drill. This wasn't his first rodeo in an interrogation room.

"Yes, Sir," Pierce answered.

"Do you have three friends that you hang out with when you are not in jail?" Blair asked.

"Yes, Sir," came the answer. Pierce had been interviewed enough that he knew in a cop interview or one with a lawyer, you answer with the minimal number of facts that will satisfy the question asked and nothing more. Volunteer nothing is the rule.

"Who are they, Pierce? I want their full names," Blair asked.

"Larry Gilbert, Joe McGuire, and Ronald Gilmore," responded Pierce.

A light bulb came on in Blair's head. Pierce admitted he was Joe McGuire's buddy. Juan, the gardener at Sunshine Casitas, said he saw a car matching Pierce's parked near the office at approximately the time of the theft, placing these four thugs at the murder scene. *Now, I need to establish who pulled the trigger.*

Observing Pierce's body language, Blair started to bore in. "Pierce, do you remember the money theft at Sunshine Casita Condo Complex seventeen years ago? You would have been about a senior in high school."

A slight hesitation from Pierce, and then, "Yes, sir."

"What can you tell me about it?"

Again, a slight hesitation, "Not much. I think there was a burglary or something, and somebody got killed."

"Who got killed, Pierce?"

Blair noticed Pierce wiggling around in his chair a little, and some positivity had left his voice. "I don't remember. That was a long time ago; all I know is what I read in the newspaper."

Blair shifted gears. "When was the first time you went to jail?"

"When I finished my senior year in high school."

"What for?"

"Robbery."

"What did you rob?"

"A convenience store."

"Why did you do it? You are from a good family."

"I thought it would be fun."

"Did you do it by yourself?" Blair asked as he had a fast pace going, but now he hoped to switch the pace quickly with a question Pierce should know was coming, but not when it would be asked.

"No."

"Who was with you?"

"Three of my friends," came a retort from Pierce.

"The three you told me their names earlier?"

"Yes."

"I saw on your rap sheet that robbery and this last one for battery have been the charges that landed you behind bars. This last one is the worst. Were your buddies on any of these other convenience store robberies with you?"

"Which ones?"

"All of them."

"Were your buddies with you when you robbed and killed Hershel Harper?"

The question caught him off guard. "No. No, I didn't kill Mr. Harper. I don't know anything about that."

"Don't try to BS me, Joel. We know you were there. Your car doesn't drive itself. You were parked right by the office."

Pierce looked down at the table and used his free hand to fiddle with the handcuffs that tied him to it. He finally looked up at Blair. "Yes, I was there."

Blair could feel Pierce's protection wall start to crumble. "Why?"

"I went to meet my friend, Joe. We were going to go out drinking."

"Were your other two friends with you?"

"So, I don't make any mistake in understanding you, you went to Sunshine Casita to meet your friend Joe. Your other two friends were with you, and you planned to go on a night of partying and drinking?"

"Yes, Sir."

"Why did you pick the condo complex as a meeting place? It seems to me a bar would have been better."

"I took my friends with me to the condo because I knew that's where Joe was hanging with his Dad. Where we went is not far from there. It is handy."

"Okay, Pierce, did you have a firearm in your car?" Blair asked as he shifted in his chair.

After a few seconds of considering his answer, Pierce answered, "Yes, my Dad keeps a gun in his car. He is afraid as he spends a lot of time out at night."

Lie number one, Blair thought. *He is nervous, and I have him on thin ice. Let's play the game and see what happens.* "Joel, where did he keep the gun in the car? Is it locked up?"

"He kept it in the glove box locked up."

"What kind of gun is it?"

"A pistol."

"No, Joel. You can't put anything bigger than a pistol in a glove box. A rifle or shotgun won't fit. What I am asking is, what brand is it? Who made it?"

"Oh, I think it is a Glock or something like that. I don't mess with guns. Knives are my choice for a defensive weapon."

"Did you guys need money for your planned drinking party?"

"No, we all had plenty of money for the night."

"How did you know there was money in the office?"

"Joe goes there with his Dad pretty often. He was walking by the office one day and heard someone through the open window say something about money. He stopped and listened to them talk. They were talking about paying condo fees. When Joe was visiting his Dad, he noticed many people going to the office around the first of the month," Joel explained. "Joe went back to the office and listened through the window as someone else came in to pay. He guessed there was a lot of money in the office the first of every month."

"How did you get in the office to steal the money?"

"We didn't go into the office. We just climbed in my car and headed for the bar when Joe showed up."

Blair thought a quick question would catch Pierce off guard. "Why did you kill Mr. Harper, Joel?"

"I didn't kill anybody. I told you all I know about that deal from what I read in the newspaper."

"Come on, Pierce. You said you would shoot straight with me. I think you are going off-script. What if I told you we have solid ballistics testing on the bullets recovered from the back of Harper's head that match them perfectly to the Glock you carry in your car? What if I tell you we have a solid eyewitness who can place you at the condo office when the murder occurred?" Blair leaned back in his chair, looked Pierce straight in the eyes, and awaited his answer.

Pierce took his eyes away from Blair, looked at the floor, and fidgeted a bit in his chair. He looked up from the floor and faced Blair. "Look, detective, I positively swear I did not shoot Harper. Yes, I was at the office but did not rob it."

"Let me get this straight, Pierce," Blair asked firmly. "You say you did not shoot Mr. Harper when we have positive proof that the gun you carry in your car did. You say you were at the office but didn't rob it. It is strange to me that you refute positive scientific proof that you did not use the Glock in your car to shoot Harper. We have positive proof you were at the office when the theft occurred, but you didn't do it. Do you realize this is starting to sound like a fairy tale? Did Yosemite Sam show up and rob the place and shoot Hershel?"

Blair sat back to watch Pierce's reactions. Pierce was starting to sweat and was becoming very nervous. Blair pressed on. He knew there was something in Pierce he needed to trip, and much would be revealed.

Pierce only sat in the chair and did not say a thing. Blair remained quiet and let him cook.

After a few minutes of total silence, Blair leaned forward and gently said, "Joel, I visited your mother. She is a kind, sweet woman, and we had a lengthy visit in your home's living room. Joel, she loves you very much, and it breaks her heart that you are in prison. She wants to see you out of here and have lunch with you."

Blair noted Pierce was getting more and more uneasy in his chair. Blair thought he could see tears forming in his eyes. His ploy was working.

"Look, Joel, if you go down for Harper's murder, you will be spending the rest of your life in this place. It ain't exactly the Hilton, as you already know. Worst of all, you will be breaking the heart of a wonderful woman. She has been all alone since your father passed. You are in here. In a few years, your term will be served. You will be out of this place. Some professionals can help you stay out of here. Your mom will be so happy. Joel, tell me the truth: did you pull the trigger on the Glock, or was it one of your friends? Did you rob the condo office?"

Pierce sat, pawing at the floor with his foot and rattling the handcuff that was hooked to the table. A long silence prevailed, and then Pierce's prison instincts kicked in. "I didn't shoot Harper, but one of the other guys did. I didn't do the robbery either. All I did was provide a ride away from the condo."

"Okay, Joel. Who pulled the trigger?"

"It was Gilbert."

"And what about stealing the money?"

"That was McQuire. He had a set of lockpicks he had taken out of his Dad's truck. He picked the lock on the door to get in and then used it to get into the desk drawer. I sat in the car and was on the lookout. Gilmore was with me. I watched one direction, and he watched the other."

"How much money was in the cashbox?"

"I think it was around $12,000. We split it four ways."

Blair made a note this time even though the interview was being recorded. "Why did Gilbert shoot Mr. Harper?"

"McQuire wanted Gilbert to stand by the door as a lookout. No one knew he had the Glock. I lied to you. We didn't keep the glovebox locked. He must have slipped the gun out while we were talking or something else. Anyway, he had the gun under his shirt. Harper walked up and wanted to know what was going on. I guess he saw McQuire with the cashbox and decided he was going to get it back. A little scuffle took place, and then Gilbert showed the gun and pushed it in Harper's face. They forced him into his car and yelled at me to follow them. We ended up down an alley, and they parked Harper's car under a little lean-to. They got Harper out of the car and had a loud argument. McQuire opened the trunk of his car, and Gilbert shot him in the back of the head. They pushed the body into the trunk, ran over to my car, and told me to get the hell out of there. And that's what I did."

"Where did you go?" asked Blair.

"We went to the bar we had planned on going to and had one hell of a party. I don't think there was much of the money McQuire stole left at the end of the night. Doubt if I ever have that big of a party again."

Pierce looked at the floor once again. This time, Blair detected relief in Pierce.

"Joel, you understand, with the evidence we have, you will go on trial for killing Mr. Harper, and the chances are very good a jury will find you guilty, and that will put you in prison for the rest of your life." Blair paused to let Joel absorb and understand fully what he had told him.

"Joel, I have something I want you to consider very carefully. There is a way for you to overcome the overpowering evidence against you. But it will take courage on your part and a willingness to give up some old friends."

Joel sat quietly and stared at the top of the table. Blair felt him reach a decision. He looked at Blair and asked, "Okay, what do I have to do?"

"Testify in court that Gilbert pulled the trigger and McQuire engineered the theft. It's up to you, Joel. You can make a good decision for yourself and your mom. Or you can take the rap for something you didn't do and spend the rest of your life in prison. If you testify against Gilbert and McQuire and prove all you did was sit in the car as a lookout, then chances are you may be convicted, but the sentence will be very light."

"What do you want to do?" Blair asked.

Pierce sat quietly for a couple of minutes, then looked at Blair.

"Okay, detective, I will do it for Mom as much as me. What do I have to do?"

****

Following an announcement and press regarding Pierce's agreement to testify in court against Gilbert, Blair had a feeling of accomplishment. When he concluded his statement to the press on the steps in front of the Police Station, he returned to his office, pulled the little chain that turned on the green desk light and sat in his chair staring out the window. There is both pride and concern in his thoughts.

There is much pride in the fact that this case is put to rest after seventeen long years. It had been a tough nut to crack. However, on the other side of the coin, Blair had great concern about the many mistakes that had been made. Those mistakes must not happen again in future investigations. It's my job to fix that!

Blair's ruminating over the wrap-up of the Harper case and the mistakes that have been made are interrupted when Betsy taps on his open-door jamb. Blair quits, staring out his window, and turns around in his chair. To his surprise, Betsy is not alone.

"Boss," Betsy says, "this is ATF Special Agent Vince Dobyns. He asked to meet with you privately as he has something important to share with you."

The two men shake hands, and Betsy leaves the office, quietly closing the door behind her. Blair motions Dobyns to the guest chair, leaves his desk, and moves across the room to the other guest chair.

Agent Dobyns starts the conversation, "Detective, I don't know whether you are aware of the rather widespread undercover operation we have been conducting here in Santa Ana."

"No," Blair responds, "at least not a specific operation. I do know of several cases you are working on for our department, but they are not large operations. By the way, thank you for the tremendous help you have given us over the years."

"No need for any thanks, Blair. Working with local law enforcement is something we do with great pleasure," Agent Dobyns says. "I think we are probably the most cooperative federal agency when it comes to working with departments like yours."

"I couldn't agree more," Blair says in a very appreciative tone. "But I know you didn't come here to get patted on the back. Sorry, I took us off subject. What can I do for you?"

"Nothing, actually; I'm here to do something for you that may be of value," comes the somewhat mysterious answer. "I know you are having growing troubles with the Mexican cartels and all the drugs they are pushing into our country. It's not many miles to the border from here."

Blair nods in agreement.

"We have located a particular very dangerous gang who have moved into Orange County. Your drug division guys are aware of these people. Still, they are having difficulty making any arrests or obtaining much intel on these bad actors and what they are up to."

Blair is very interested in what is being said and shifts in his chair to get more comfortable. He does not want to miss anything Agent Dobyns has to say.

"We decided this is a gang that needs to be irradicated before it gets a stronger hold on the drug dealers in Orange County and the only way to do that is to cut the head off the snake, and the only way to find the snake's head is to go undercover and infiltrate the gang with our people. But you already know that."

"You have helped us do that a time or two in the past," Blair agrees. "But I will admit you have my curiosity piqued. You didn't come here to have a discussion over law enforcement techniques."

"No," Agent Dobyns replies, "Do you know anything about a Mexican cartel known as "Los Siete Assientos"?"

"I don't recall ever hearing that name," Blair answers with much curiosity in his voice.

"It is a new gang, and they have targeted Orange County as their territory. We want to wipe them out before they get a foothold. This UC operation is put together quickly. That's probably why you haven't heard about it yet. Anyway, what I need to discuss with you is a situation that occurred a couple of days ago.

"One of our UC Agents has worked his way into the private meetings of the gang. I might add, at great danger to himself, as these dudes are as violent as any I have ever seen. They hang out In the backroom of a crappy little bar.

"The agent working this detail made several buys over the past few months. Each buy has been bigger than the last. As a result, he gained more and more trust with the gang.

"Last night, we took them down. We cut off the head of the snake."

Blair is fascinated with the story, but he is starting to wonder what it has to do with him and why he is telling this story. He should be talking to the drug enforcement officers.

"Did you arrest them?" Blair wants to know.

"Yes, we did. All seven of the so-called assassins. They are in jail and facing Federal charges. And that's the reason I came to see you."

Blair is totally stumped regarding what this is all about. He could get this story from his drug enforcement officers. They always communicated with ATF, and there is little doubt the story will be shared. What's Dobyns's point, Blair thinks?

"When we took them down, there was quite a cache of drugs and several firearms. Dobyns reaches down and picks up a small black bag he brought with him off the floor and places it in his lap. Looks at Blair and unzips the bag with an almost theatrical motion.

"Detective Blair, here is something I think you will want to see."

With that, Agent Dobyns withdraws a marked clear plastic evidence bag and hands it to Blair.

Blair holds up the bag to view its contents. "It's a Glock," Blair says with great, yet quiet surprise."

"I've been following your inheritance of and interest in the old Harper cold case. Now you can totally close the door and lock it on that case. You are holding the Glock you never found. That's your murder weapon."

Blair is speechless as he holds it up in front of him and turns and examines the Glock through the clear plastic of the evidence bag. He studies all the way around the bag and then does it again.

"We don't know how the gun came into the gang's possession. We will work that one out. We ran the serial number through our database at the National Tracing Center in Martinsburg, West Virginia. It is standard procedure for law enforcement to recover a firearm at a crime scene. We use it to determine the background of the firearm to develop investigative leads."

"Yeah," Blair says. "I know you do that. You can pretty much learn a gun's life history."

"That's right. Every gun has a life history of movement and possession," Agent Dobyns says. Still, he believes Blair should have a good understanding of ATF's process. Maybe not, Dobyns thinks. I might as well finish my explanation. "We can determine everything starting with the birthplace of the manufacturer. Sometimes an importer. Then Wholesalers, retailers, FFLs, and Initial Purchasers complete paperwork and background checks. If we're lucky, we might have a chain of possession beyond the initial buyer.

"As you probably know, most folks don't keep records or receipts. All that information can help to link a suspect to a firearm in a criminal investigation and identify potential traffickers."

"It's too bad people don't keep better records," Blair adds. "It could save us a lot of trouble in several types of investigations. I think it's human nature to not keep records if there isn't a requirement."

Agent Dobyns laughs. "Yeah, we all got fed up with that paper stuff in high school."

Dobyns then returned to his story about putting together the history of a crime gun. "The end of the line is the gun's graveyard when we destroy it.

"The good news for you is we had a NIBIN hit on the stolen Glock from the pawnshop in Phoenix. That fingerprint a fired gun creates on shell casings and bullets is science. It's unique and individually identifiable. Those tracks left in the brass are a traceable signature.

"Then the lights started to come on. I am aware of your hunt for the gun used to shoot Hershel Harper. Blair, you and Soper have made that case famous. Our lab test fired the gun, and the bullets matched up with one that your firearms examiner entered in NIBIN."

Blair just sat holding the Glock in the plastic evidence bag. He turned it over almost tenderly in his hands. "This gun matched O'Neill's IBIS exam of the bullets removed from Mr. Harper?"

"Yes," Agent Dobyns answers quietly. "That is your illusive murder weapon."

Blair continues to examine the package in his hands. "I don't know how to thank you enough for bringing this to me.

It has been seventeen long years. In all honesty, I thought this gun was somewhere out there in the Pacific Ocean."

"Sorry, I can't leave it with you; I know you understand the chain of custody. It is evidence in our Federal case, and I must take it with me. I might be bending the rules a bit by bringing it by, but I thought you might like to see it, even if you had to look through a plastic bag."

"Agent Dobyns, you will never know what this means to me. I can put the final stamp on this case. It's closed!"

Agent Dobyns allowed Detective Blair to take a picture of the clear plastic evidence bag with the Glock inside. Blair happened to have his personal 35mm camera in a bag under his desk. He had picked it up that morning from a local repair shop.

The men bid each other a warm farewell.

As the office door closed silently behind Agent Dobyns as he left the office, Blair sat back down in his chair and resumed his stare out the window, his mind rolling over a mix of totally different ideas.

It is nearly thirty minutes before Blair can forget this crazy but as happy as possible ending to the Harper cold case and get his mind back onto the challenges he is facing with managing the Santa Ana Police Department Detective Bureau.

Mistakes, serious mistakes had been made, but he could not fix them all tonight. In fact, he could not fix any of them tonight; it is going to take much work and coordination with the detectives he supervised.

Blair decides it is time to go home. He pulls the little chain and turns off the green desk light, gets up from his chair, walks slowly to the door, places his hand on the doorknob, and then pauses a moment before opening it. Yes, I can think about this at home. I haven't spent much time there lately, Blair thinks as he finally opens the door, leaves his office, and heads to the garage to get his car and drive home.

Traffic is light and Blair makes good time on his way home. When he arrives, he walks into the house and decides he is not going to do a thing, just relax. He owes it to himself; he has earned it.

Blair relaxes on his couch doing something he seldom does; he has a cold beer in his hand. Even though it is time to focus on the future, his thoughts return to the old, now-closed Harper murder case. I hope Soper is watching from Heaven, Blair thinks. It took seventeen years to solve this case. Many people had been hurt, Hershel Harper's family the most. Carlos Morales had been falsely accused, and it cost him his job at the condo. Thousands of hours had been devoted to the case by detectives from my department. That has to change are some of the things running through his mind. Mistakes had been made. Information gathered never got to the place it was supposed to. I'm going to work on fixing that, is his paramount thought.

Joel Pierce had followed through, and his testimony had resulted in the conviction of Larry Gilbert for Hershel Harper's murder and Joe McQuire's accessory to murder. Joel and his friend Ron Gilmore received felony grand theft charges. A good lawyer argued that Joel and Gilmore had not played a role in the committing of the murder and theft and were, in fact, victims themselves of McQuire and Gilbert.

The Harper family finally had closure. Carlos Morales had flourished at the car dealership, and now, the black cloud of suspicion that had hung over him all these years is gone. The new technology of IBIS and NIBIN provided critical clues for the case, they identified the crime gun lost for so many years.

And I got to hold that damn Glock that played hide and seek for seventeen years.

Now I can put that terrible file away forever. That feels good!

Things have even gotten a little better here at home. Blair indulges in a pleasure he seldom has time to do. He sits on the couch and enjoys a cold beer. After he finishes the beer, he sits quietly for a while, going over the closure of the case. Blair decides he wants one final cup of coffee for the day. It would wash the beer taste out of his mouth.

Barbara had not come to meet him when he came in the door. What the heck, he thought, she's here somewhere. Instead of getting up and going to the kitchen to brew the coffee himself, he hollered, "Barbara." No answer, so he tries again, "Barbara."

Maybe she's upstairs in the back bedroom and can't hear me, Blair tells himself. Blair gets off the couch and goes to the kitchen.

While the coffee is brewing, he checks the rest of the house for his wife. He cannot find her anywhere downstairs.

He climbs the stairs and walks into their bedroom. Nobody here. Maybe she is in the bathroom and didn't hear me, Blair thinks.

As he starts to walk across the bedroom to the bathroom, what he sees causes him to come to an immediate stop. The bathroom door is open, and the lights inside are off. However, the empty bathroom did not cause Blair to slam on his brakes. No, she had several of her favorite outfits lying on the bed.

Where the hell did she go?

Disgusted with her, Blair turns to leave the bedroom and return back to his coffee and the couch downstairs. He reaches for the switch to turn off the lights and notices a small paper note on the nightstand on his side of the bed.

Blair picks it up and starts to read, "I thought you were having a good time at work, so I decided I would have a good time, too. Don't look for me; I will be home before sunrise. Barb."

Blair rereads the note.

Well, I guess she must be tired of bitching at me about not making enough money and has found her a sugar daddy somewhere, Blair thinks as his anger and disappointment start to build at the same time. She has been riding me about not making enough money for years. She doesn't think my being a detective is a good enough job for her husband. Maybe it's time for me to leave? She's been getting worse and worse, and I think she has someone she is monkeying around with. Perhaps it's time for me to get out of here.

Blair crunches the note in his hand into a ball and throws it across the room. He angrily turns off the bedroom lights and returns to the kitchen, pours himself a cup of delicious Brazilian coffee, and returns to the living room, where he sits alone, pondering his situation. Blair attempts to relax and get his mind back on the satisfaction of putting the final nail into the Harper cold case. He even got to hold the gun no one could find for seventeen years. However, he cannot enjoy his moment of victory. The thought that has angered him for years pushes everything else out of his mind. Not much has changed. She has constantly been on my case. I guess I need to go find a job that pays more money and has prestige. Not!

Blair sits for a few more minutes; the negative thoughts continue to overtake his mind. I gotta get out of here and finally move him to action. Blair gets up from the couch, goes to the kitchen, removes a large thermos from a cabinet, and fills it with his freshly brewed coffee.

This isn't a home anymore; it's a hellhole, Blair thinks as he grabs his thermos of coffee and storms out the door.

Twenty minutes later, he is at his desk in a deserted detective department.

Blair sets his thermos on his desk, takes a seat in his chair, and pulls the little chain that turns on his green desk light. His mind has turned his anger into positive action. Barbara and her nagging over money are pushed into the garbage can for now. There are cases to be solved and a detective bureau to run. The first order of business is to find out why the interview on the Harper case never made it to the proper destination.

Detective Blair has no idea of the dramatic change that is about to take place in his life.

THE

AUTHOR

Jim Ross Lightfoot was born in 1938 in Sioux City, Iowa, to an unwed mother and was adopted when he was a few months old. A wonderful farm couple adopted him, and he grew up on a farm in Southwest Iowa.

His fascinating life career began upon graduation from high school. He enlisted in the US Army and served in the active reserve from 1956 — 1968. His business career began as an IBM Customer Engineer. He was a police officer in Tulsa, Oklahoma, before entering the broadcast business for 24 years. KMA Radio, an old-line powerhouse radio station in the Midwest, was home for 19 years. He was an award-winning Farm Broadcaster, speaker, and rodeo announcer.

In 1984, he launched a successful bid for a seat as a US Congressman. During his twelve-year tenure, he focused on agriculture and the infrastructure of the highways, airports, and waterways that provide the shipping capabilities to export farm products overseas. As Chairman of an Appropriations Sub-committee, he had oversight of 40% of Federal Law Enforcement's budget. The agencies included the Bureau of Alcohol, Firearms, and Explosives, ATF, The United States Secret Service, USSS, Federal Law Enforcement Training Center, FLETC, US Customs Service, IRS and other minor agencies in the Treasury Department. He served twelve years and retired being a strong believer in term limits.

He finished his career as VP of Forensic Technology Inc., FTI, the founder and developer of a system that has become the World standard in ballistic forensics, now utilized in more than 88 countries around the World. He served as VP for 14 years before retiring.

He is a licensed Commercial Pilot and holds Twin-engine Flight Instructor, Instrument Instructor, and Ground Instructor Ratings.

Lightfoot and wife Nancy live in White Oak, Texas.